Also by Jennifer L. Schiff

THE CRISIS BEFORE CHRISTMAS

Jennifer Lonoff Schiff

Shovel
& Pail
Press

This is a work of fiction. Names, characters, businesses, places, events, and incidents are either the products of the author's imagination or used in a fictitious manner. Any resemblance to actual persons, living or dead, or actual events is purely coincidental.

THE CRISIS BEFORE CHRISTMAS: A SANIBEL ISLAND MYSTERY
by Jennifer Lonoff Schiff

Book Nine in the Sanibel Island Mystery series

https://www.SanibelIslandMysteries.com

Cover design by Rita Sri Harningsih

Formatting by Polgarus Studio

ISBN: 979-8-218-03741-3

Library of Congress Control Number: 2022913365

There are three stages of man:
he believes in Santa Claus;
he does not believe in Santa Claus;
he is Santa Claus.
—Bob Phillips

I don't think Christmas is necessarily about things.
It's about being good to one another.
—Carrie Fisher

The main reason Santa is so jolly
is because he knows where all the bad girls live.
—George Carlin

PROLOGUE

Things had been quiet on Sanibel since Guin had returned from Italy at the end of July. Of course, things were normally quiet on Sanibel in August and September, in October too. A good thing. Guin had had her fill with covering crime, especially murder. And she was relieved that there hadn't been a reason for her to visit the Sanibel Police Department. It would have been odd being there without him. Him being Detective William O'Loughlin, her erstwhile beau. He had abruptly retired in June, returning to Boston to help take care of his grandson—leaving Guin behind.

Guin had been hurt by his refusal to even consider a long-distance relationship. And she had gone off to England and Italy* with a bruised heart. But while she was learning to make authentic Tuscan food in the hills of Chianti (and suss out a killer), her heart had begun to heal. Good food and wine and beautiful scenery had a way of doing that. But it wasn't just Italy. It was Glen. The two had been working side by side at the *Sanibel-Captiva Sun-Times* for over two years now, she as a reporter, he as a photographer. And they had become friends. Good friends. And in Italy, they had become something more.

But as November wound down, and the island went into holiday mode, Guin couldn't help feeling a sense of foreboding.

---

* Read *Something's Cooking in Chianti*.

Though her friend Shelly told her she was being silly. Nothing bad ever happened on Sanibel at Christmastime. But Guin couldn't help it. Her instincts were rarely wrong.

And sure enough, she was right.

It was a few days after Thanksgiving. Guin had just returned from visiting her family in New York. And Shelly had called her to see if she had heard the news. What news? Guin had asked her. About the San Ybel Resort & Spa, a popular family-owned vacation spot on the island. It was being sold.

Guin hadn't known the hotel was for sale. And neither, it seemed, had anyone else. Except apparently for Suzy Seashell, the woman who ran Shellapalooza, a local blog devoted to shelling and island gossip. That's where Shelly had read the news.

Guin immediately pulled up the blog and began to read. The deal had been done in secret. No doubt because many people would be upset by the news. Especially when they heard who the Thompsons had sold the resort to—the Mandelli Group, a New York-based investment firm run by notorious financier and real estate developer Anthony Mandelli, a man with a less than sterling reputation when it came to business and women.

How could the Thompsons have sold the resort to someone like him? Guin wondered. It didn't make sense. And the article didn't say. Just that the sale was scheduled to close right before Christmas.

Guin told Shelly she needed to go and immediately called her boss, Virginia "Ginny" Prescott. Did she know about the sale? Ginny knew everything that happened on the island. But she hadn't known about the sale of the San Ybel until that morning. And she was furious at being scooped by Suzy Seashell.

Guin was scheduled to cover the upcoming holiday lighting event at the San Ybel for the paper, along with Glen.

It was an annual tradition that brought people from across the United States and Canada and even farther away to Sanibel. And she had been looking forward to it. But now she had a new mission: to find out how Anthony Mandelli had managed to finagle his way into the San Ybel and if he could be stopped.

CHAPTER 1

"Are you saying he's not your boyfriend?" said Shelly. She and Guin were having a drink at 400 Rabbits, a new Mexican restaurant that had recently opened at the corner of Rabbit and Sanibel-Captiva roads, where Doc Ford's used to be.

"No, I just don't like the word. *Boyfriend* sounds so… I don't know, high school."

"It's just a word, Guin."

"Words have power."

"Fine. How should I refer to him then?"

"As Glen."

Shelly pursed her lips.

"And how does Glen refer to you?"

"I don't know."

"I bet he calls you his girlfriend."

"Why is it so important to you?"

"I just don't understand why you won't refer to him as your boyfriend. You've been seeing the guy for months now."

"I told you. I don't like the word."

"Is it because of the detective?"

"No. I've barely thought about him since Glen and I returned from Italy."

"Uh-huh. So you two haven't texted?"

"No." However, that wasn't entirely true. Guin had texted the detective to wish him a happy birthday. But he hadn't responded. And she had then deleted him from her phone.

Shelly was about to say something when they heard someone clear his throat. They turned to find Marty Nesbitt, Sanibel's resident sixty- or seventy-something lothario, grinning at them. As usual, he was dressed in a Hawaiian shirt, his thinning gray hair pulled back in a ponytail.

"Ladies!" he said, a smile cracking the leathery skin on his face. "Fancy seeing you here!"

Guin grit her teeth.

"Hey, Marty," said Shelly, clearly not excited to see him.

Marty looked at Guin's drink.

"Is that a margarita?"

Though it obviously was.

Guin turned to face him.

"It is."

"Any good?"

She nodded.

Marty signaled to the bartender.

"I'll have what she's having," he said, grinning.

Guin rolled her eyes.

"I hate to be rude, Marty," said Shelly. "But Guin and I were in the middle of a private conversation."

"Private, eh?" he said. "But you're sitting at the bar."

Though until Marty had come over, there had been no one sitting next to them.

"Good point," said Guin. "Hey, Shell, shall we grab our table?"

"Table?"

Guin gave her a look.

"Oh, right! Our table!"

They got up, but Marty stopped them.

"Hey, you don't need to run off on my account. I know how to be discreet. Your secrets are safe with me. They don't call me Mum's the Word Marty for nothing."

Guin suppressed a snort. Everyone knew Marty had some of the loosest lips on the island.

"I'm sure," said Guin. "But we have a reservation."

"Oh," said Marty. "Well, that's okay. Sandy should be along any second."

"Sandy?"

"My new lady friend."

"What happened to Eunice?"

"She wasn't doing it for me."

No doubt Eunice had seen the light and dumped Marty. But Guin didn't say anything.

"Does Sandy live on Sanibel?" Shelly asked.

Marty nodded.

"Just moved here from Upstate New York."

That explained it, thought Guin. Any woman who lived on Sanibel would know to avoid Marty. Though, to be fair, he did have a few redeeming qualities. He wasn't horrible looking. And he was known to be generous, supporting several local nonprofits and those in need. He was just incredibly annoying.

"Well, I hope you and Sandy enjoy your dinner," said Guin.

"I'm sure we will," he said. "Especially dessert," he added, waggling his bushy eyebrows.

Guin wanted to throw up. Instead, she smiled politely and quickly headed to the hostess stand, asking the hostess if they could have the empty booth at the end (far away from Marty).

The busboy had just poured them water when Shelly opened her mouth.

"So, what do your mother and brother think about you and Glen?" Guin didn't say anything. "You still haven't told them that the two of you are dating?"

"Lance knows."

"But not your mother?"

"It's complicated."

"What's so complicated?"

"You know how my mother is."

"Doesn't she want you to be happy?"

"She wants me to be married."

"Still?"

"What can I say? She's old-fashioned. And I don't think she's entirely forgiven me for divorcing Art."

"But he cheated on you with your hairdresser!"

"I know. But all of her friends' children are married and have kids, and…"

"You know, you and Glen could still technically…"

"Can we please change the subject? What are you going to have?"

"I haven't looked at the menu."

"Well, get whatever you want. My treat."

Shelly looked at her.

"Does that mean you're writing about 400 Rabbits for the paper?"

Guin looked around, to make sure no one was listening, then nodded.

Shelly grinned.

"Well, in that case…"

"Just don't say anything."

"My lips are sealed. So, how many times have you eaten here?"

"Just once before tonight. And I should come back one more time. I've been working my way through the menu."

"Well, if you need help. You know Steve will eat practically anything."

"Actually, that's a great idea. You and Steve can join me. Is he around next week?"

"I think so. What about Glen?"

"I was planning on including him."

"Are you ladies ready to order?"

It was their server.

"Could you give us a minute?" said Shelly.

"Sure," said the server. "I'll come back in a few."

"That was yummy," said Shelly.

Guin agreed. They had shared an order of the hand-crafted guacamole to start, then Guin had had the grouper street tacos and Shelly the al pastor burrito. And they had shared a piece of key lime pie for dessert.

"Can I get you anything else?" asked their server.

"Just a check," said Guin.

"The paper paying?" asked Shelly.

"Sh!" Guin admonished her.

"Oops. My bad. Probably shouldn't have had that second margarita."

"You okay to drive?"

"I'm fine. I'm sure the beans and rice sucked the alcohol right up."

Guin wasn't so sure about that but didn't say anything.

The server returned with the check a minute later, and Guin handed him her credit card. The paper would reimburse her after she turned in her article and expense report.

A breeze swept by as they stood outside the restaurant. The cool night air felt good. Refreshing. The sky was clear. And as Guin looked up, she could see hundreds of stars as well as several planets.

"What are you looking at?" asked Shelly.

"The sky. I never get tired of seeing all the stars."

"I know how you feel."

They stood looking at the sky for another minute.

"That reminds me," said Shelly. "Are you going to the holiday lighting Saturday?"

"The one at the San Ybel?"

"Is there another one?"

"Glen and I are covering it for the paper."

"I still can't believe the place is being sold."

"I know," said Guin. "Though it's not a done deal yet."

"Suzy seems to think so."

"Well, you can't believe everything Suzy writes." However, Guin hadn't heard of any reason why the sale wouldn't go through. "You and Steve going to be there?"

"We wouldn't miss it. Say, you want to go shelling Saturday? There's going to be a negative tide around seven."

"Sure. Let me know where you want to meet."

Shelly said she'd send her a text and they said their goodbyes.

Guin walked in the door and was immediately accosted by her cat, Fauna, a sleek black rescue.

"What?" said Guin, looking down at the feline, who was glaring up at her. "I gave you food before I left."

Fauna followed Guin into the kitchen. Guin looked down at Fauna's bowl. It was empty.

"I'm not giving you more food."

Fauna started to meow.

"Okay, just a couple of treats. But that's it."

Guin could have sworn Fauna smiled as she opened the door to the pantry. She dropped two cat treats into Fauna's bowl. Then she headed to her office to type up her notes from dinner, realizing along the way that she had left her phone in her bag. She turned around and went back to the kitchen to retrieve it. When she took it out, she saw she had two texts and a voicemail.

The first text was from Glen. He wanted to know if Guin was free for dinner tomorrow. He was making some of Bridget's recipes and wanted her to try them.

Bridget was the woman who had taught the cooking course in Italy and was an old friend of Glen's. She and her husband Dante, a butcher and restauranteur in Chianti, were about to publish their first cookbook, and Glen had volunteered to test some of their recipes.

"Which ones are you making?" Guin texted him.

A minute later, he replied.

"Does it matter?"

Did it? Not really. Everything Glen had made from Bridget and Dante's cookbook so far had been delicious.

"What time?"

"That depends. You want to help me cook?"

Guin thought about it. She had helped him a few times and enjoyed it. Though sometimes she just preferred to be fed.

"Sure," she wrote back. "Can I bring anything?"

"Just yourself. Be here at 6."

"OK. A domani." (That meant *until tomorrow* in Italian.)

"Ciao," Glen replied, adding a kiss emoji.

Guin smiled. Then she opened the text from her brother.

"Just checking in," he had written. "Everything okay? Mom says she hasn't heard from you since you left."

Guin rolled her eyes. She had texted her mother as soon as she had gotten back to Sanibel, letting her know she had arrived safely. But she hadn't actually spoken to her.

"Everything's fine," Guin typed. "Just busy. Tell Mom I'll call her this weekend."

"They're going away," Lance replied. "Call her tomorrow."

Guin frowned. She was having dinner with Glen tomorrow. And no way was she calling her mother from Glen's place.

"You good?" Guin texted him.

"Yup. Just busy."

"OK. Well, thanks for checking in. Send Owen my love." Owen was Lance's husband.

"I will. Love you."

"Love you too."

Guin looked down at her phone. She was about to play the voicemail message but decided to check her call history first. There was her mother's number. The voicemail was undoubtedly from her. Her finger hovered over the voicemail icon. Then she removed it. She would listen to her mother's message and call her in the morning. Right now, she had work to do.

CHAPTER 2

"So, what are we making?" Guin asked Glen, following him into the kitchen.

Glen lived in a modest two-bedroom house in Fort Myers, which he had bought to be near his parents. The house was located on a canal, and Glen had spent the last two years fixing it up. His most recent project, just completed, was updating the kitchen.

"The kitchen looks great, by the way."

"Thanks. I'm pretty happy with it."

"So, what are we making? I'm guessing not *Bistecca alla Fiorentina*," she said, not seeing a large steak.

"Nope, not making steak."

"*Peposo*?"

Peposo was a Tuscan beef stew they had made in their Italian cooking class.

"Nope, not *peposo*. Though it is a stew of sorts."

"Did we have it when we were in Italy?"

Glen nodded.

"On our second night in Chianti. It's a Tuscan seafood stew called *cacciucco*."

"*Cacciucco*," Guin repeated. "Remind me, what's in it? And don't say *seafood*."

Glen smiled.

"There's snapper, grouper, shrimp, mussels, calamari, chopped tomatoes, tomato paste, wine…"

"Whoa. That's a lot of seafood. Is it difficult to make?"

"Not really. I'll show you the recipe."

Glen held up his tablet for Guin to see.

"Have you made it before?"

"Once."

"How did it turn out?"

"Pretty good."

"Just pretty good?"

Glen smiled.

"I knew I could do better."

Guin looked at the recipe again.

"I don't see snapper and grouper in Bridget's recipe."

"I decided to use local fish."

"How does Bridget feel about that?"

"She said she was fine with it. Actually, she thought it was a great idea."

"Oh, did she now?"

"You don't believe me?" Guin looked like she didn't. "You want to call her?"

"That's okay." Italy was six hours ahead. And Guin didn't want Glen to feel that she didn't trust him.

"The point is to use fish that's fresh. And she said she would add a note to that effect."

"Got it."

"So, shall we begin?"

"What do you want me to do?"

"Get out the bottle of white wine I have in the fridge."

Guin went over to the refrigerator and took out a bottle of white wine.

"This one?"

Glen nodded.

"It's Italian," said Guin. "From that winery we went to. I didn't know you had any left."

"A couple of bottles."

He got out a corkscrew and opened the wine. Then he poured some into each of their glasses.

Guin swirled it and took a sniff.

"Smells good."

"It tastes even better."

Guin took a sip.

"Mm."

"Was I right?"

Guin nodded. Then she took another sip.

"Very good. But let's save the rest for dinner."

Glen took another sip. Then he put down his glass.

"Okay. Now the first thing we need to do is cut the fish into large cubes."

It took around an hour to make the *cacciucco*. While it was cooking, they made garlic bread. Then, when everything was ready, they took the stew and the bread over to the new kitchen island.

"*Buon appetito!*" said Glen.

Guin leaned over her bowl and breathed in the tomatoey aroma.

"It smells amazing."

Glen leaned over his bowl and inhaled.

"It does smell pretty good."

Guin dipped her spoon in, making sure to get as much seafood on it as possible. Then she raised it to her mouth.

"Mm…" she said as she chewed. "This is really good."

"I agree."

They continued to eat, making small talk as they did. When only the broth was left, they soaked it up with the garlic bread.

"I enjoyed that," said Guin. "The seafood was done perfectly. And that broth…"

"I know," said Glen. "We make a good team."

"We do," said Guin, smiling at him.

"Speaking of teamwork, what's the game plan for Saturday? Shall I pick you up?"

Guin looked confused.

"For the holiday lighting event. It's going to be pretty crowded at the hotel, and the parking lot's bound to get full early."

"True, but you don't have to get me. I'm not exactly on the way."

Guin's house was on the West End of Sanibel and the San Ybel was in an area known as Middle Gulf, located closer to the Causeway.

"It's no big deal."

"If you don't mind…"

"Not at all. Shall we say seven?" The ceremony began at eight.

"That's fine. I can always interview a few people while we're waiting for the event to begin. I wonder…"

"Yes?" said Glen.

"Do you think Mandelli will be there?"

"I'd say there's a good chance he will be. You going to be okay if he is?"

Guin had had a couple of run-ins with the randy developer, who thought pawing women was his right.

"I'll be fine."

"Though if he says or does anything inappropriate…"

Guin smiled.

"I'll knee him."

Glen looked at her.

"Kidding." Sort of.

"Well, I'll be watching your back in case he tries anything."

"Thank you. However, I would hope, as the new owner of the hotel and with people watching him, he'd behave himself." But Guin wasn't so sure that would make a difference. He had misbehaved in public before.

"All right. Enough about Anthony Mandelli. You ready for some dessert?"

"Dessert? But we didn't make anything."

Glen smiled.

"I made it earlier."

"What did you make?"

"Guess."

"Just tell me."

Glen shook his head.

"At least give me a clue."

"Come on, take a guess. It's something I know you'll like."

"That could be a dozen things." Glen knew Guin had a sweet tooth. "Is it something from Bridget's cookbook?"

"Partly."

Guin looked thoughtful.

"Did you make tiramisu?"

Guin loved tiramisu.

"Nope, though I thought about it."

"Hm… Did you make a *torta della nonna*?"

A *torta della nonna* was an Italian custard tart.

"Nope."

"I give up."

"So easily? Come on, take one more guess, then I'll tell you."

Guin sighed.

"Fine. Did you make *cantucci*?"

Cantucci were almond cookies—little biscotti—that were popular in Tuscany.

Glen smiled.

"Excellent detective work. You're partly right."

Guin cocked her head.

"Partly right?"

"I guess I technically made two desserts. Though they go together."

"You made two desserts?" Guin was impressed. Barely a year ago Glen's repertoire pretty much consisted of mac and cheese, grilled cheese, and pasta. "What's the other one?"

"Guess."

"I'm tired of guessing. Just tell me."

"Fine. I made gelato."

"You made gelato?"

"Don't look so surprised. Gelato is easy to make."

"Maybe if you have a gelato maker."

"Which I bought this very week."

"You bought a gelato maker?"

"Technically, an ice-cream maker."

"So, what kind of gelato did you make?"

"Well, I thought about making *bacio* [dark chocolate hazelnut] or *pistacchio*, but I wound up making coconut."

"I'm down with coconut."

"I thought you would be. So, shall we have some?"

"Let's clean up first."

"Oh my God," said Guin, taking another bite of the coconut gelato. "This is amazing. And the *cantucci* are really good too. The flavors totally complement each other."

"I'm glad you like everything."

"Like doesn't begin to cover it. You've really upped your game, Glen Anderson."

He smiled.

"Bridget and Italy inspired me."

"So, what else do you have up your sleeve?"

"Actually," he said. "How do you feel about French food?"

"I love French food. Why?"

"I was thinking we could go to Paris."

"Paris, as in Paris, France?"

"I wasn't referring to the one in Texas."

"Why Paris? Is there a cooking course there you want to attend?"

"Actually…" Guin waited for him to go. "I was brainstorming ideas with Ginny…"

"You were brainstorming ideas with Ginny?"

Guin knew Ginny enjoyed Glen's company, but she usually brainstormed article ideas with her reporters, not freelance photographers.

"Would you let me finish?"

"Sorry. Go on."

"As I was saying, Ginny's been wanting to do more travel pieces. And I suggested she send the two of us to Paris for Valentine's Day."

Guin stared at him.

"You asked Ginny to send us to Paris for Valentine's Day?"

"I did."

"And what did she say?"

"She thought it was a great idea."

"She did?"

"Yup."

"Did she say if the paper would pay? Paris isn't cheap, you know."

"She said the paper would subsidize the trip."

"What does that mean? Knowing Ginny, that means they'll pay for breakfast and not much else."

Glen smiled.

"A little bit more than that. We just have to cover the flight and lodging."

"Oh, is that all?"

"I have plenty of points."

"Enough to cover our flights and a hotel?"

"Maybe not that many. But doesn't your brother have a corporate apartment there?"

"He does, but… Did you already ask him if we could stay there?"

"Not yet. But even if we can't stay there, I'm sure we can

find a reasonably priced hotel."

"And what about meals?"

"The paper will pay for meals. Though we probably won't be dining at Guy Savoy or L'Orangerie. Still, there are plenty of romantic places to eat and things to do there that don't cost a fortune."

"Romantic places, eh?"

"Well, the article is for Valentine's Day."

"Valentine's Day is not exactly my favorite holiday."

"I know. But this trip will change that."

Guin wasn't so sure.

"So, when would we go? If Ginny wants to run the article around Valentine's Day, we'll need to go before then."

"I was thinking the end of January."

Guin looked thoughtful.

"That's not that far away. We should probably look into flights and hotels."

"Does that mean you'll go?"

Did it? Guin loved Paris. But to spend a romantic week there with Glen? Sure, it sounded great on the surface. But what if something went wrong? What if they argued? Then she might never want to go to Paris again.

"I need to think about it."

"Okay. Just don't take too long. As you said, we'll need to book soon if we plan on going."

"I said I'll think about it," Guin snapped. Then she immediately apologized, claiming the wine had made her tired.

They finished cleaning the kitchen, and Guin said she should head back to Sanibel.

Glen took her hand.

"You don't have to go."

Guin looked up at him. She was tempted to stay, but she

had work to do in the morning.

"Thanks, but I need to be up early tomorrow, and you know what traffic getting on to Sanibel can be like."

He did, but he didn't want Guin to leave just yet.

"Stay, just a little while longer."

Guin saw the look in his eyes. And again, she was tempted. Very tempted. But she knew that if she didn't leave now, she wouldn't leave until the morning.

"I should go. I don't want to nod off on the Causeway."

"All the more reason for you to stay. You can head home in the morning, before the traffic."

Guin smiled up at him.

"You're not making this easy."

Glen gave her a wicked grin.

"I know how to make it harder."

He took her in his arms and kissed her.

Several minutes went by. Then Guin gently pushed him away.

"I should go."

"Must you?"

"I must."

He walked her to the door.

"Thanks for helping me make dinner."

"It was my pleasure."

"Do you mean that?"

"Why would I lie?"

"Well, if you're serious, I have some more recipes I need to test."

"Just let me know when."

They stood in front of the door.

"Well, goodnight. I'll see you Saturday."

Glen leaned down and gently kissed Guin goodnight. She looked up at him, a part of her wanting to stay. Then she turned and opened the door.

CHAPTER 3

Guin arose at six-thirty Saturday. She and Shelly were going shelling along West Gulf Drive, and Guin needed to get dressed quickly as Shelly would be there any minute. Sure enough, Guin found a message from her friend as soon as she had finished throwing clothes on. Shelly was outside her door.

"I'll be right there," Guin replied.

She grabbed her shelling bag, gave Fauna some food and water, and left.

"Looks like a nice day!" Guin said, looking up at the sky as they headed to the beach. Though the sun had yet to fully rise.

"There was a northwest wind earlier," said Shelly. "So there should be lots of shells."

"Here's hoping."

"You're such a pessimist."

"I'm not a pessimist. I'm a realist."

"Toe-MAY-toe, toe-MAH-toe."

"Look, I'd be thrilled if we found lots of good shells. But my track record isn't great."

"That's because you don't visualize."

"Visualize?"

"You must envision yourself finding good shells," said Shelly, closing her eyes and extending her arms. "Picture a junonia just lying there waiting for you."

"Uh-huh. So the problem isn't the tide or the wind or that I'm shelling in the wrong spot but me not picturing myself finding the shells I want?"

Shelly kept her eyes closed, her arms still extended, as though she was in a trance.

"Mock me all you like, but I'm telling you, this works."

Guin glanced at her.

"So what are you visualizing?"

"Some lovely orange and purple scallops and rose petal tellins."

"You don't have to visualize to find scallops." There were usually plenty on the beach. "Are they for a project?"

Shelly nodded.

"You going to tell me about it?"

"Not yet. It's a secret."

"Are you going to open your eyes? I wouldn't want you to trip."

Shelly opened her eyes.

"Come on," said Guin. "Let's go look for shells."

They headed down to the water.

"Which way?" asked Guin.

"Hm," said Shelly, glancing around. "Let's head east."

They headed east, their eyes cast downward.

"I'm not seeing anything," said Guin. And she doubted Shelly was either. The beach was pretty bare. So much for visualization.

Suddenly, Shelly darted into the water.

"You see something?" called Guin.

Shelly didn't answer. She was too busy digging. Guin took a few steps closer. A few seconds later, Shelly held up her prize, a large horse conch. She was beaming.

"Wow!" said Guin. "That's one big orange scallop."

Shelly pursed her lips.

"Haha. Very funny."

(Guin knew it was a horse conch.)

"What are you going to do with it?"

"I don't know. But I'll figure out something!"

Guin had no doubt she would. Shelly was very creative.

"You want to stash it someplace? It looks too heavy to carry around."

"I'll manage," said Shelly, stuffing it into her bag.

They continued to walk, stopping occasionally to examine shells. The shells had become more plentiful the further east they went. And although Guin hadn't found a junonia or a Scotch bonnet or a true tulip, she had found several small horse conchs, a few banded tulips, a couple of nutmeg shells, a Florida cone, and an alphabet cone. But she left most of them on the beach for someone else to find.

"Why aren't you taking them?" asked Shelly.

"Because I don't really need them."

"*Need*?" said Shelly. "No one really needs more shells, Guin. Well, I do, because of my jewelry. But you know what I mean."

"I do. I just promised myself I would only take shells that are perfect or that I don't have."

"You need to stop being such a perfectionist."

"I'm not a perfectionist."

Shelly eyed her.

"Aren't you? You just said you'd only take perfect shells. And I know how you edit your articles a zillion times before you send them to Ginny."

"I don't edit them a zillion times. I just want to make sure they're—"

"Perfect?"

"I was going to say well written. And as far as shells are concerned, I'm not looking for perfection. I just don't choose to take ones with cracks or missing pieces or blemishes."

"But those blemishes or imperfections are what make them interesting."

"Maybe. But then how come you don't use damaged shells in your jewelry?"

"Sometimes I do. But jewelry is different. People want shells that look nice."

"Aha! My point exactly."

Shelly made a face.

They had passed Beach Access #1 and were near the West Wind Island Resort when Guin said she should turn around.

"I should probably turn around too," said Shelly. "I've got a lot of work to do."

"Still making jewelry for Christmas?"

Shelly nodded.

"I'm back-ordered."

"Wow, that's great!"

"I guess."

They were nearly back to where they had started when Guin saw something with brown spots rolling in with the tide. She immediately dropped her bag and ran into the water, grabbing for the shell before the tide could pull it back into the Gulf.

"What is it?" called Shelly, hurrying over. "Is it a junonia?"

Guin was standing in the water, examining her find.

"No, it's an alphabet cone. Check it out." She held it up for Shelly to see. "I've never seen one quite like this before. See? It's like each time it got injured or had a growth spurt, it changed color."

She handed the alphabet cone to Shelly, who studied it and then handed it back to Guin.

"Please tell me you're not going to throw it back."

"Nope. It's definitely a keeper."

"Good. You should enter it in the Shell Show."

"I don't know about that. I don't think it would win a prize."

"It would if you entered it in the Misfits category."

"Misfits? I didn't know there was such a category."

"There is. Though it may have a different name. But you should definitely enter it."

Guin studied the alphabet cone.

"Maybe I will," she said. She paused. "I know! I could call it the Rosetta Cone."

"The Rosetta Cone?"

"You know, like the Rosetta Stone."

"I love it!"

They headed back to Guin's place, and Guin invited Shelly in for coffee. But she declined, telling Guin that she needed to get back to her workroom. So they said goodbye and that they'd look for each other later at the holiday lighting.

Guin spent the rest of the day doing work. As the paper's general assignment reporter, Guin was tasked with covering everything from restaurant and store openings to human interest stories to crime and whatever else Ginny wanted her to write about. And this was the busy season on Sanibel and Captiva. Which meant no days off. However, Guin took a break for lunch and closed her laptop a little after five, so she could get in a walk before the holiday lighting.

She stepped outside and saw several of her neighbors and their dogs gathered down the block. No doubt they were out for their evening stroll. Guin hurried to catch up.

Guin had become an unofficial member of the dog pack, often joining them for their evening walk. She often thought about getting a dog. But she had a feeling Fauna wouldn't approve. So this was the next best thing.

She listened as they talked among themselves, petting the dogs that came up to her. Then a little before six, she excused herself and said goodbye. She needed to get changed. And she should probably eat something. Although there would be food at the holiday lighting, she'd probably be too busy interviewing people to eat. This way she wouldn't be starving later.

She took a quick shower and went into her closet to get dressed. She thought about wearing something red and green. Then she changed her mind. Too cliché. Instead, she slipped on a pair of white jeans and a pretty blue top. It was more Hanukkah than Christmas, but the holiday lighting wasn't just about Christmas.

She checked herself out in the full-length mirror. Then she went into the kitchen to eat a little something. When she was done, she went into the bathroom to apply a little makeup. She was just finishing up when the doorbell rang. No doubt it was Glen.

"Coming!" she called.

She opened the door to find Glen looking handsome in a pair of form-fitting jeans and a white button-down shirt. It was almost like they had coordinated.

"You look very nice," he said, eyeing her appreciatively.

"Thank you. You do too. I just need to grab my bag."

She went over to where she had left it.

"All set," she said.

Fauna came over and started rubbing herself against Guin's leg. Guin frowned as black fur covered her white jeans.

"Let me give her some food and grab the lint roller."

She poured some dry food into Fauna's bowl, which Fauna immediately began to eat. Then she took the lint roller and removed the cat hair from her jeans.

"Okay," she said to Glen. "Let's go."

He smiled and led her out to his car.

Even though they had gotten to the hotel a half-hour before the festivities started, there was not a parking spot to be had.

And Glen refused to leave his BMW with the valet, preferring to park the car himself.

"I'll drop you off in front and go around one more time," he told Guin.

"Just give the car to the valet."

"I will if I don't find anything. But I thought I saw someone pulling out over there."

Guin sighed. What was it with men and their cars? She knew the BMW was his baby, but really. He was just as protective with his SUV.

"Fine. But don't take too long."

"I won't."

Guin looked like she didn't believe him.

"I promise I'll let the valet park it if I don't find anything."

"Okay. I'm going to take a look around. Come find me."

"I will."

Guin got out and walked around the hotel. There were holiday decorations everywhere. You could probably see them from space when they were all lit. She went inside, where there were more decorations and dozens of people milling around. Guin looked to see if Shelly and Steve were there, but she didn't see them.

She made her way back to the entrance, figuring she'd intercept Glen. When he didn't appear, she moved to the side and sent him a text. She had just finished typing when she felt someone looming over her.

"You're standing under the mistletoe." She turned to see Anthony Mandelli leering at her. "Hoping to be kissed?"

Guin frowned.

"No."

But Mandelli didn't seem to notice.

"Come on, baby, one little kiss."

Was he drunk? He had a drink in his hand and looked a little glassy-eyed.

"I said no."

He reached out to grab her, and Guin stepped away. She didn't want to cause a scene, but no way was she kissing Mandelli.

He seemed amused.

"Playing hard to get, I see."

"I'm working, Mr. Mandelli."

"Please, call me Tony. All my friends do."

Guin wanted to tell him she was not his friend, but she kept her mouth shut. Where was Glen?

Mandelli reached for her again. And again Guin stepped away. Time to try a different tactic.

"While you're here, can you tell me why you decided to purchase the San Ybel?" she asked him.

"I'd be happy to. Why don't we go up to my suite, and I'll tell you all about it?"

Guin was about to tell him what she thought of that idea when Glen appeared.

"You okay?" he asked her.

"Yes, fine."

He looked at Mandelli, more like glared at him.

"Take it easy, cowboy. The lady and I were having a private conversation."

Glen scowled.

"I was just asking Mr. Mandelli why he wanted to purchase the San Ybel," Guin explained.

"And I told Gwen I'd be happy to tell her… someplace a bit more private."

"It's Guin, and she's not going anywhere with you," said Glen, taking a step toward Mandelli.

Mandelli smiled, clearly not the least bit intimidated.

"Isn't that up to Gwen?" He placed a hand on her arm. "Come on," he said.

Glen looked like he was about to punch Mandelli.

Much as Guin might like that, it would not do for Glen to punch the new owner of the hotel.

She was about to say something when a member of the hotel staff came over to Mandelli and whispered something in his ear.

"I'll be right there," he told the man. Then he turned back to Guin. "I have to go," he informed her. "But drop by the Presidential Suite later, and I'll tell you anything you want to know." He gave her a last lascivious grin and then walked away.

"I don't understand how the Thompsons could have sold the resort to that creep."

"Neither do I," said Guin. "So, did you find a place to park, or did you surrender your car to the valet?"

"I found a spot."

Guin was about to make a crack when she saw Shelly charging toward them, Steve a few feet behind her.

"Sorry we're late! I wasn't paying attention to the time, and then there was a line for the valet, and…"

"You're not late," said Guin. "The ceremony hasn't begun."

"I know, but I wanted to get here before it got too crowded." She looked around. "There must be over a hundred people here."

"More than that," said Glen. "I should go take some pictures before the place fills up."

"Okay," said Guin. "You want me to come with you?"

"You don't have to. You sure you're okay?"

"I'm fine. I'll catch up with you later."

Glen excused himself, and Shelly turned to Guin.

"What was that about?"

"I had a run-in with Anthony Mandelli."

"You okay?"

"I'm fine."

Shelly looked like she didn't believe her.

"Really, Shell."

"If you say so. You want to grab a drink?"

"Can't. I'm working. Speaking of which, I should interview a few people."

"You can interview us."

Guin smiled.

"Thanks, but it'd be best if it was people I didn't know."

"Suit yourself. You sure I can't get you something?"

"Positive. I'll get something after the lighting ceremony. But thank you."

Shelly then went with Steve to the bar.

CHAPTER 4

It was time for the lighting ceremony. Everyone was gathered outside. The grounds looked like a winter wonderland. Well, a winter wonderland if Santa's workshop had relocated to Southwest Florida. The palm trees surrounding the hotel had been strung with lights. Santa's sled graced the roof of the hotel, complete with eight reindeer. And there were giant candy canes and ornaments everywhere, as well as snowmen and a menorah.

The general manager of the resort, Laurence Washburn, welcomed everyone. Then he gave a short speech, talking about the history of the resort and the lighting ceremony. When he was done, he looked over at Anthony Mandelli, who was standing near the makeshift stage. Was that a pained expression on Washburn's face? Well, it was quickly gone as he turned back to face the crowd.

"As many of you probably know, the San Ybel will soon be under new ownership." There was mumbling and grumbling in the crowd, and Guin was pretty sure she heard a few boos. "And we are fortunate to have the head of the new ownership group here with us this evening." He turned again to Mandelli. "Mr. Mandelli, would you join me on the stage?"

Mandelli smiled at the crowd and took his place next to Washburn. No one in the crowd was smiling. But that didn't faze Mandelli.

"Good evening," he said to the audience. "It's a pleasure to be here with all of you this evening. I know how much the San Ybel means to Sanibel. And I promise you, my partners and I are planning great things for the resort."

"He'll probably run the place into the ground like he did that resort in the Hamptons," Guin heard a man near her mumble.

"And that other resort," his companion said.

"But tonight is the famous—or should I say infamous?" he said with a grin—"lighting ceremony, where we kick off the Christmas season, one of my favorite times of the year. So what do you say? Shall we get lit?"

A solo voice shouted "Yeah!" And there were a few chuckles. But Guin felt more like she was at a funeral than at a joyous event.

Someone handed Washburn a box with a big red button.

"Shall we?" he said to Mandelli.

He held the box and began counting down from ten, the crowd counting down with him. When they got to one, Mandelli pressed the button and all of the decorations lit up.

There were lots of oohs and aahs, and Guin had to admit, the display was impressive. It also made her suddenly homesick for New York. When she was little, her father would take her and Lance to the tree lighting at Rockefeller Center. It was one of her fondest memories.

"Now let's continue this party inside!" said Mandelli. "Drinks are on me!"

The crowd of onlookers streamed into the hotel, and Guin followed them inside.

Guin had been busy interviewing people. She spoke with a family that had been coming to the San Ybel for years, a young couple on their honeymoon, and a group of friends who said this was their first time to the island. Guin particularly enjoyed speaking with a man named Walter, a grandfather, who had been coming to Sanibel since he was a kid and now took his extended family to the island to attend the lighting ceremony.

Guin wanted Glen to take a picture of Walter and his family. But he was nowhere to be found. So Guin took a few pictures of the family with her phone and asked if the paper's photographer could take a proper picture of them later. Walter said he'd be delighted, and they exchanged phone numbers.

Guin had just said goodbye to Walter and his family when Shelly came over.

"Have you been to the ballroom yet?" she asked Guin.

"Not yet," said Guin. "I was about to head over there."

"You should definitely go have a look."

Guin studied her friend's face.

"Is there something I should know?"

The ballroom was supposed to look like Santa's workshop and include a toy train that ran on a small circular track around the room.

"Just go have a look. I'll go with you."

They started to head to the ballroom. But Guin noticed that Steve hadn't moved.

"You not coming?" Guin asked him.

"I already got an eyeful."

Guin wondered what that meant. But Shelly was already pulling her toward the ballroom. There was a sign on the door with the words *Santa's Workshop* written in a child's hand. Or maybe an elf's. Shelly pulled open the door and they went inside.

Guin glanced around. It certainly looked like Santa's workshop, or how Guin imagined Santa's workshop to look. And the train was a nice touch.

Shelly nudged her and pointed up at the stage. Guin's mouth fell open. There, sitting in Santa's chair, with a drink in his hand and a blonde in his lap, was Anthony Mandelli. What did he think he was doing? Guin was furious.

She looked around the room to see if anyone else was appalled. But most people were too busy mingling to pay much attention to what was going on on the stage or didn't care. Though not everyone. Guin saw Patrick Finney staring, a scowl on his face, clearly displeased with the scene.

Finney was a real estate agent on the island. He and his now ex-wife Audra Linwood used to run a successful real estate practice on the island. Then they had a falling out after Audra decided to go out on her own and the two of them divorced. They were now rivals. And making matters worse, at least to Finney, Audra had been doing business with Mandelli—and getting the business from him, if rumors or appearances were to be believed.

Guin returned her gaze to the stage where Mandelli was whispering something to the blonde.

"I wonder what he said to her," said Shelly.

"I don't want to know," Guin replied. "I'm surprised no one's said something."

"Someone probably has. But do you want to be the guy to tell the new owner of the hotel he's behaving inappropriately?"

Shelly had a point. But enough was enough. Guin started to move toward the stage, but Shelly grabbed her arm. Guin turned and looked at her.

"Why are you stopping me?"

"It's for your own good. You don't want to cause a scene."

"Like he hasn't already caused one?"

Guin looked back up at the stage.

"I just know I've seen her someplace," said Shelly.

Guin turned to her friend.

"You mean the blonde?"

Shelly nodded.

"You've seen her on the island?" asked Guin.

"No, I don't think that's where I've seen her. But I'm sure I've seen her before."

They both stared at the blonde. She was attractive, with honey-colored hair, a heart-shaped face, and an ample bosom. Guin thought her to be in her late twenties, possibly early thirties.

"I can't believe she's putting up with this," said Guin. "It's Santa's chair, for Pete's sake!"

"Maybe he paid her to sit in his lap."

"You couldn't pay me enough."

"Maybe she works for him."

"If so, she should sue him for sexual harassment."

"Maybe he said he'd give her a bonus."

"More like a boner."

Shelly snickered.

Guin glanced around the room again. She didn't see Finney. Had he left? She sure wanted to. She wondered if Audra knew about the blonde and hoped she would step into the ballroom. No doubt she'd put a stop to the shocking display.

"I've seen enough," said Guin. "Let's go."

Shelly reluctantly followed her to the door. Just as they got there, however, Glen entered.

"You leaving?" he asked them.

"Yes," said Guin. "Where've you been?"

"Taking pictures."

Duh. Guin should've known he'd say that.

"I was looking for you. I met this nice older man named Walter who's been coming to the San Ybel for years, and I'd love you to take a picture of him with his kids and grandchildren. They're all here for the holiday lighting."

"I'd be happy to. Just tell me when and where."

Guin glanced around. They weren't in the ballroom. Probably a good thing.

"Let me send Walter a text."

She took out her phone and asked Walter where he was and if Glen could photograph his family. She finished typing and looked up to see Glen staring at the stage. Mandelli and the blonde were still there. Glen raised his camera and took a picture.

"Why'd you do that?"

"I'm a photographer. And it's an interesting composition."

"Take another one. But zoom in this time."

Guin turned to see Ginny. Where had she come from?

"You're here."

"How very observant of you." She turned to Glen. "Get me some close-ups of the happy couple."

Glen obeyed. But Guin was disgusted.

"Why?" she asked her boss.

"You never know when it could come in handy."

"You planning on blackmailing him?"

Ginny didn't reply.

"Is Joel here with you?" Guin asked her.

"You know Joel hates these kinds of things."

Joel was Ginny's common-law husband, an introvert who hated crowds and preferred reading books and solving crossword puzzles to socializing. Pretty much the opposite of Ginny. But the two of them loved each other and made it work.

"Who's the blonde?" asked Ginny. "She looks familiar."

"I thought the same thing!" said Shelly.

Ginny continued to study the woman on Mandelli's lap.

"Do you think she's from around here?" Guin asked her.

"I doubt it. You see many women on Sanibel who look like that?"

Guin studied the blonde. Ginny had a point.

"Do you think he brought her with him from New York?"

"Maybe. Or he hired her."

Guin thought that quite likely.

"I wonder if Audra knows about her."

Ginny grinned.

"I have half a mind to go get her."

"Where is she?"

"Last I saw, she was just outside the ballroom speaking with some people, probably trying to sell them a house."

Just then, the blonde got up. Mandelli handed her his glass and patted her on the behind. Guin frowned, as did the blonde. Then the blonde made her way off the stage.

"So, did Glen tell you?" said Ginny, turning to Guin.

"Tell me what?"

"About Paris."

"He did."

"You don't seem excited."

"You know how I feel about Valentine's Day."

"I know, but I'm sure a week in Paris with Glen will change your mind."

Guin was about to say something sarcastic when she heard someone shout "Watch out!" A second later, they heard a crash. A woman screamed. They turned toward the stage, where the crash had come from, and saw Anthony Mandelli lying face down, a large spotlight next to him.

"Someone call nine-one-one!" a man shouted.

Guin looked around the room. People were acting as if a gun had gone off, hurrying to leave the ballroom, though many lingered, gazing up at the stage.

There was a commotion by the door. It burst open. It was Audra. She hurried to the stage, shoving people aside and shouting for someone to get a doctor.

"I'm a doctor," said a man who looked to be in his late sixties.

Audra studied him.

"What kind of doctor?"

"A radiologist."

Audra frowned.

"I assume you can tell if he's okay or not?"

"I think I can manage it," said the radiologist, not the least cowed by Audra.

He climbed the short flight of stairs to the stage and knelt next to Mandelli's prostrate form.

"You think he's dead?" Ginny asked Guin.

"He doesn't appear to be moving. Though it's hard to tell from here."

"Come on," said Ginny, taking Guin's hand.

"Where are we going?"

"To get a closer look."

Guin didn't want to go, but she had no choice. Ginny stopped near the stage where a small crowd had gathered.

Guin turned to the man next to her.

"Did you see what happened?"

"One of the spotlights fell," he replied.

"I meant, did you actually see the spotlight fall?"

"No. I was talking to my wife."

Guin wanted to ask if anyone had seen the spotlight fall. Then she spied Glen. Maybe he had seen it. She went over to him.

"Did you see what happened?"

"No, I was photographing the train."

Guin frowned.

"Someone must have seen what happened." And where was the blonde? Guin scanned the room, but she didn't see her. She looked back up at the stage. Mandelli still hadn't moved. "Do you think he's dead?" she asked Glen.

"I don't know. Though if he was, I don't think the doctor would still be examining him."

He had a point.

The doors to the ballroom flew open and two EMTs came rushing in. Guin watched as they made their way to the stage and spoke with the doctor and Audra.

"Where are the police?" Guin asked no one in particular.

"They're probably on their way," Ginny replied. Guin hadn't realized she was just behind her.

"I haven't worked with Detective Brown. What do you know about her? And how does she feel about reporters?" Detective O'Loughlin had disliked discussing cases with the media, even or especially with Guin.

"She's not coming."

Guin turned to her boss.

"What do you mean she's not coming? They're not sending a detective?"

"Detective Brown is on leave."

"On leave? Did she do something?" Guin hadn't heard anything.

"No, she's taken a leave of absence to be with her father. He's not well."

"What's the matter with him?"

"Cancer."

"Oh," said Guin. "I hope he's okay."

"Pretty sure it's terminal."

Guin didn't know what to say.

"How long will she be gone?"

"I don't know. I suppose until her father dies or goes into remission."

"So the island doesn't have a detective?"

"The chief was looking to get someone to cover for her."

Guin was about to ask Ginny another question when the doors to the ballroom flew open again. Guin stared as Detective O'Loughlin entered, accompanied by Officers Pettit and Rodriguez. What was the detective doing here? He was supposed to be in Boston.

She turned to Ginny.

"What's he doing here?"

Ginny didn't answer. She was too busy watching the detective and the two uniformed officers make their way onto the stage.

Guin grabbed her boss's arm.

"Answer me, Ginny." Ginny turned to face her. "Did you know Detective O'Loughlin was back on Sanibel?"

Ginny looked down at Guin's hand on her arm then back up at Guin's face. Guin immediately took her hand off her boss.

"I did not know."

"Don't lie to me, Ginny."

"I'm telling you the truth. I assumed they'd pull someone from Lee County, not Massachusetts."

"Which proves what happens when you assume," Guin mumbled.

They watched as the detective spoke with the EMTs. When he was done, he turned and addressed the crowd.

"Ladies and gentlemen, if I could have your attention." Everyone in the room quieted. "We'd like to speak to everyone here." There were groans from the audience. "So please don't leave the room without talking to me or one of my officers first."

"What about the people who were here and left already?" someone shouted.

"We've notified management. No one's to leave the hotel without speaking with me or Officers Pettit or Rodriguez."

Guin heard lots of grumbling.

"Please," said Detective O'Loughlin. "We know it's late." Well, late for Sanibel. "If you'd form two lines, we'll get your information and you can leave."

There were more groans and grumbling as everyone in the ballroom formed two lines. Fortunately, there weren't that many people. But who knew how many people had left. Would the detective and his crew be interviewing everyone who attended the lighting ceremony?

"You okay?" Ginny asked Guin.

"Perfectly fine," Guin replied. Though she was not

perfectly fine. She was shocked to see the detective. And angry. How could he show up on Sanibel without letting her know? She turned to Ginny. "I should go speak to him, find out what's up."

Ginny put a hand on Guin's arm.

"You sure?"

"You don't want me to write about this for the paper?"

"I can always get Craig."

"Craig's not here, and I am."

Craig was Craig Jeffers, an award-winning crime reporter from Chicago who had retired to Sanibel with his wife Betty. He was an avid fisherman who Ginny had coaxed out of retirement to become the paper's fishing reporter. Then she had cajoled him into covering crime for the paper. Not that there was a lot of crime on Sanibel or Captiva. Mostly people getting ticketed for going over the 35 mph speed limit. Though there was the occasional burglary and murder.

Ginny studied her.

"If you're sure."

"I am."

Ginny smiled.

"Then go get him, Tiger."

Guin put her shoulders back and was heading to the stage when Glen intercepted her.

"What?" she said, looking up at him.

"Are you okay?"

"Perfectly fine. Now if you'll excuse me, I have a job to do."

"Did you know he was back?"

"No. Now I really should get up there."

Glen looked like he was about to say something but instead gestured for her to go.

"Thank you," she said. Then she headed to the stage.

CHAPTER 5

Guin tried to go up on the stage, but Officer Rodriguez told her the stage was off-limits, so she waited below. The EMTs had placed Mandelli on a gurney and were now slowly lowering it to the ground. Mandelli didn't move, and his eyes were closed. Was he unconscious? Probably. If that spotlight had hit him on the head, it was a wonder he was alive.

Detective O'Loughlin was saying something to Officer Pettit. Pettit nodded and left the stage. Then the detective saw her. Guin wondered if he would come over or ignore her. She studied him. He seemed a bit thinner and paler. Well, living up north and taking care of a baby could do that. Not that Guin knew what it was like to take care of a baby, not having had one of her own. Though she had babysat several when she was younger.

They stared at each other for several more seconds, then the detective moved toward her. Guin braced herself.

"Ms. Jones."

"Detective O'Loughlin, what a surprise to see you here on Sanibel. Retirement not agree with you?"

It came out snarkier than Guin had intended.

"Just helping out the chief while Detective Brown is on leave." He examined her. "You look good."

"Thank you. Wish I could say the same about you. Little Frankie wearing you out?"

Frankie was the detective's grandson.

"I see you haven't lost that sharp tongue of yours."

"Yes, well," she said. She hadn't meant to snipe at him. She tamped down her anger and told herself to get over it. She had a job to do. "Could I get a quote from you?"

"I have nothing to say."

"Really? The new owner of the hotel is nearly killed by a spotlight, and you have nothing to say?"

The detective didn't reply.

"What about his status? I assume he's still alive or else the EMTs would have draped a sheet over him or something."

Still nothing.

"Oh, come on! Surely, you can tell me if he was alive when they wheeled him out of here."

"Fine. He was alive when the EMTs took him, though not conscious."

"Will he live?"

"Not for me to say. I'm not a doctor."

"What did the doctor and the EMTs say?"

"You'll have to ask them."

Guin frowned.

"What about the light?"

"What about it?"

Guin groaned inwardly. This was like old times. Clearly, spending time with an infant hadn't made him easier to deal with.

"Did it fall on its own or did someone deliberately drop it?"

"No comment."

"No comment? You don't seriously think that light just happened to fall, do you?"

The detective was about to say something, but Guin interrupted.

"Never mind. I know what you're going to say: *you're investigating.*" It's what he always said.

The detective's lips curled into the approximation of a smile.

Guin looked up at the rigging.

"There must be a ladder or something to get up there."

The detective didn't say anything.

Guin returned her gaze to him.

"So, you going to ask everyone if they saw anything?"

"That's the plan." He looked at her. "You see anything?"

"And if I did?"

"Look, I get that you're angry with me—"

"I'm not angry," Guin said, cutting him off. Though she was angry.

"But this isn't the time or the place," said the detective. "A man's been seriously injured. And I have a job to do."

"I have a job to do too," said Guin.

They eyed each other. Then the detective ran a hand over his face.

"I've been meaning to talk to you."

"So talk."

"Not now."

"When?"

"Soon. I'll text you." Guin didn't believe him but didn't say anything. "However, right now, I need you to answer my question. Did you see anything?"

Guin sighed.

"No. I was talking to Ginny when it happened. I heard someone shout, 'Watch out!' Then we heard a crash, and there was Mandelli, sprawled on the stage."

"Did you happen to see anyone else on or near the stage?"

"No. But he had a rather attractive blonde in his lap just before."

"Female?"

Guin nodded.

"Can you describe her?"

Guin did.

"And you say she was sitting in his lap until a few minutes before the light fell?"

"That's right."

"Did you see where she went?"

"No. I think she had gone to get him another drink. But I didn't see her afterwards."

The detective was scribbling in his little notebook.

"You see anyone else?"

"Not on the stage. Though I saw Patrick Finney earlier. He was here in the ballroom. And he looked none too pleased to see Mandelli."

"Finney the real estate guy?"

"That's the one."

"You see anything else?"

Guin thought.

"Audra Linwood came rushing in right after the accident. It was almost as though she knew something had happened."

The detective continued to take notes. Then he looked back at Guin.

"But you didn't see anyone other than the blonde up on the stage with him before the accident?"

"No. But I supposed someone could have been standing in the wings, out of sight."

The detective looked like he was going to ask her another question, but Officer Pettit had come over. He whispered something in the detective's ear. The detective nodded.

"I need to go."

"Of course."

He left her and followed Officer Pettit.

"How did it go?"

Guin hadn't seen Ginny approach.

"I was more helpful to him than he was to me." Typical.

Ginny was about to say something when they heard Detective O'Loughlin calling for everyone's attention. He reminded them that they were not to leave the premises without speaking to him or one of his officers first. Guin wondered if that reminder was a result of Officer Pettit's whisper. She guessed he had told the detective that people had been trying to sneak out.

Guin looked over at the detective and saw a man and a woman approach him. She had seen them earlier. Had they seen the light fall? She wanted to eavesdrop, but the detective would notice her. She would wait and go up to them after.

She was so busy watching them she didn't see Glen come over and jumped when he laid a hand on her shoulder.

"Sorry, I didn't mean to scare you."

Guin placed her hand over her heart and controlled her breathing.

"It's okay. What's up?"

Before he could answer, Ginny interrupted.

"You get pictures of the scene?"

He nodded.

"Good."

"The police didn't stop you?" asked Guin.

"I don't think they noticed."

"You get backstage?" asked Ginny.

Glen nodded again. And Ginny smiled.

"Good man."

"I also got pictures of the EMTs taking Mandelli away."

"Better hide your camera. We don't want the police to confiscate it."

"I can download the photos."

"But you don't have your computer," said Guin.

"This camera has Wi-Fi, so I can download the images to my phone."

"Here comes O'Loughlin," said Ginny. "Go download those photos. We'll distract him."

Glen nodded and left.

"Where's he going?" asked the detective.

"To the little boys' room," said Ginny. "He'll be right back."

The detective frowned.

"I have to admit, I'm surprised to see you here, detective. I thought you were nestled in the bosom of your family up north."

Guin thought that Ginny was laying it on a bit thick, but she didn't say anything.

"I take it you're here to help out while Detective Brown is away? Though I'm curious to know why they didn't just borrow someone from Lee County."

The detective was about to answer when Officer Rodriguez came over and pulled him away.

"I wonder what that's about?" said Guin as they watched the detective and Officer Rodriguez converse.

"Only one way to find out," said Ginny.

"You want me to eavesdrop?"

Ginny gave her a look that said, "Yes! Go eavesdrop!"

"Okay, I'm going."

She had nearly reached the detective when he turned and looked at her. Guin stopped.

"What's happened? Is everything all right?"

"No. Mandelli's dead."

"What?" said Guin. "But… you said he was alive."

"He was when he left here. He died just before they got to the hospital."

"What happened?"

The detective looked around.

"Where's the photographer? He's taking an awfully long time."

"His name is Glen, and he'll be back any minute."

Officer Rodriguez stood near the detective as if awaiting orders.

"Rodriguez, go look for him if he's not back here in the next two minutes." Officer Rodriguez nodded. Then the detective turned his attention to Guin.

"If you see him first, tell him to come find me."

"Of course," said Guin.

The detective and Officer Rodriguez moved away.

"What was that about?" It was Ginny.

"Mandelli's dead."

"Dead?"

"Died en route to the hospital."

"What happened?"

"The detective didn't say."

They watched as O'Loughlin spoke with a man, another guest who had been in the ballroom at the time of the accident. Had he seen something? Then Guin spied Glen coming towards them.

"You able to download those pictures?" Ginny asked him.

Glen nodded.

"Good."

"Detective O'Loughlin wants to speak with you," Guin told him.

"Okay," he said.

"Be careful." Glen gave her a questioning look. "Mandelli died on the way to the hospital."

"Ah."

Officer Rodriguez had spied them and was heading their way.

"Go talk to the detective," said Guin. "I'll wait for you."

"You don't have to."

She smiled.

"So I should walk home?"

"Right. I forgot. Though… Ginny, could you drive Guin home?"

"I'm fine waiting for you," said Guin.

"Well, I'm going," said Ginny.

"You going to speak with the detective?"

"If he wants to speak with me, he knows how to find me."

She said goodnight and made her way to the exit. No one stopped her.

"Mr. Anderson." It was Officer Rodriguez.

"I was just going to speak with Detective O'Loughlin," Glen informed her.

"I'm going to mill about," said Guin. "I'll meet you by the bar."

"Sounds good," said Glen. Then he followed Officer Rodriguez.

Guin looked for the couple who had spoken with the detective, but she couldn't find them. They must have left. She spoke with several other people, but none of them had seen the light fall or anyone lurking around the stage. She was heading to the bar when she ran into Shelly. She had forgotten all about her.

"You're still here," she said.

"I couldn't leave when I saw the detective was back! Are you okay?"

"I'm fine. Where were you?"

"I went to the little girls' room when you were chatting with Ginny. The next thing I knew the place was chaos, and they wouldn't let me back into the ballroom or leave. Then I saw the detective. Did you know he was back?"

"I had no idea."

"Huh. I wonder what he's doing here."

"Covering for Detective Brown."

"They couldn't find someone closer?"

"Apparently not."

"Does Glen know he's back?"

"He does."

"And he's okay with it?"

"I don't know. We haven't had a chance to discuss it. Not that it matters or makes any difference. It's over between me and the detective, Shell."

Shelly looked like she didn't believe her.

"Really."

"If you say so."

"I do."

"So what happened in there?"

"I'm not sure. All I know is a spotlight came loose and knocked Mandelli out of that chair. And now he's dead."

"Wow, talk about karma."

"Karma?"

"Mandelli always wanted the spotlight on him, and he finally got it."

Guin shook her head.

"What about the blonde?" asked Shelly. "Was she injured too?"

"No, she had gotten up just before the spotlight fell."

"Huh."

"You wouldn't happen to have seen her around, would you?"

"No. Though I just know I've seen her somewhere. It's driving me crazy. I never forget a face."

"Where's Steve?"

"Last I saw him, he was talking to Jimbo and Sally."

"Well, I'm going to go find Glen. We said we'd meet up at the bar."

"I'll go with you."

"Shouldn't you go find Steve?"

"He's probably at the bar."

They were just outside the bar when Shelly stopped and grabbed Guin's arm.

"What?" said Guin.

"Over there," Shelly pointed.

Guin saw where Shelly was pointing. It was the blonde all right. And Glen was next to her.

What were they doing together?

But before they got any further, Steve stopped them.

"There you are!" he said.

"I told you I was going to look for Guin," said Shelly.

"Looks like you found her. Can we go now?"

Shelly saw Guin looking at the blonde and Glen.

"You go," she said.

"But how will you get home?"

"I'll hitch a ride with Guin."

"But…" Shelly silenced him with a look. "Fine," he said. "Just don't get into any trouble."

"I wouldn't dream of it."

He looked unsure but left.

"Okay, now let's go find out who our mystery blonde is," said Shelly.

CHAPTER 6

They were now just a couple of feet away from Glen and the blonde, who were seated next to each other.

"Do you think her boobs are real?" asked Shelly. "They look too perfect to be real."

Guin gave her friend a dirty look. Then she turned to Glen and the blonde and cleared her throat.

"Oh, hey!" Glen said, smiling up at her.

"Hey, yourself," said Guin. "Who's your friend?"

Glen looked confused for a second. Then he smiled.

"This is Honey Lamb."

"Honey Lamb?" *That couldn't be her real name*, thought Guin.

"And you are?" said Honey, looking up at Guin.

"I'm Guin, Glen's partner."

The two women eyed each other.

"And I'm Shelly!" said Shelly. "Their friend."

"And how did you two happen to find each other?" Guin asked Glen and Honey, ignoring Shelly.

"We just ran into each other," said Glen.

"I was rather upset, and Glen offered to buy me a drink," Honey explained.

"How gallant of you," Guin said to him.

"Is your name really Honey?" asked Shelly.

Honey didn't seem bothered by the question.

"Technically, it's Henrietta. But no one calls me that.

And before you ask, I got the nickname when I was a baby. My daddy used to say I was sweet as honey, and my brother thought Honey was my name. Pretty soon, everyone started calling me that."

"Cute," said Shelly. "Guin's name's really Guinivere."

"Guinivere?" said Honey.

"My mother was into Arthurian legends," Guin explained.

Honey looked confused.

"You know, King Arthur and the Knights of the Round Table?"

"Never heard of them."

Figured.

"And how do you two know each other?" asked Honey, looking from Guin to Glen.

Had she not heard Guin tell her they were partners?

"We work together," said Glen.

"Oh, is she your assistant?"

Glen smiled.

"No, we both work for the local paper. She's a reporter, and I'm a photographer. We're here covering the lighting ceremony."

"I just love photographers," purred Honey.

Guin frowned.

"And I make jewelry!" Shelly blurted. "You can buy it on Etsy."

Honey gave her a condescending smile.

"And what do you do?" Guin asked Honey.

"I work for Mr. Mandelli."

Guin wondered if Honey knew that Mandelli had died. She guessed not.

"Doing what?"

"I guess you could say I'm his special assistant."

"Special assistant?" Immediately, she had unkind thoughts but squelched them. "And what does a special assistant do?"

"Oh, this and that."

"And how long have you been working for Mr. Mandelli?"

"A few months. He was teaching me about the business."

More like giving her the business, Guin thought.

"Oh? So you're interested in real estate?"

"Sure. Who wouldn't be?"

Well, Guin for one. But she didn't say anything.

"Have you spoken with Detective O'Loughlin? I know he was looking for you."

"We spoke."

"What did the two of you talk about?"

"I don't think that's any of your business."

"Actually, it is. I'm covering the story for the paper."

"I thought you were here for the holiday lighting."

"I'm a general assignment reporter. I cover whatever is considered newsworthy here on the island."

"I see," said Honey, appraising her. "Well then. He wanted to know where I was when the accident occurred and what my relationship was to Tony."

"And what did you tell him?"

"I told him I had gone to the ladies' room and that I was Tony's special assistant."

Guin found it interesting that Honey referred to Mandelli as Tony.

"Did he ask you anything else?"

"He asked me if Tony had any enemies, anyone who disliked him, especially here on the island." She gave Guin a look as she said the last part. Guin ignored it.

"And what did you tell him?"

"I told him I'd only been working for Tony for a few months, but I didn't doubt he had enemies. Men like Tony usually did."

"Did you give him any names?"

Honey looked at her. Had Mandelli told Honey about Guin? Not that there was much to tell.

"I said I'd get back to him."

"Were you sleeping with him?"

"Excuse me?"

"Guin!" It was Glen.

"It's okay," said Honey, laying a hand on Glen's arm. She looked back at Guin.

"No, I was not sleeping with him."

"Just sitting in his lap."

"That was just Tony having some fun. He wanted to play Santa."

"And you were fine with him pawing you?"

Honey sighed.

"Look, I know what you're thinking, but our relationship was strictly professional." Guin raised her eyebrows. "He was drunk, and I didn't want to cause a scene."

"So you let him have his way with you."

"He's harmless."

Guin disagreed but didn't say anything.

"And you say you were in the ladies' room when the light fell?"

"That's right."

"Can anyone vouch for that?"

Honey gave her a look, as did Glen. Was he defending her? She turned back to Honey.

"Did you happen to see anyone backstage when you were on Mr. Mandelli's… on the stage?" She had been about to say *lap* but stopped herself.

"Just the maintenance guy."

"Maintenance guy? How did you know it was someone from Maintenance?"

Honey shrugged.

"Who else would be backstage? And he didn't look like a guest."

"What did he look like?"

"I can't really say. It was dark back there. But if I had to describe him, I'd say he was medium height with dark hair."

That could describe nearly anyone.

Honey drained the last of her drink and got up.

"This has been fun, but I should get going."

"Where are you going?" asked Guin.

"To my room."

"Are you staying at the hotel?"

Honey looked at her as though Guin had asked a stupid question.

"Tony booked the Presidential Suite."

"The Presidential Suite? You were staying there together?"

"It has two bedrooms. And now if you'd excuse me?" She turned to Glen. "Thanks for the drink."

She had only taken a couple of steps when Audra Linwood stormed into the bar.

"You!" she said, pointing a finger at Honey. "Where do you think you're going?"

"Hello, Audra."

"Don't *Hello, Audra* me!" said Audra. "And you're not going anywhere until you answer a few questions."

"I'm rather tired, Audra. Can it wait? I was just heading to my room."

"*Your* room? Don't you mean Tony's room?"

Honey didn't respond. But Audra wasn't done.

"I know all about you, Missy."

"I sincerely doubt that," said Honey.

"Well, Tony's not here. And I want you gone."

"Sorry to disappoint you, but Detective O'Loughlin asked me to stay."

"Find somewhere else."

"Tony reserved the suite for a week."

"We'll see about that."

"I'm going," said Honey.

"We should go too," Glen said to Guin. He got up and went over to where Audra and Honey were standing.

"Ladies," he said, acknowledging the two women. They turned to look at him. "It's been a long evening, and I think we could all do with some rest."

Guin knew what Glen was doing, diffusing the situation. He was good at that.

"I am pretty tired," said Shelly, letting out a loud (possibly fake) yawn.

Everyone turned and looked at her.

"What? It's been a long day."

Guin smiled at her friend.

"Fine," said Audra. "But we're not done," she said to Honey.

CHAPTER 7

"I don't think Audra likes Honey very much," said Shelly as they stepped outside.

"Ya think?" said Guin sarcastically.

"Do you think she's jealous?"

"Quite possibly. Where'd you park?" Guin asked Glen.

"Over there," he said, pointing to the other side of the lot.

"Do you mind giving me a lift?" Shelly asked him.

"What happened to Steve?"

"He left."

"You don't mind dropping Shelly off, do you?" Guin asked him.

"Not at all."

Glen said he'd go get the car. As they waited for him, Guin saw Audra emerge from the hotel. She was talking on her phone. Guin wondered who she was talking to so late. Audra handed her ticket to the valet, continuing to talk into her phone.

"I'll be right back," Guin said to Shelly.

"You're not going over there."

"I am."

"But why?"

"I want to ask her about Mandelli."

"Can't it wait?"

"I'll just be a minute."

Audra was putting her phone in her bag when she saw Guin approach.

"What do you want?" she snapped.

"I just had a few questions."

"About?"

"Anthony Mandelli."

"I'm rather tired, Ms. Jones."

"This'll only take a minute."

"Call my office Monday and schedule an appointment."

"Fine," said Guin, knowing she wouldn't get anything out of the real estate agent that evening.

She had turned to go when Audra called out to her.

"Tony told me about the two of you, you know."

Guin stopped and turned back around.

"Excuse me?"

"He told me how you flirted with him and then got mad when he rejected you."

Guin knew she was staring but couldn't help it. What kind of story had Mandelli told Audra? While it was true Guin may have flirted with him to get information for a story she was working on. Something she had immediately regretted. She had had zero interest in the man. And when she had told him that he had accosted her. Indeed, if the detective hadn't miraculously appeared when he had, it was quite likely Mandelli would have dragged her away and raped her.

"What he told you was a lie," Guin calmly told her.

Audra didn't look convinced.

"Look, I just want to know how the Mandelli Group came to purchase the San Ybel. No one even knew the hotel was for sale."

"I knew."

"How?"

The valet pulled up in Audra's car.

"I'm afraid that's confidential."

"Did you broker the deal?"

Audra looked at her.

"You think I'd let someone else handle the sale?" She made to go to her car, but Guin stopped her.

"Please. Our readers would love to know how one of Sanibel's preeminent hotels came to be sold."

Guin knew she was laying it on a bit thick, but she hoped to appeal to Audra's ego.

Audra regarded Guin.

"Call my office Monday."

"I'll do that. By the way, where were you when the light fell?"

"Speaking with some VIPs outside the ballroom. Now I really must be going. Good night, Ms. Jones."

Guin watched as Audra drove away.

"Guin!" It was Shelly. She was squeezed into the backseat of Glen's BMW. "We've been waiting for you!"

"Sorry," Guin said as she got in the car.

"How did it go with Audra?"

"She told me to arrange an appointment."

They drove out of the San Ybel and onto Middle Gulf Drive.

"So who do you think did it?" asked Shelly.

"You don't think it was an accident?" said Glen.

"Please," said Shelly. She turned to Guin. "Do you think Audra could have done it?"

"Why would she want to kill him?" asked Guin.

"Hello? You saw him and Honey up on that stage. If I saw some hot blonde giving Steve a lap dance in public, I'd sure as heck want to kill him. Her too. Wait!" Glen hit the brake. "Sorry. Keep driving. I just had another thought. What if Audra had intended for the light to fall on Honey?"

"But Audra wasn't in the ballroom. She was speaking with some VIPs."

"Is that what she told you?"

"Yes. And I saw her rush in."

"Well, she could have paid someone to loosen the light."

"Paid someone?"

"Sure, why not? It happens all the time in movies."

Guin didn't know what to say. Shelly turned to Glen.

"So, what do you think of Detective O'Loughlin being back?"

"Shelly," warned Guin.

"I wonder why he's here," Shelly continued.

"Don't look at me," said Guin. "I haven't heard from the man in months. Though…"

"Yes?"

"I could ask Craig. I bet he'll know."

"Or you could ask the detective."

No one spoke for several seconds.

"You really didn't know he was back?" Glen asked Guin.

"I really didn't know."

They pulled up in front of Shelly's house. Guin got out and folded down the seat so Shelly could get out.

"Thanks for the lift," said Shelly. She got out and stopped. "Hey, I know it's short notice but are you guys free tomorrow evening? Steve just got a shipment of brats and is planning on grilling them up. We'd love for you to join us."

Steve was from Wisconsin and had missed the bratwursts he grew up eating so much that he had the butcher from his hometown send him a care package every fall and winter. Then he'd share the sausages with friends.

"I'm free," said Glen. He looked over at Guin.

"I don't think I'm doing anything, but let me check." Guin wasn't a big fan of sausage, but she didn't mind Steve's brats.

"I'll take that as a yes," said Shelly. "See you two tomorrow!"

"Wait," said Glen. "What time?"

"The usual, six o'clock. But you're welcome to come earlier."

Guin wondered if Steve would invite the detective. The two were fishing buddies. Had Steve known the detective was back in town? Though if he had, wouldn't he have said something?

"Goodnight, Glenivere!" Shelly called from the door.

Guin frowned.

"I should have never told her about that."

Glen smiled.

"I don't know. I kind of like it. It has a certain ring to it."

Guin didn't say anything.

They headed west and Guin began to nod off.

"You tired?"

"It's been a long day."

"Well, we'll be back at your place soon."

Ten minutes later, they arrived. Guin had fallen asleep. Glen nudged her.

"Hm?" she said.

"We're home."

Guin got out and headed to the front door. Glen followed her.

"It's late," she told him.

"Does that mean you don't want me to come in?"

"Do you mind?"

Glen looked like he did but said that he didn't.

"Thanks. I just really need to get some sleep."

Truth be told, she was thinking about the detective and wanted to be alone with her thoughts.

"So, shall I pick you up at five-thirty tomorrow?"

Guin looked confused.

"For the barbecue… at Shelly and Steve's?"

"Right. Sorry. I can just meet you there."

"It's no big deal."

"Fine, but make it five-forty-five."

"You got it." He leaned down and kissed her on the forehead. "Good night," he said. Then he headed to his car.

"Wait," said Guin, running after him.

He stopped and waited. Guin rose on her toes and kissed him. He immediately pulled her close.

"You sure you don't want me to stay?" he whispered in her ear several minutes later.

Guin hesitated.

"You better not."

"Better why?"

"I need sleep."

"I could sleep next to you."

Guin smiled.

"I doubt either of us would get much sleep if you were lying next to me."

Glen grinned.

"Probably not."

"You should go."

"You sure?"

Guin nodded.

"Okay, see you tomorrow then."

He gave Guin another kiss. Then he got in his car.

CHAPTER 8

Guin woke up a little before seven. Sunlight was filtering into her room, and Fauna was asleep at the foot of her bed. Guin got up and headed to the bathroom. Then she went to the kitchen to make herself coffee.

As the coffee was steeping in her French press, she thought about her father. She had been thinking about him a lot recently. She always did around Christmastime. She remembered him taking all of them to Rockefeller Center to see the tree and go skating. Then they would check out the windows along Fifth Avenue.

She also remembered how he used to make coffee for himself and her mother every morning. Guin would ask if she could have some. She loved how it smelled. But her father said she couldn't have any until she had finished growing, saying it would stunt her growth. Guin hadn't believed him and would get Lance to sneak her a cup. He was older than Guin and a prize sneak. But maybe there had been some truth to what her father said as Guin had topped out at five-foot-four and her brother wasn't much taller.

Thinking about her father made her think of the detective for some reason. He too would make a fresh pot of coffee in the morning, making it strong the way she liked it whenever she stayed over. That wasn't the only thing both men shared. They were both men of few words who didn't like to discuss their feelings.

Guin had thought her father cold when she was young. Then they had started going to baseball games together, and she had seen another side of him.

Her father had played baseball in his youth and had dreamed of playing professionally. But he wasn't good enough. Still, he had loved the game. And when Lance was old enough, he would offer to take him to games. But Lance hated baseball and refused to go with his father. Guin, sensing an opportunity, told her father she would go. So he took her instead.

Soon it became a regular thing. They would take the subway to Shea Stadium; get hot dogs, fries, and sodas; and sit in the stands and cheer. In between innings, her father would ask Guin things. And she would ask him things. And in this way, father and daughter got to know one another.

He'd been dead for over twenty years now, but she still thought about him whenever she watched a baseball game. And at Christmastime. And sometimes when she made coffee. Speaking of which, she poured her coffee into a mug and took a sip. She took another sip and looked out the window. A flock of ibis was nibbling the grass.

She thought about the detective. Had she been attracted to him because he reminded her of her father? Though that was absurd. True, the detective was much older than she was. But he looked nothing like her father. However, temperamentally, they were quite similar. Guin frowned. Then she remembered, today was the farmers' market. And it was best to get there early. She poured the rest of her coffee into a to-go cup and quickly got dressed.

The market was busy. Not a surprise. The holiday season was a busy time on Sanibel. Good thing Guin had gotten there early. She spied the Jean-Luc's Bakery booth and made a beeline for it. Jo and Jake were there as usual and smiled as Guin approached.

"You save me a *pain au chocolat*?" she asked them. Jean-Luc's breakfast pastries were known to go fast.

"Of course!" said Jake. "Anything else?"

Guin looked over the assortment of pastries, quiches, and baguettes, all of which looked delicious.

"Throw in an almond croissant and a baguette."

Then she noticed a tray full of colorful French macarons.

"Are those new?" she asked.

Jake nodded.

"Jo made them."

Guin looked at the young woman.

"I'm impressed! I didn't know you could make macarons."

"I'm still learning," said Jo.

"Taste one," said Jake. "What flavor would you like?"

Guin eyed the macarons.

"Is that pistachio?" she said, pointing to a green one.

"It is!"

"I'll have one of those."

He took a pistachio macaron out of the tray and handed it to her. Guin took a bite.

"Wow!" she said. "This is really good."

Jake beamed.

"Told you. Jean-Luc says they're even better than his."

"He's just being kind," said Jo.

"He wouldn't say something like that unless he meant it," said Jake. He leaned forward and spoke confidentially to Guin. "I think he's grooming her to take over the business."

Jo shot Jake a disapproving look.

"Oh?" said Guin. "Is he thinking about retiring?" Though Jean-Luc couldn't be more than fifty.

"He's been going to Montreal a lot," said Jake.

"To see Angelique? Is he thinking about moving there?"

Angelique was an old flame who lived in Montreal with her two children. Though she spent part of the winter on Captiva, where her parents had a place.

"Don't go spreading rumors," Jo admonished Jake. She turned to Guin. "He'll be back any day. And he's not retiring anytime soon."

Well, that was a relief.

Guin looked over at the macarons again.

"You know what? I'll take a box of macarons too." She'd bring them to the barbecue, to share with Shelly and Steve.

"What size?" asked Jo.

"One that'll fit a dozen, three of each kind."

Jo assembled a box and began placing the macarons inside. When she was done, Guin paid for everything. Then she went to explore the rest of the market.

Fauna was waiting for Guin by the door when she got home.

"What?" said Guin.

She could have sworn Fauna was glaring at her.

"Don't look at me like that."

Fauna meowed.

"Sorry, but I don't speak cat."

She headed to the kitchen, Fauna following her. She placed the *pain au chocolat* and the almond croissant on a plate. She was tempted to eat both of them, but she'd probably go into sugar shock if she did. But which one to eat now and which one to save? After hemming and hawing for over a minute, she decided to cut them in half and have one half of each now and the other halves tomorrow.

She took a bite of the *pain au chocolat* first. So good. Then she took a bite of the almond croissant. Also delicious. She sighed with pleasure. When she was done, she washed her plate.

"Time to get to work," she said. She poured herself a glass of water and took it to her office.

Guin had been working on her piece about the lighting ceremony when her phone started buzzing. She had forgotten to silence it. She tried to ignore it, but it continued to buzz. Exasperated, she picked it up to see who was calling or messaging her. It was Shelly. Of course. Guin opened the message. Shelly wanted to know if Guin had seen the new edition of Shellapalooza.

Guin was almost afraid to look.

She typed in the URL and frowned when she saw the headline: "New Owner of San Ybel Resort & Spa Murdered at Holiday Lighting as Dozens Watch!" *Uh-oh*, thought Guin. Ginny must be fit to be tied.

Guin tried to remember if she had seen Suzy Seashell— real name Susan Hastings—at the holiday lighting ceremony. She didn't recall seeing her, but it was likely Susan and her husband Karl had been there. After all, it was a big event. Had they been in the ballroom when the spotlight had fallen on Mandelli? Again, Guin didn't remember seeing them there. But she could have missed them. Or Susan could have learned what happened from someone who had been there.

Guin began to read.

The article quoted the head of special events for the hotel, Hermione Potter, saying she had no idea how the spotlight had come loose, that it was an accident. Yet "Suzy" claimed it was no accident, that someone had deliberately set out to hurt the new owner of the San Ybel and that the police would be shining the light of justice on the case to reveal the culprit.

Guin cringed at the purple prose. Then she mentally kicked herself. Why hadn't she sought out Hermione? After all, they were friends, or friendly. Well, she would call her first thing Monday.

Suzy also mentioned Honey in the article, referring to her as Mandelli's *very special assistant*. And she made Audra sound like a hero when all she did was ask if there was a doctor in the house. Was that because Audra was an advertiser?

Guin's phone was buzzing again. It was Shelly. Instead of texting her back, Guin called her.

"Did you read the article?" Shelly asked her.

"I just did."

"And?"

"It's very Suzy."

"Meaning?"

"Meaning it's full of gossip and innuendo."

"Well, gossip and innuendo are Suzy's stock-in-trade."

"True. Did you happen to see her and Karl there?"

"I did, briefly."

"Where did you see them?"

"Outside."

"Outside the hotel or outside the ballroom?"

"Outside the hotel. Why?"

"She made it sound as though she was there in the ballroom."

"Maybe she was."

"Well, if she was, I didn't see her."

"Though she could have had someone on the inside feed her the information," said Shelly.

"True."

"Did you see what she wrote about Honey?"

"I did."

"Do you think she could have done it?"

"But why would she want to kill Mandelli? Wait, check that."

"I wonder if Suzy knows who did it."

Guin frowned. Ginny would be furious if Suzy disclosed the killer—no way it had been an accident—before the paper did.

"If she does, she should tell the police before publishing it on her blog."

"And risk getting scooped by you and Ginny?"

"Better that than having the killer target her next." Shelly didn't say anything. "Well, thanks for letting me know about Suzy's latest."

"You should really read Shellapalooza."

"I'm a bit busy. Speaking of which, I should get back to work."

"Okay," said Shelly. "See you later."

They ended the call and Guin's phone began to buzz again. She really needed to remember to turn off the ringer. She was going to ignore it but saw that it was Ginny, so she picked up.

"Hey, Ginny. What's up?"

"Did you see what that woman published on Shellapalooza this morning?! She has no journalistic integrity! None. And how did she get those quotes?"

"I have no idea."

"Did you speak with Hermione Potter?"

"Not yet."

"What are you waiting for?"

"It's Sunday."

"So? I doubt she has the day off after what happened."

She had a point.

"I'll text her as soon we're done."

"Good. Do that."

"And I was going to reach out to Craig, see if he's heard anything."

"Good idea. Do whatever you need to do. We can't have Shellapalooza scooping us and, God forbid, printing the name of the murderer before we do."

"We don't actually know if Mandelli was murdered."

"You don't honestly think that spotlight just happened to come crashing down on him on its own, do you?"

"No, but…"

"I have to go," said Ginny. "Just find out what happened. Before Suzy Seashell does."

"I'm on it," said Guin. But Ginny had already hung up.

CHAPTER 9

Guin texted Hermione as soon as she got off the phone with Ginny, asking if she had a few minutes to chat. Then she stared at her phone, waiting for a reply. However, the telltale dots failed to appear. Hermione was probably busy. After all, she was in charge of special events for the hotel, and this was peak event season. And one of her events had just gone horribly wrong.

Guin waited a few more minutes then called the San Ybel, asking for Special Events. No one picked up. She waited for voicemail but was informed that the mailbox was full. Not a surprise. She thought about calling Hermione's cell phone, but she had already texted her. She would just have to wait for Hermione to get back to her.

Guin again wished she had sought out Hermione the night before, as Suzy or one of her minions had done. But she couldn't go back in time. She sighed and looked at her phone again. Still no reply from Hermione.

She stared out the window. She thought about calling Craig, but he was probably out fishing. But who else was there to call? Well, there was the detective. But she doubted he'd tell her anything.

She picked up her phone and entered Craig's number. She'd leave him a voicemail if he didn't pick up. She waited as the phone rang. She was preparing to leave a message when he picked up.

"Craig?" she said.

"You sound surprised. Did you butt-dial me?"

"No, I meant to call you. I just thought you'd be out fishing."

"If you thought I was out fishing, why did you call me?"

"I was going to leave a message. I need help with a story. Where are you?"

"I'm out fishing."

"Then why'd you pick up?"

"The fish aren't biting, and I figured you wouldn't be calling me on a Sunday morning unless it was important. So, what's up?"

"You hear about what happened at the San Ybel last night?"

"You mean about your friend Mandelli?"

"He wasn't my friend. What did you hear?"

"That a light fell on him."

"Anything else?"

"He didn't make it."

"You hear anything about the light, whether it was an accident or if someone made it fall?"

There was silence on the line.

"Craig? Are you there?"

"Sorry, we're moving the boat. What were you saying?"

"I asked if your source or sources thought it was an accident or if someone deliberately loosened the light."

"Too early to say."

"You don't really think that light could have come loose and fallen on its own, do you?"

"I'm guessing you don't think it was an accident."

"I do not. Lights don't just fall from the sky. And the timing is suspicious."

There was silence again. Though Guin thought she heard someone talking to Craig.

"Craig?"

"Sorry. Someone was asking me something."

Maybe she should have waited to call him.

"Well, I'm planning on going to the hotel later and taking a look for myself."

"They've probably closed off the ballroom."

Guin frowned.

"Maybe Hermione, the head of Special Events, could sneak me in."

"I'd wait until the police were done. You don't want to be accused of anything."

"What do you mean?"

"I mean you and Mandelli had a history, and you were in the ballroom when the light fell. If I were you, I'd steer clear of the place until the police say it's okay."

"You don't think I had anything to do with it, do you?"

"No, but no point in taking any chances."

Guin frowned. As much as she hated to admit it, Craig had a point. But she still wanted to check out the stage and the rigging.

"Speaking of Mandelli, you hear anything from the medical examiner's office?"

"Just that they've scheduled an autopsy."

"For when?"

"Tomorrow."

"That was fast. But why are they conducting an autopsy?"

"Standard procedure."

"Right."

Guin heard shouting in the background.

"I need to go," said Craig.

"Did someone catch something?"

"Looks that way."

"Just one more thing." Craig waited. "Did you know that O'Loughlin was back?" No answer. "I'll take that as a yes. You know what he's doing here?"

There was more shouting on Craig's end of the line.

"I've gotta go," he said.

"Can you just…"

But the line had gone dead.

Guin sighed and checked her text messages. Still no reply from Hermione. Not that it had been that long. Should she try calling her? Though if she hadn't replied to her text… Guin mulled it over and then called. Hermione's phone rang several times and Guin was preparing to leave a message when Hermione picked up.

"Guin?"

"Hey, Hermione. I'm sorry to bother you on a Sunday, but I was hoping you could spare me a few minutes to talk about last night."

"I'm a bit busy at present," she replied in her clipped British accent, Hermione being English. "Though… are you free for lunch?"

Guin had just eaten half of a *pain au chocolat* and an almond croissant, so she wasn't hungry. But she accepted Hermione's invitation.

"Excellent. Meet me in my office at twelve-thirty and drag me out if I refuse to leave."

"Have you been there all morning?"

"More like all night and all morning."

"You must be exhausted. Can't you go home and take a nap?"

"No rest for the weary, I'm afraid. I've got to go, but I'll see you here at twelve-thirty."

They ended the call and Guin put *Lunch with Hermione* on her calendar. Then she turned off the ringer on her phone and placed it in her desk drawer. She needed to work and didn't want to be interrupted.

At noon, a notification popped up on Guin's computer monitor, informing her that she had a lunch date with

Hermione in thirty minutes. She saved the document she was working on, got up, and stretched. Then she headed to the bathroom to freshen up.

She had gathered her bag and her car keys and was nearly out the door when Fauna came trotting over to her looking upset.

"What?" said Guin, looking down at the cat.

Fauna meowed.

"You don't want me to go?"

Another meow.

"I'll be back soon. I promise."

Fauna frowned. Or so it seemed to Guin. Then she meowed again. Guin sighed.

"I wish you could tell me what it is you wanted."

Fauna let out another loud meow and then trotted to the kitchen. Guin followed her. Fauna's food bowl was empty.

"You need to pace yourself, Fauna."

More meowing.

"Look, I'll give you a little more food but then no more until later."

Fauna watched as Guin went into the cupboard, removed the bag of cat food, and poured a little bit into her bowl. Fauna sniffed the food and meowed.

"Sorry, kitty cat. That's what's on offer. Take it or leave it."

Fauna sniffed again at the food. Then she began to eat. Guin shook her head. Then, before Fauna could complain again, Guin hastily left.

Guin arrived at the San Ybel and was able to find a parking spot. She got out, locked the Mini, and headed inside, pausing to admire the holiday decorations. They weren't lit up during the day, but they were still pretty.

The lobby was busy, full of guests as well as locals who

had come to check out the holiday decorations and have Sunday brunch. Guin made her way to the stairs and went up to the second floor where the executive offices were located. Hermione's door was ajar, but Guin knocked anyway. There was no answer.

"Hermione?" she said, poking her head inside. But Hermione wasn't there. Guin checked her phone. It was just past twelve-thirty. She checked her messages. Nothing from Hermione. Had she forgotten about their lunch date?

She was about to send Hermione a text when she heard her voice down the hall. And she wasn't alone. Guin scowled at the sight of Detective O'Loughlin.

"Guin!" said Hermione spotting her. "Have you been waiting long? Detective O'Loughlin arrived a bit unexpectedly and…"

"No need to explain," said Guin. She looked at O'Loughlin. "Detective."

"Ms. Jones."

Guin turned back to Hermione.

"Is now not a good time? I can come back later."

"No, no. We were just finishing up. Weren't we, Detective O'Loughlin?"

"How's the investigation going?" Guin asked him.

"It's going," he said. Guin thought he looked tired. Was he not sleeping?

"You discover how that light came loose?"

He didn't answer.

"I hear there's going to be an autopsy tomorrow. Do you suspect foul play?"

"Foul play?" *Was that a smile? Or was it a smirk on the detective's face?* "You been watching those mystery movies again?"

"I'll have you know those *mystery movies*, as you like to call them, can be very informative," Guin replied.

"Please. The only mystery is how people can believe that stuff. If I had a nickel for every inaccurate, ridiculous…"

Guin cut him off. "I know, you'd be a millionaire."

The detective turned to Hermione.

"Thanks for your help, Ms. Potter. We'll be in touch."

"Just let me know when we can reopen the ballroom. We have several events scheduled in there."

"You may want to move them."

Hermione opened her mouth to say something then thought better of it.

The detective turned to Guin.

"Ms. Jones."

"Detective."

Guin watched as he headed toward the stairs.

"I'll be right back," she told Hermione.

"Detective!" she called.

He stopped and turned to look at her.

"I could use a quote from you for the paper, about what happened last night."

"No comment."

"Not that again. There must be something you can say."

"You can tell your readers that the police are investigating."

"I should think that's a given. What about the light?"

"What about it?"

"Did it fall on its own or did someone loosen it?"

"I'm not at liberty to say."

Guin studied him. He had definitely lost some weight since she had last seen him, and he looked older.

"Are you okay?" she asked him.

"Why?"

"It's a normal thing to ask someone."

"I'm fine."

"You just seem a bit…" She didn't know what word to use.

"I'm fine," he repeated. But he didn't look fine.

He turned to go, but Guin stopped him.

"Yes?" he said.

"Can you at least tell me who you've spoken to or if you have any suspects?"

"You know I can't do that."

"What about why you're on Sanibel? Can you at least tell me that?"

"I was visiting a friend."

Guin was about to ask him another question, but he stopped her, saying he had to go. She watched as he went down the stairs. Then she turned and walked back to Hermione's office.

CHAPTER 10

"I hope you don't mind eating in the Mermaid Lounge," said Hermione, taking a bite of her chopped salad.

"Not at all," said Guin. She had also ordered the chopped salad, but she wasn't hungry.

"I've just been so busy of late, and now this." Hermione sighed. "This was supposed to have been my day off."

"No rest for the weary, eh?"

"None at all," said Hermione. "Though my husband and I have a lovely vacation planned for May. If I last that long."

"Oh? Where are you going?"

"To Majorca. His brother has a place there."

"Sounds wonderful."

"It is. I haven't been in ages. So, you wanted to ask me about last night."

"I did."

"Well, fire away. Though I don't know how much help I'll be."

"Do you have any idea how that spotlight came loose?"

"None at all. And Luis swears he checked the ballroom that afternoon and nothing was amiss. But the police said it looked like someone had loosened the clamp and the cable that held up the spotlight."

"Who's Luis?"

"Sorry. He works in Maintenance."

"So the police think it was sabotage?"

"That's what it sounded like."

"So it wasn't an accident," Guin said more to herself. "Who had access to the ballroom?"

"It wasn't locked. At least not during the day. Anyone could have gone in there."

"Did you know Mr. Mandelli would be playing Santa?"

"No, I had no idea, nor did anyone else."

Then it couldn't have been premeditated.

"So whoever loosened the light had to be quick and know what they were doing."

"I suppose," said Hermione.

"And you say Luis had checked the ballroom beforehand?"

Hermione nodded.

"Including the lights?"

"He said he did."

"Do you know where he was when the light fell?"

"I don't. Why?"

"Ms. Lamb, Mr. Mandelli's assistant, swore that she saw a maintenance worker backstage just before she got up. She said the man was around medium height with dark hair."

"That describes Luis, but I can't imagine him intentionally harming anyone."

"Did the police speak with him?"

"I believe so."

"Could I speak with him?"

"I don't think he's working today, but I'll check."

"I'd appreciate that."

They continued to pick at their salads.

"Were any employees unhappy about Mr. Mandelli taking over the San Ybel?"

"Honestly?" said Hermione.

"Please. No need to sugarcoat with me."

"Well, to be frank, no one here was very happy about the Thompsons selling the place. It's a bit like a family here. And the Thompsons have been good owners. Though they're getting on in years. And there was talk of them retiring. But to sell the place to a group of faceless New York investors? That just seemed wrong."

"Had you heard of the Mandelli Group?"

"I looked them up."

"So you know about their track record."

"Mm," said Hermione.

"So why did the Thompsons sell to them?"

"I'm guessing they offered the Thompsons a lot of money."

They were silent for several seconds. Then Guin spoke again.

"Do you think others knew about the Mandelli Group's track record?"

"Probably."

"Were they worried about losing their jobs?" The Mandelli Group had a history of firing people.

"I'm sure some were. But we were told at the staff meeting that Mr. Mandelli personally guaranteed no layoffs, only improvements."

"Did he now? And did people believe him?"

Hermione sighed.

"I don't know."

"What about Anthony Mandelli? Did you ever hear anyone at the hotel say anything negative about him?"

Hermione picked at her salad. Then she looked up at Guin. "This is strictly off the record." Guin nodded. "He wasn't very nice to the staff." That was not a surprise. "He acted as though he owned the place already."

"I see," said Guin.

"And there was a rumor that he had attacked two of the maids."

"A rumor?"

"I heard it from a reliable source, but I don't have proof."

"When you say attacked, do you mean...?"

Hermione nodded.

"Did they go to HR?"

"They were afraid to. One of them is waiting to get her green card and the other is new here. Neither wanted to get in trouble with the new boss."

"Do you know the maids in question?"

"I do, and I believe them."

Guin sat back, digesting the information. Then she leaned forward again.

"Could either of them have loosened that light?"

"Neither of them was working last night."

"Maybe they had someone do it for them, a husband or boyfriend who works at the hotel, perhaps?"

Hermione was about to reply when her phone began belting "Never Gonna Give You Up" by Rick Astley. Guin grinned as Hermione quickly silenced her phone.

"Sorry, that was my husband."

"I love it," said Guin. She wondered if she should get a special ringtone for Glen. But what song would she choose?

Hermione's phone began to ring again. No song this time. She looked down at it and frowned.

"I need to get this," she said, swiping to answer. "Yes?" she said. Guin saw her nod her head and say that she'd be right there. Then she hung up. "I need to go. But please stay and finish your salad. Lunch is on me."

"Thank you. Is everything okay?"

"Just the usual."

"I know you're in a hurry, but, when you have a minute, could you arrange for me to speak with Luis and those two maids?"

"I don't know about the two maids. I'm probably not supposed to know. But I'll speak with Luis."

"Thank you."

"Say, when the holidays are over, let's have a proper girls' night out."

"I'd like that," said Guin.

Hermione's phone was ringing again. She sighed, not answering it.

"Go," said Guin.

She watched as Hermione hurried out of the Mermaid Lounge, her salad only half-eaten. Guin looked down at her own salad. She had only picked at it. She could always take it home and eat it for lunch tomorrow. She signaled to a waiter and asked for a to-go box.

Guin spent the rest of the afternoon working on her article about the holiday lighting, unsure if she should include the part about the spotlight falling on Mandelli. She had sent Ginny a text, asking if she should include it, but Ginny hadn't gotten back to her.

She was still working when the doorbell rang. She looked at the clock on her monitor. It was five-thirty. She went to the front door and peered outside. It was Glen.

"You're early," she said, letting him in.

"I was worried about traffic."

"I need a few minutes. Make yourself at home."

Glen took a seat in the living room while Guin went to get changed. Not that Shelly and Steve's barbecues had a dress code. But Guin was feeling a bit grungy. When she emerged a few minutes later, she smiled to find Fauna curled up in Glen's lap.

"Aw," she said.

Glen looked up at her.

"I think she's lonely."

"Lonely?"

"She seemed desperate for attention."

"She's always desperate for attention."

"I think she needs a buddy."

"A buddy?"

"You know, another cat."

"Another cat?"

"I think she misses Flora."

Guin regarded Fauna.

"I don't know. She seems pretty happy to me."

Fauna had her eyes closed and was purring.

"Sure, now. But what about when you're not here?"

"Cats are solitary creatures."

"Says who?"

Guin didn't say anything.

"You should get another one."

"Oh, you do, do you?"

"Wouldn't you like another cat?"

"I've thought about it, but…"

"But what?"

"What if Fauna doesn't like the new kitty? What if she enjoys being an only child?"

"I think she'd like having a friend to play with."

"Speaking of friends, we should head to Shelly and Steve's."

"Sorry, Fauna," said Glen, gently removing the cat from his lap. Fauna meowed in protest.

"I should give her some food," said Guin.

She went to the pantry and took out a can of cat food, scooping the contents into Fauna's bowl. Fauna lunged.

Guin sighed and then turned to Glen.

"Let's go."

Shelly and Steve's door was unlocked, and Guin and Glen let themselves in. They had only taken two steps inside when Shelly rushed over and pulled them aside.

"Is everything okay?" asked Guin.

"There's something I need to tell you."

"Did something happen? Did Steve burn the brats?"

"As if that would ever happen," said Shelly.

"Then what is it?"

"*He's* here."

"He who?" said Guin.

"The detective!" said Shelly. "I had no idea Steve invited him."

"It's fine, Shell."

Shelly stared at her.

"Really?"

"Yep. Totally okay."

"You're not mad?"

"Nope."

Shelly gave her a funny look.

"Huh. I was sure you'd be upset."

"Why would I be upset?"

"Well…"

"Look, I've made my peace with Detective O'Loughlin being here." Though that wasn't entirely true. "And we're all adults."

Shelly studied her.

"Okay then. If you don't care…"

"Not in the least." Though Guin felt her nails digging into the palm of her right hand.

"All righty then. You guys want to grab a beer? They're in the cooler out back on the lanai."

"Shall we?" said Guin, looking at Glen.

"After you."

They had started to head back when Shelly pulled Guin aside again. Glen stopped, but Guin told him to go on ahead.

"Yes?" she said, looking at Shelly.

"I found out what he's doing here. He's visiting his old boss, the former chief."

"Who told you that?"

"Steve. He heard it from one of his fishing buddies. Apparently the old chief has cancer, and they don't think he's going to make it. The detective flew down to pay his respects."

Guin didn't know what to say.

"Steve said the two of them were pretty close and it hit the detective pretty hard."

Again, Guin didn't know what to say.

"So, you're really okay with the detective being here?"

"I told you, I'm fine."

"What about Glen? Is he okay with it?"

"You'd have to ask Glen. Speaking of Glen, I should go and find him."

They headed out to the lanai. Glen had a beer in his hand and was chatting with Steve.

"Hey," she said, laying a hand on Glen's arm.

He turned and smiled at her.

"Everything all right?"

"Everything's fine."

"Can I get you a beer?" he asked her.

"Sure."

He went over to the cooler.

"There's High Five, Funky Buddha…"

"I'll have a High Five."

Glen pulled out a bottle of the IPA, opened it, and handed it to Guin.

"Thank you," she said.

Guin took a sip and looked around. The detective was speaking with one of Steve's fishing buddies. She had seen him here before but had forgotten his name. It was Burt or Bruce or something.

"You going to talk to him?"

Guin turned and looked at Glen.

"Who?"

"The detective. You going to talk to him?"

"You mean about the case?"

Glen gave her a look. Fortunately, she was saved from

further talk about the detective by Jimbo and Sally, neighbors of Guin's who were friends with Steve and Shelly. Sally needed a new camera and wanted to pick Glen's brain. While the two of them discussed cameras, Guin asked Jimbo how he was doing. A few minutes later, Steve announced that the brats were ready.

CHAPTER 11

"You're avoiding him."

Guin looked up at Glen.

"I am not avoiding him."

"Then why haven't you talked to him?"

"Because I have nothing to say to him."

"I don't believe that."

"Do you want me to talk to him?"

"I just don't want you to think that you can't talk to him with me around."

Guin regarded him.

"If I wanted to talk to him, I'd go talk to him."

"Okay. Just checking."

"Anyway, I saw him earlier, and he had nothing to say."

"You saw him earlier?"

"At the San Ybel. He was speaking with Hermione when I got there. I asked him about the case, but he said *no comment*."

"Did you ask him about his family?"

"Why would I ask him about his family?"

"To break the ice?"

"Look," Guin began.

"You know he's been eyeing you all evening."

"He has?"

"And I've seen you stealing glances at him."

"I have not been stealing glances at him."

Glen made a face.

"Just go over there and talk to him."

"And say what?"

"Ask him how he's doing."

"Fine, if it makes you happy, I'll go talk to him. But it'll be a short conversation."

She turned and made her way over to the detective. He was talking to Steve. But they both stopped as Guin approached.

"I should go help Shelly," said Steve and scooted away.

Guin shot him a look. Then she turned to face the detective.

"I just heard about the old chief," she said. "Sorry."

"Thanks," said the detective.

"You two were close?"

He nodded. As Guin knew, the detective didn't like discussing his personal life, but she persevered.

"How bad's the cancer?"

"Pretty bad."

He clearly didn't want to talk about the chief. Time to change subjects.

"How's Frankie?"

"Good."

"You have any pictures of him? He must be getting big."

The detective looked like he was trying to decide if Guin really wanted to see pictures of his grandson or not.

"Come on. Show me a picture of him," she prodded. "Unless you don't have any."

The detective regarded her. Then he took out his phone, swiped, and handed it to her.

"These are the latest ones."

Guin began to swipe.

"He's adorable," she said. And she meant it. He was a cute kid. "He's going to be one soon, yes?"

The detective nodded.

"At Christmas."

She continued to swipe through the photos, several of which included the detective's son Joey and his wife.

"You going back up to celebrate with them?"

"That's the plan."

She looked back down at the detective's phone. There was a photo of him with his family. He was smiling. A rarity. She looked up at him.

"You happy there?"

He nodded.

"You ever miss Sanibel?" Though what she really meant was, *Do you ever miss me?*

He held out his hand. Guin looked at it.

"My phone."

"Right." She handed it back to him.

The detective looked over her shoulder.

"So, you with the photographer now?"

It took a second for Guin to realize he was referring to Glen.

"I am."

"You happy?"

She thought for a second.

"I am."

"Good," he replied.

The two looked at each other and Guin wondered what would have happened if he hadn't left.

"So, you're going to work this case and then head back to Boston? What if Detective Brown doesn't come back?"

"Then they'll have to find a replacement."

"You won't stay?"

"I can't."

Guin was going to ask him why not, but Shelly had appeared.

"I need you in the kitchen."

"Excuse me," Guin said to the detective.

He nodded, and she followed Shelly to the kitchen.

"What's up?"

"Things looked pretty intense over there. You okay?"

"I'm fine. Is that why you got me?"

Shelly nodded.

"So, what were you two talking about?"

"This and that."

Shelly's expression said she was not satisfied with that answer.

"He was showing me pictures of his family."

"And?"

"I asked him if he was planning on sticking around."

"And?"

"He said he wasn't."

"Even if…"

"I don't think there's anything that'll change his mind."

"Sorry."

"Don't be. It's for the best."

"Well, I'm sure Glen will be relieved."

"Maybe. I don't think he was worried. He's the one who told me to go speak with the detective."

"Oh?"

"He thought we needed to clear the air."

Steve came into the kitchen.

"You getting dessert?"

"Yup," said Shelly.

Steve left, and Shelly opened the refrigerator. She grabbed a large platter of fruit and handed it to Guin.

"Take this out to the lanai. I'll take out the cookies."

"Don't forget my macarons!"

Guin walked out to the lanai and placed the fruit platter on the table.

"Everything okay?" asked Glen.

"Yep."

Shelly arrived with a large platter of cookies and

brownies and placed it on the table next to the fruit.

"Where's the box of macarons I gave you?" asked Guin.

"I was going to save them."

"Bring them out. They don't keep that long."

Shelly went to get them. When she returned, she told everyone to help themselves. Soon there was a line.

"Be sure to take a macaron," Guin told Glen. "Jo made them. And they're delicious."

Glen picked up a coffee macaron, and Guin picked up a raspberry one. Then they found a spot off to the side.

Guin watched as Glen bit into his macaron.

"Mm!" he said.

Guin smiled.

"Told you."

Guin bit into hers.

"The raspberry is good too."

"So, you have a good chat with O'Loughlin?"

"Uh-huh," said Guin, eating a piece of pineapple.

People were starting to leave.

"We should get going," said Glen. "I told my mother I'd stop by and see her."

"You didn't tell me you were going to see your mother. Isn't it late?"

"It's not that late, and she's a night owl. But we should get going."

"You should have told me. I could have met you here."

"It's not a big deal. I told her I might not get there until after eight."

Guin looked at her watch. It was eight o'clock.

"Okay, let's go."

"Everything okay?" asked Shelly.

"Everything's fine," said Guin. "Except that Glen forgot to tell me he needed to go see his mother."

Shelly looked confused.

"He drove me here."

Shelly continued to look confused.

"I told my mother I'd stop by on my way home from the barbecue."

"I'm still not following," said Shelly.

"Glen insisted on picking me up. And if he drives me back to my place, he'll be late to see his mother."

"I can drive you home," said Shelly.

"There, problem solved," said Guin. "Go."

"I don't want to inconvenience you," Glen said to Shelly.

"It's not an inconvenience."

Guin saw Jimbo chatting with Steve.

"Let me go ask Jimbo."

She went over to him.

"Hey, Jimbo, would you and Sally mind giving me a lift?"

"Sure," he said. "We were about to leave. You ready?"

"Ready when you are."

She went back over to Glen.

"All set."

"You sure?"

"Jimbo said no problem."

"Okay."

He leaned down and kissed her.

"Though I could have driven you home."

"No need. Tell your mom I said hello."

"I'll do that."

He left, and Guin glanced around. There was no sign of the detective.

"He left a while ago," said Shelly.

"Who?" said Guin innocently.

"You know who I mean, the detective."

"I wasn't…"

Shelly held up a hand to stop her.

Jimbo and Sally came over.

"Thanks for having us," Sally said to Shelly. "Everything was delicious."

Shelly smiled at her.

"You and Jimbo are always welcome."

Jimbo looked at Guin.

"You ready?"

"Yup," she said. She gave Shelly a peck on the cheek and told her she'd talk to her soon.

CHAPTER 12

Guin yawned and looked over at the alarm clock. It was just past six-thirty. She had a lot to do, but the beach was calling. She turned on her phone and checked the weather. It was cool—well, cool for Sanibel, meaning in the low 60s—but sunny. And the wind was from the northwest. Which was good for shelling. Next, she checked her tide chart. It was just past low tide. But the tide wouldn't be high for several hours.

She got out of bed and quickly threw on a pair of capris and a rash guard. Then she went to the kitchen, put dry food in Fauna's bowl and gave her fresh water, and hurried out the door.

Dawn was breaking as she stepped onto the beach, and the sky was pale blue. She glanced around, trying to decide which way to walk. There were other people on the beach. And no doubt others had been and gone home already. Guin just hoped they hadn't taken all the good shells.

She walked down to the water's edge and closed her eyes. She imagined finding a true tulip and a king's crown conch. Though she'd be happy finding a gaudy nautica or a lace murex. She opened her eyes and looked to the right and then to the left. There seemed to be more people to the right, and on the way home last night, Sally had told her there had been a big shell pile just past Beach Access #1. So she headed east.

She was staring intently at the waterline, looking for shells, when she heard her name being called. She looked up to see her friend Lenny coming toward her. She hadn't seen him since before Thanksgiving.

She smiled as he approached.

Lenny was a retired middle school science teacher from Brooklyn who had moved to Sanibel several years before Guin. He was a Shell Ambassador, someone who helped beachcombers identify sea life, and also a bit of a curmudgeon. But Guin had a soft spot for curmudgeons, especially ones who were fellow Mets fans.

"Long time no see," she said. "How are you?"

"I can't complain." Though he often did.

"What have you been up to? I feel as though I haven't seen you in ages."

"I've been helping out at the Shell Museum. They're a bit short-staffed."

"That's nice of you. So you've been skipping your morning beach walk?"

"Never. Gotta get in my steps. I've just been mixing it up, going to different beaches."

Guin used to mix it up too. But since she moved into her house, she'd been sticking to the beaches along West Gulf. After all, why drive when you could walk to the beach in under ten minutes? However, she'd been meaning to go to Lighthouse Beach and Blind Pass, two of her favorite Sanibel beaches, which typically had more shells than West Gulf.

"Well, I'm happy to see you. You find anything?"

Lenny reached into his pocket and pulled out a big chocolate alphabet cone.

"Whoa! You find that near here?"

"Down by Tarpon," he said.

"You think there are more?"

"Only one way to find out."

"You mean you didn't grab all the good shells?"

Lenny frowned.

"Shell Ambassadors aren't supposed to grab shells. And I'm donating this one to the museum."

"I was teasing, Len." Though the first time she encountered Lenny, he was grabbing a shell she had had her eye on. But she didn't bring it up.

"I'm heading east," she told him.

"I'll join you. I was about to turn around anyway."

They walked in silence for several minutes. Then Guin asked him if he had gone to the holiday lighting that weekend. She hadn't seen him there.

"Nah, too many people. You go?"

She nodded.

"Glen and I were covering it for the paper."

"I heard about that guy who got whacked."

"What did you hear?"

"That a light fell on him. You knew him, right? Mancini?"

"Mandelli."

"You there when it happened?"

"As a matter of fact, I was. But I didn't see the spotlight fall."

"You think someone did it on purpose? That's what Suzy seems to think."

Did everyone read Shellapalooza? Probably.

"I think it unlikely that the light just happened to fall when it did."

"Who do you think did it?"

"I don't know. I don't think a lot of people were happy about him buying the hotel."

"You think someone from the hotel killed him?"

"I don't know." Though who else could have loosened the light?

"I heard your friend the detective was back."

Guin didn't say anything.

"You speak with him?"

"Briefly."

"He back for good?"

"I don't think so."

They walked in silence for several minutes, until Guin said she should turn around.

"Where'd you park?" she asked him.

"By West Wind."

"They don't mind?"

"You going to tell them I'm not a guest?"

Guin smiled.

"Take care of yourself, Len."

"You too, kiddo."

Guin made herself a pot of coffee as soon as she got home and took her mug to her office. She had made a list of the people she wanted to speak to. On it were Audra Linwood and Patrick Finney, Luis, and Honey Lamb.

She called Audra's office a little after nine. A man answered. And for a second she thought she had dialed the wrong number. She had been expecting Candy, Audra's usual receptionist/Gal Friday.

"Can I help you?" said the man.

"Sorry," said Guin. "Is Candy there?"

"She's off this week. Is there something I can help you with?"

"I was calling to schedule an appointment with Audra."

"Are you a client or looking to purchase or sell a home here on Sanibel?"

"No, I work for the paper. I'm a reporter. Does she have some time later today?"

"Let me check. Could you hold?"

She listened as hold music began to play. Several minutes

went by, and Guin was about to hang up when the man came back on the line.

"Sorry to make you wait. She has some time today at two."

"Great," said Guin.

"What is your name, please?"

"Guinivere Jones."

"Could you spell that for me?"

"Just put down Guin. That's G-U-I-N. And Jones is spelled the usual way."

"Got it."

"And I didn't catch your name."

"Fletcher, Fletcher Reid."   .

Guin immediately pictured a preppy-looking twenty-something.

"Are you new?"

"I am."

"Well, see you at two."

They ended the call, and Guin called Patrick Finney's office. He worked for a large real estate company on the island, as opposed to having his own firm. A receptionist picked up, and Guin asked if Finney was available, but she was told he was with a client. Would she like to leave a message? Guin said she would and was put through to his voicemail.

"Patrick," she said. "It's Guinivere Jones. I'd love to get a moment of your time to discuss an article I'm working on. Let me know when you're free."

She deliberately kept it vague, not wanting to reveal her true purpose. He might not agree to meet with her if he thought she was accusing him of murder. She gazed out the window. The lake behind her house looked like a mirror. She stared out at it for several seconds. Then she turned back to her computer.

She needed to send Ginny her article about the holiday

lighting ceremony, but which one? The first version of the article was upbeat and didn't mention what had happened to Mandelli. The second version ended with Mandelli being hit with the light and the police investigating. As Ginny hadn't gotten back to her, Guin would send her both versions and let her choose.

She made a couple of tweaks and then sent the articles to Ginny. Now what? She hadn't heard from Hermione. Should she just go to the San Ybel and see if Luis was around? No, she should give Hermione a little more time. She said she'd reach out to him. But if she hadn't heard back from Hermione by late afternoon, she'd seek out Luis on her own—and talk to Honey too.

Guin was eating lunch in the kitchen when her phone started to vibrate. She quickly unlocked it, hoping it was Hermione. But it was an email from Ginny.

She was letting Guin know that she had received both versions of the holiday lighting article and would get back to her. She also wanted Guin to check out a new restaurant, a new Italian place that would be replacing Matzaluna. The restaurant, called Tutti Pazzi, would be having a soft opening that Friday. And she had told the owners that someone from the paper would be there to cover it.

Guin frowned. She was already reviewing one restaurant. Now Ginny wanted her to review another one on top of everything else? Though covering a soft opening wasn't the same as reviewing a place.

She wrote Ginny back, asking for details about the soft opening and who would be photographing it for the paper. Then she finished her sandwich.

Ginny got right back to her. The event started at five-thirty with cocktails and appetizers, followed by dinner. And she was planning on sending Glen. Was that all right? Guin smiled. It was more than all right.

"And when can I expect your review of 400 Rabbits?" Ginny added.

Right. Guin had forgotten about 400 Rabbits in all of the chaos. She needed to go there one more time.

She texted Glen.

"Hey, I need to go to 400 Rabbits this week. Care to join me? I'm inviting Steve and Shelly too."

"When?" he wrote back.

"Wednesday?"

"I'll put it on my calendar."

"Let me just double-check with Shelly first. And did Ginny tell you about the Tutti Pazzi soft opening Friday?"

"She just did. Shall I pick you up at 5?"

"That's silly. I'll just meet you there."

Tutti Pazzi was close to the Causeway, some 15 or 20 minutes east of Guin's, depending on traffic.

"I don't mind."

"Well, I do," wrote Guin. "I'm going to text Shelly and see if she and Steve are free Wednesday and I'll get back to you."

"OK," he replied and added a kiss emoji.

Guin sent one back to him. Then she texted Shelly.

"You and Steve free for dinner Wednesday?"

"You cooking?" Shelly wrote back.

"No, going to 400 Rabbits."

"Let me check with Steve."

Guin put down her phone and went to the bathroom. When she came back, she found she had a missed call from Patrick Finney. Of course, the two minutes she was away from her phone, he calls her. She listened to her voicemail. Finney said he could see her at four. No need to call him back if that worked. She quickly checked her calendar. That worked.

Her phone began to buzz. It was a reminder about her appointment with Audra. Guin looked down at what she was wearing. She was still dressed in her beach attire. She definitely couldn't go see Audra looking like that. Fortunately, she had just enough time to change.

Audra was always impeccably dressed. And Guin knew she would command more respect if she looked more like a professional and less like a beachcomber. Though she had gotten rid of nearly all of her suits and business attire when she moved to Sanibel. Still, she had a few items that she thought would pass muster.

She went into her closet and picked out a skirt and top. She added some jewelry and went to put on a little makeup and comb her hair.

She looked at herself in the mirror. She had put on foundation to hide her freckles. Every day it seemed she got a few more, even though she liberally applied sunblock to her face. The perils of having fair skin. She removed her hair from the ponytail holder and frowned. Too frizzy. So she twirled it into a kind of French twist.

"Better," she said.

She went back into her closet and pulled out a pair of high-heeled sandals. Then she exchanged them for a more modest pair. She slipped them on and looked at herself in the full-length mirror.

"I'd say I looked professional," she said to her reflection.

She felt something furry rubbing against her leg. She looked down.

"What do you think, Fauna? Do I look like a professional?"

"Meow," said Fauna, looking up at her.

Guin knelt and stroked the side of Fauna's face. Fauna purred.

"Okay, gotta go. I'll be back later."

She straightened and looked down at her skirt.

"Guess I should get out the lint roller first."

She grabbed the one she kept in her nightstand and removed the cat hair from her skirt. Then she went to get her bag and her keys.

CHAPTER 13

Guin parked in front of Audra Linwood's office and looked at the time. It was just two o'clock. She went inside and headed to the reception desk. A young man was seated there. He looked like something out of the pages of *GQ* or *The Preppy Handbook*. *This must be Fletcher.* He was speaking on the phone. Guin waited.

"Can I help you?" said the young man when he was done with the caller.

"Are you Fletcher?" asked Guin.

"I am."

"I'm Guin Jones, from the paper. I spoke with you on the phone earlier. I have a two o'clock appointment with Ms. Linwood."

"Right," he said. "She's running a bit late, but she should be here any minute. Please, have a seat."

Guin remained standing.

"When did you start working here?"

"Last month."

"Are you from around here?"

"No, Miami."

"What brought you to Sanibel?"

"Audra."

"Audra?"

"She and my mother are old friends. I was selling real estate in Miami and doing okay, but I wanted a change. And Audra suggested I come here."

"You weren't worried about being bored? Sanibel's not exactly Miami."

Fletcher smiled.

"That's fine by me. I'm not what you'd call a party animal. I like to work hard then go for a walk or a run and relax at home with a good book or a movie."

"Wow," said Guin. "I don't think I know many people your age like that." Though, in fact, Guin hardly knew any twenty-somethings. Maybe there were more like Fletcher than the ones she read about online or saw on social media.

"You'd be surprised. Not everyone my age wants to be a social media influencer."

The phone began to ring, and Fletcher immediately answered it. As he chatted with the caller, Guin looked out the large plate-glass window and wondered how much longer Audra would be. She took out her phone to check her messages. Still no word from Hermione.

She sat down on one of the overstuffed couches and was flipping through the latest issue of *Times of the Islands* when Audra sailed through the door.

"You would not believe the day I've had!" she said to Fletcher, completely ignoring Guin. "I keep having to explain to people that they're not going to get the beach cottage of their dreams for half a million dollars. This isn't HGTV. I swear, no one has realistic expectations anymore."

"I'm sorry you've had a bad day, Audra," said Fletcher sympathetically.

"Well, it wasn't all bad. I beat out Patrick for that listing up on Captiva. And Mrs. Blaisdell put in an offer on that condo I showed her."

Fletcher smiled up at her.

"You're amazing!"

Audra smiled back at him, and Guin wondered if their relationship was more than just professional. But that was silly. Fletcher was practically the same age as Audra's daughter. Though she knew plenty of men dated much younger women. Why couldn't a woman date a younger man? Still, Audra wouldn't date someone who worked for her, would she? Especially the son of an old friend.

Suddenly, Audra noticed Guin sitting there.

"What do you want?" she said.

"She's your two o'clock," said Fletcher.

"I thought you said I had an appointment with a real estate reporter."

"I…" Fletcher looked at Guin.

"It's my fault," she said. "I wasn't clear. However, you did say the other night that I should call the office and arrange an appointment."

"I did?"

"On Saturday? At the San Ybel? To talk about the sale?" Audra sighed.

"Fine. But I only have a few minutes."

"That's fine," said Guin.

"Come," said Audra imperiously. "Let's go to my office."

Audra seated herself behind her big desk.

"So, what is it you wanted to know?"

"I wanted to know about your role in the Mandelli Group's acquisition of the San Ybel."

"I brokered the deal."

"How did you know the hotel was for sale? No one else seemed to."

Audra smiled.

"I have my sources."

"Can you reveal them?"

"I'm afraid not."

"Were there other bidders?"

"Not really."

"But there were others interested in acquiring the hotel."

Audra sighed.

"Why do you care?"

"I'm covering the sale. So, who were the other bidders?"

"The great Ginny Prescott doesn't know?"

Guin didn't reply.

Audra sighed again.

"Very well. There were two other parties that were interested, Julian Hornsby and the Victor Group."

"Julian Hornsby and the Victor Group?"

"Really? You've never heard of Julian Hornsby, the eccentric British billionaire, or the Victor Group?"

Guin shook her head.

"Does the Victor Group own hotels?"

Audra gave Guin a pitying look.

"Do they own hotels? Yes, they own hotels. Several, in fact. They're French. Maybe that's why you haven't heard of them. Though they have outposts in New York and L.A. Patrick represented them."

"Patrick as in your ex?"

Another look.

"Yet the Thompsons chose the Mandelli Group. Why?"

"Why not?"

"Did they offer the Thompsons a lot of money?"

Audra didn't reply.

"What happens now that Mr. Mandelli's no longer involved? Will the deal still close?"

"Of course," said Audra. "Why wouldn't it?"

"Well…" Guin began. But Audra cut her off.

"It may have been Tony's name on the company, but he wasn't the only investor."

"I see," said Guin. "Getting back to the other bidders, were they angry about losing out?"

"I wouldn't say they were pleased. But that's life. To the victor belongs the spoils."

"Speaking of victors, you said your ex-husband, Patrick

Finney, represented the Victor Group."

"So?"

"He wasn't exactly a fan of Mr. Mandelli."

"That's putting it mildly."

"What makes you say that?"

"He loathed Tony and accused him of not playing fair."

"Why did he say that?"

"Because he's a sore loser."

"And what about your relationship with Anthony Mandelli?"

"What about it?"

"Were the two of you on good terms?"

"Of course we were on good terms. We were partners."

"What about Ms. Lamb?"

Audra frowned.

"What about her?"

"You didn't seem very fond of her. Were you upset that Mr. Mandelli brought her with him to Florida?"

"Who Tony brings to Florida is his business. Though…" She stopped herself.

"You were going to say?"

"Nothing. It doesn't matter."

"And you say Mr. Mandelli's death won't affect the sale?"

"As I told you, no."

"Any idea who benefits from his death?"

"What do you mean?"

"I mean, do you know who stands to inherit?"

"I've no idea. He didn't discuss such things with me."

"What about family?"

"As far as I know, he didn't have any children. But I believe there was a niece or a nephew."

Guin made a mental note to ask Honey. Maybe she knew. Though she said she'd only been working for Mandelli a few months. Still.

"What about enemies?"

"Enemies?"

"Anyone here on the island who disliked him enough to…"

"Drop a large spotlight on him?"

Guin nodded.

"I already gave the police a list."

"Can you tell me who was on it?"

"Other than Patrick?"

Was Audra really throwing the father of her child under the bus? Though Guin also suspected him.

"If you wouldn't mind."

"Well, there was Hugo, of course. He was quite irate."

"Hugo?"

"Hugo Blanchet? The head of the Victor Group?"

Guin made a mental note to look him up and was about to ask Audra another question when Audra's phone began to ring. Audra immediately answered it.

"Yes?" she said. "Okay, put him through." There was a brief pause. "Roger, darling! Can you hold for a minute? I'm just finishing up something." She covered the phone with her hand and looked at Guin. "I trust you can see yourself out?"

Guin opened her mouth and then closed it. She would follow up with Audra later.

"Thanks for your time," she said. Then she let herself out.

She walked back to the reception area and said goodbye to Fletcher.

"You wouldn't happen to need a house or a condo?" he asked her.

Guin smiled.

"No, I recently bought a place."

"Oh. Are you interested in selling it? You know, the market's heating up."

"But where would I go?"

Fletcher didn't have an answer.

"Good luck to you," said Guin. "If you'd like, you can give me a few of your cards. And if I happen to know of anyone who's looking to buy or sell…"

Fletcher immediately reached into the drawer and pulled out a small stack of cards.

"Here," he said, handing them to her.

Guin looked at the one on top and then tucked them into her bag.

"Have a good rest of your day," she said.

"You too," said Fletcher.

Guin stepped outside and pulled out her phone. There was a text from Hermione. She apologized for not getting back to her. It had been another crazy day. But she promised to talk to Luis and get back to her.

Guin sighed and thanked her.

She looked at the time. It was nearly three. She had an hour until her appointment with Patrick Finney. Should she stop by the Sanibel Police Department and see if a certain detective was available? Not that he would tell her anything if he was. Though wasn't the autopsy supposed to be today? But the results wouldn't be available for at least a day or two.

She stared across the road. It didn't make sense to go home. But where should she go? The San Ybel wasn't far away. She could always drive over there and see if Honey was around.

CHAPTER 14

Guin parked in front of the San Ybel and headed inside. As she approached the front desk, she saw Honey arguing with one of the clerks.

"I don't understand," Honey said. "The suite was reserved through Friday."

"I'm terribly sorry, Ms. Lamb. We can move you to another room."

Honey looked angry.

"I don't want to be moved. Mr. Mandelli reserved the suite, and I plan on staying there."

"I'm afraid you can't do that."

"Why not?"

"We have a lovely room with a view of the Gulf."

"Is it as nice as the Presidential Suite?"

"No, but…"

"I'd like to speak with the manager."

"I'm afraid Mr. Washburn's in a meeting."

"Then let me speak with someone else."

"I'm afraid there is no one else."

Honey fumed.

"This is unacceptable."

The front desk clerk tried to appease her.

"Allow us to offer you a complimentary spa treatment."

"Make it several spa treatments. This place is starting to get on my nerves."

"I'll take care of it."

"Do that. And arrange for someone to move my things to my new room."

"Of course," said the clerk. "Thank you for being so understanding."

"I'd still like to speak with the manager."

"I'll let him know."

Honey didn't move.

"Is there something else I can help you with?"

"The key? To my new room?"

"Of course, my apologies." The clerk quickly got the key. "It's on the top floor."

Honey snatched the key and was headed toward the elevators when her phone started ringing. She immediately answered. Guin hid behind a nearby column and listened.

"I can't talk right now," Honey told the caller. "They're kicking me out of the suite, and I have to pack…. I don't know why. Though I have my suspicions…. They've put me in a new room on the top floor…. I'll see you later."

Honey ended the call and continued to the elevator bank. Guin needed to snag her before the elevator came.

"Honey!" she called.

Honey stopped and turned.

"What do you want?"

"I was hoping to speak to you. I had a few questions about Mr. Mandelli and the other evening."

"Sorry, but I have to go pack my things."

"Oh, are you leaving?" said Guin, playing dumb.

"No, they're kicking me out of the Presidential Suite and moving me to another room."

"I thought you said Mr. Mandelli had reserved the suite for a week."

"I thought so too."

"So, will they be moving Mr. Mandelli's things too?"

"I don't know. I suppose so. I need to speak with the manager."

"Could I possibly meet with you after you've moved, maybe buy you a drink?"

Guin sensed Honey was judging her.

"You don't secretly work for one of those tabloids, do you?"

"No, just the local paper here."

"Okay. I could use a drink. What time is it?"

Guin looked down at her watch.

"Nearly three-thirty."

"I'll meet you at the bar at five-thirty."

"Great!" said Guin. "See you then."

Guin had said she would wait to hear back from Hermione before contacting Luis. But she was at the hotel with time to kill. She picked up a house phone and asked to be connected to Maintenance.

The phone rang, and a man answered.

"Maintenance."

"Is Luis available?"

"He's not. Is there something I can help you with?"

Guin wondered if she should tell him the truth or make something up. She decided on the former.

"Actually, I'm a reporter with the *Sanibel-Captiva Sun-Times*. And I wanted to speak with Luis about what happened on Saturday."

"He's not talking to reporters."

"Tell him I'm a friend of Hermione Potter's and that I'm not looking to get him into trouble."

No response.

"Can I just give you my name and my number? Tell him he can speak to me off the record. That means I won't print what he tells me. I'm just trying to find out how the light could have come loose."

"Luis had nothing to do with that," said the man.

"I believe you, but I'd still like to speak with him. May I give you my name and number?"

The man sighed.

"You can, but I don't know if he'll talk to you."

Guin gave him her information, spelling her name for him.

"And you are?"

"Nick."

"Thank you, Nick."

Guin wondered if Nick would tell Luis that she called. Well, if she didn't hear from him by tomorrow afternoon, she'd follow up. And Hermione said she'd speak with him. Maybe that would help.

She looked at her watch. She needed to get going, but she speed-dialed Craig instead.

"Did they do the autopsy?" she asked as soon as he answered.

"I assume so."

"Can you check and see?" Guin knew not to assume.

Craig said he would.

"Thanks. Also, have you heard of a billionaire named Julian Hornsby or the Victor Group?"

"Heard of Hornsby, not the other one. Why?"

"They both supposedly wanted to buy the San Ybel. I don't know who represented Hornsby, but Patrick Finney was representing the Victor Group. He hated Mandelli and was at the holiday lighting event. I saw him in the ballroom."

"You think he could have dropped that light on him?"

"Maybe. Or paid someone to do it. I'm heading to his office now to speak with him."

"Be careful."

"I will. While I'm there, could you do some digging into the Victor Group and Hugo Blanchet? He heads it."

"I'll see what I can dig up."

"Thanks."

Guin heard someone speaking to Craig. It sounded like Betty.

"Everything all right?"

"Betty wants to know when you're coming over for dinner."

"When I'm invited," said Guin.

"You know you don't need an invitation."

"You wouldn't want me to just show up and expect you to feed me, would you?"

"There's plenty of food."

Guin smiled.

"Well, ask Betty when's a good night and let me know."

She heard Betty saying something to Craig.

"I'll do that. And she says to bring Glen."

"Gotta run. Let me know what you find out."

It was a relatively quick drive from the San Ybel to Patrick Finney's office. She was a few minutes late, but hopefully he wouldn't care. She went up to the reception desk and told the young woman seated there that she had an appointment with Mr. Finney.

"Your name?"

"Guinivere Jones. I'm with the *Sanibel-Captiva Sun-Times.*"

The young woman picked up the phone.

"I have a Ms. Jones here to see you." She listened, nodded her head, and hung up. Then she turned to Guin. "He'll be out in a minute."

"Thank you."

Guin glanced around the reception area. It looked like nearly every other real estate office on Sanibel and Captiva, with paintings and photographs of beach scenes, white or pastel-colored sofas and armchairs, bleached wood or porcelain tile floors, and a coffee table stacked with decorating, real estate, and lifestyle magazines.

She took a seat on one of the overstuffed sofas and picked up a magazine. She was about halfway through it when Finney came out. She immediately put the magazine down and stood up.

"Ms. Jones," he said. "Sorry to keep you waiting."

"No problem. Thank you for taking the time to see me."

"Shall we go back to my office?"

Guin nodded and followed him back.

CHAPTER 15

"So, what did you want to talk to me about?"

"The San Ybel and Anthony Mandelli."

Finney frowned.

"I understand you represented the Victor Group, one of the bidders."

"That's right."

"But you lost out to the Mandelli Group."

"Because they cheated."

"What makes you say that?"

"We made the Thompsons an all-cash offer, but that lowlife and my ex-wife told them a pack of lies and convinced the Thompsons not to sell to us."

"What kind of lies?"

"They made Hugo and the Victor Group out to be evil foreigners who didn't really care about the hotel and would turn it into a playground for rich foreign playboys. As though that would be a bad thing."

"I see. And that wasn't the case?"

"The Victor Group has an impeccable reputation. Unlike the Mandelli Group. And they planned to revitalize the San Ybel. Hugo even bought a house here, so he could personally supervise the renovation."

"But the Thompsons chose the Mandelli Group. Did Mandelli offer them more money?"

"What do you think?"

"Was it a lot more?"

"I don't know how much they offered the Thompsons, but I know it wasn't cash like ours."

"So Mandelli was going to finance the deal?"

"Supposedly. Though I heard he was having trouble raising the money."

"Where'd you here that?"

"It's no secret that the man's leveraged up to his eyeballs."

"But it wasn't just his money."

"True. Though why risk doing business with someone with Mandelli's track record when you have an all-cash offer on the table?"

Guin didn't have an answer.

"What about Julian Hornsby? I heard he also bid on the hotel."

Finney snorted.

"That old coot? He wanted to turn the place into a golf resort. Can you imagine? It would never have gotten past the city council."

"Was he upset when he lost out?"

"He's buying up some place in Naples instead, so I doubt it."

Guin mentally scratched him off her list of suspects and returned to Mandelli.

"Did the Thompsons tell you why they went with the Mandelli Group?"

"No, but I told you: they didn't play fair."

"You mean they lied about the Victor Group's intentions."

"That and Mandelli practically gift-wrapped that assistant of his and delivered her to Fred."

"You mean Honey Lamb?"

"What kind of name is that anyway? Where did he pick her up, Hooters?"

"And what did you mean by gift-wrapping her and delivering her to Fred?"

Finney gave her a look, and Guin understood.

"Oh," she said.

"Fred couldn't keep his eyes off of her, or his hands for that matter."

"What about his wife?"

"She mostly ignored his boorish behavior. I guess she was used to it."

Guin immediately felt sorry for Mrs. Thompson.

"Yet despite losing out, you were at the holiday lighting."

"So?"

"I saw you in the ballroom. You were there just before that light fell. But I didn't see you afterward."

"What are you implying?"

"Where were you when the light fell on Mr. Mandelli?"

"In the lobby."

"Did anyone see you?"

"Lots of people saw me."

"Anyone in particular?"

"Hugo, for one."

"Hugo as in Hugo Blanchet? He was with you at the holiday lighting?"

"He was."

"Why?"

"The Thompsons had invited us. It would have been bad form not to attend."

"I see. And did the two of you speak with anyone?"

"What do you mean? We spoke with lots of people."

"Sorry. I meant, is there anyone who can vouch for you and Monsieur Blanchet being in the lobby when the light fell?"

"Are you accusing me and Monsieur Blanchet of something, Ms. Jones?"

"No. I was just trying to ascertain where you were when the incident occurred, if anyone had seen the two of you in the lobby."

"Talk to the Monteros."

"The Monteros?"

"You don't know Raphael and Nicole? They're in the paper often enough."

Guin felt embarrassed. The names sounded familiar, but she couldn't place them.

Finney sighed.

"They support a number of nonprofits here on the island and are always hosting or attending parties. Hugo and I were chatting with them. Nicole's from France, like Hugo, and they were discussing some art exhibit they had both seen in Paris. I'm sure she'll remember speaking with us."

Guin made a note to talk to them. Surely, Ginny had their information if they'd been in the paper.

"You said Hugo—Monsieur Blanchet—was there that evening. Do you know if he interacted with Mr. Mandelli?"

"I don't. You'd have to ask him."

"Could you give me his contact information?"

"No."

"No?"

"I'd need his permission."

"Can you get it?"

"I could, but…"

Guin frowned. Finney clearly didn't want to help her. Though how hard could it be to find the rich Frenchman, especially if he just bought a house on the island?

"What about you? Did you speak with Mr. Mandelli that evening?"

"Briefly."

"What did you say to him?"

"That's really none of your business."

"What about your ex-wife?"

"What about her?"

"How did you feel about her working with Anthony Mandelli?"

"I told her she was a fool to trust him."

"How did she react?"

"She told me I was just jealous."

"Were you?"

"Me, jealous of a guy like Anthony Mandelli? You've got to be kidding. The guy's a con artist, a shyster. Everyone who does business with him loses money or goes broke."

"So you tried to warn her, and she ignored you. You must still care about her."

"I don't, but I care about our daughter. I worried Mandelli would take all of Audra's money and she'd have nothing to leave Cassie."

"And now Mandelli's dead, and her money's safe."

Finney's phone pinged. He picked it up, looked at it, and then put it back down.

"If you would excuse me, Ms. Jones, I have an important meeting with a client."

"I just had a couple more questions."

"I'm afraid I don't have the time."

"Then I'll make it quick. Now that Mandelli's dead, could the Thompsons cancel their deal with the Mandelli Group?"

"You'd have to ask their lawyer. And now I really must..."

"Just one more question."

"I'm sorry, but I must ask you to leave."

Guin thanked him for his time and left, pausing outside Finney's door. She was about to head back to the reception area when she heard Finney on his phone. She leaned in to listen.

"Sorry. There was a reporter here asking me questions.... No, nothing for you to worry about. I handled her. I'll arrange a meeting with the Thompsons."

Was Finney speaking with Hugo Blanchet? Guin wanted to stay and hear more, but someone was coming down the hall. So she quickly made her way out to the reception area.

It was now a little before five. Guin needed to be back at the San Ybel at five-thirty to meet Honey. But the hotel was just a few minutes away. As was the Sanibel Police Department. She was tempted to go there and see if Detective O'Loughlin was around. Decisions, decisions.

After mulling it over, she got into her Mini and headed to the SPD.

She looked for the detective's car in the lot. But of course, it wasn't there. No doubt it was still in Boston.

She climbed the stairs and went inside. She hadn't been to the police department in months and smiled when she saw a familiar face behind the plexiglass window.

"Hi, Sue," she said.

"Hey, Guin. Haven't seen you around here in a while."

"I know. But that's a good thing, right?"

Sue smiled.

"Yeah, things have been pretty quiet. Though we had a break-in at the Dunes over Thanksgiving that was pretty exciting."

"Oh?"

"You didn't hear about it?"

Guin shook her head.

"I was up north over Thanksgiving."

"Well, you missed a doozy. This guy visiting his in-laws got wasted and went to the wrong house. Busted a window then made himself at home, stripping his clothes off and climbing into their bed."

"Wow."

"Oh yeah," Sue continued. "Then the next morning, the owners come back, and the wife sees this naked man in her bed and freaks out."

"I'd freak out too if I found a strange man in my bed. So, what happened? Did you arrest the guy?"

"Nah. The owners were friends with his in-laws. And the guy agreed to pay to replace the window and have the bedding dry cleaned. So they let him off."

Guin thought Sue seemed disappointed.

"So, what brings you here? Wait, let me guess: you want to speak with Detective O'Loughlin." Sue grinned.

"Am I that predictable? Wait, don't answer. Is he here?"

"He was earlier. Let me check."

Guin waited as Sue called back to the detective's office. Or Guin assumed that was what she was doing. She returned to the window a short time later.

"He said to give him a few minutes."

"Okay."

Well, at least he was there and willing to speak with her.

The waiting area was small, and there wasn't a place to sit. But the detective said he'd just be a few minutes. So Guin stood in the corner and waited. But after five minutes, she began to feel claustrophobic.

"I'll just be outside," she told Sue.

Ten more minutes went by, and Guin wondered if the detective had forgotten about her. Or maybe he was just hoping she'd go away. She frowned. She needed to go to the hotel. She went back inside and waited for Sue to get off the phone.

"Hey, Sue, any word from the detective?"

"Sorry, he must be busy."

Guin looked down at her watch again then back up at Sue.

"Can you tell him I had to go and ask him to give me a call when he's free?"

"Sure thing," said Sue.

"Thanks."

Guin jogged down the stairs. Should she text the detective? She had deleted his contact information, but she still knew his number by heart. Unless he had changed it.

She reached the bottom of the stairs and looked up. For a second she thought about blowing off Honey and waiting for the detective. But that would be foolish. Instead, she unlocked the Mini and got in.

The decorations outside the San Ybel lit up just as Guin approached the entrance. She stopped to admire them. They really were impressive. She thought about the windows along New York's Fifth Avenue, and how festive they looked this time of year, and felt a pang of homesickness. But as beautiful as the windows along Fifth Avenue were, ditto the rink at Rockefeller Center, she'd take palm trees and seventy-degree weather over freezing temps and icy sidewalks any day.

She stepped inside the hotel and looked around. The lobby was busy. Clearly, the incident on Saturday hadn't dissuaded people from visiting. She went over to the bar, but Honey wasn't there. She looked at her watch. It was nearly five-thirty.

"Can I get you something to drink?" asked the bartender.

Guin wanted a margarita, but she was working. So she ordered a club soda with lime instead. As she waited, she checked her messages. Shelly had gotten back to her about 400 Rabbits. Wednesday was fine. What time?

"Let's meet there at 7," Guin wrote her back. "Would you mind making the reservation?" Then she sent a text to Ginny, asking her if she could give her Raphael and Nicole Montero's contact information.

"Here you go!" said the bartender, depositing a club soda in front of her. "Can I get you anything else?"

"Thanks. I'm good for now."

Guin took a sip and looked around. There was the general manager, Laurence Washburn, speaking with someone just outside the bar. She should go talk to him. She told the bartender she'd be right back and got up. She had nearly reached Washburn when a familiar figure stopped her.

"Ris," she said.

Dr. Harrison "Ris" Hartwick was the science director at the Bailey-Matthews National Shell Museum and Guin's former beau, who until recently she suspected still had feelings for her.

"Well, this is a pleasant surprise," he said, smiling at her. "What are you doing here?"

"I'm meeting someone."

"Oh?"

"It's for work. What are you doing here?"

"I'm meeting Val. She wanted to see all the decorations."

"Val as in the owner of that new yoga studio?"

"She's the one!"

Rumor had it the two were dating. And Guin thought them a perfect match.

"Well, enjoy. Now if you would excuse me?"

"Must you rush off? I feel like I haven't seen you in ages."

Guin had been keeping an eye on Laurence Washburn, but he had disappeared. She frowned. Then she saw Honey out of the corner of her eye. She was wearing a form-fitting dress that was more appropriate for cocktails in Manhattan or the Hamptons than a drink on Sanibel.

"I really must go," she said.

She turned and saw Honey heading their way.

"Well, hello there," said Honey, taking Ris in.

Even though Ris was probably old enough to be Honey's father, he was quite attractive—and had been voted one of Southwest Florida's sexiest men not that long ago.

"I don't think I've seen you around," she continued.

Guin thought about taking Honey's arm and dragging her to the bar. But that would be rude. Instead, she made introductions.

"Honey, this is Dr. Harrison Hartwick, the science director at the Bailey-Matthews National Shell Museum. Honey works for the Mandelli Group. I'm interviewing her for an article I'm working on."

Ris smiled.

"Nice to meet you, Honey."

"The pleasure's all mine," said Honey.

Guin wanted to roll her eyes.

"Ris is meeting his girlfriend."

"Is he?"

"Yes," said Ris. "And, as a matter of fact, I see her now."

He waved, and Guin and Honey turned to see an attractive, very fit brunette heading their way.

"Would you excuse me?" he said to the two of them. "Nice meeting you, Honey." Then he headed off to intercept Val.

Honey sighed.

"Why is it all the good ones are taken?"

"Good question," said Guin. "Come on, let's go get a drink."

They headed to the bar. Guin's club soda was still there, but the ice had melted.

"What can I get you?" the bartender asked Honey.

"I'll have a Cosmo."

"And for you?" he asked Guin.

Guin looked longingly at the bottles of tequila behind the bar.

"Another club soda."

"Let's go sit at one of those tables," said Guin as they waited for their drinks. "We'll be just over there," she told the bartender.

He nodded, and they went to grab the empty table.

CHAPTER 16

The bartender brought over Honey's Cosmo and Guin's club soda. Guin waited until Honey had had a couple of sips of her drink and seemed to relax. Then she asked her how the move to the new room had gone.

Honey clearly wasn't happy about the move but said she had stayed in worse places. Though Guin imagined the new room was quite nice.

"Were you able to speak to Mr. Washburn to find out what happened?"

"No. But I've got a good guess who's responsible."

"Who?" asked Guin.

"Her initials are A. L."

"You think Audra Linwood had you removed from the Presidential Suite?"

"She was furious that Tony brought me. I heard her telling him to send me back to wherever he found me. Like he just picked me up off the street." She took another sip of her Cosmo. "But he told her to forget about it."

Interesting, thought Guin.

"I bet she told them to move me."

"But she doesn't own the hotel."

"Not yet."

"Is she part of the Mandelli Group?"

"I know she gave Tony a lot of money."

"How much did she give him?"

"I don't know for sure, but enough to make her think she could tell Tony what to do. Like that would ever happen."

"Will the deal still go through now that Mr. Mandelli's dead?"

Honey shrugged.

"You don't know?"

"Not my concern."

"But you work for the Mandelli Group."

"I worked for Tony."

"Isn't that the same thing?"

"Tony's gone. And I doubt they'll keep me on, even though I was instrumental in helping them get the hotel deal."

"Oh?" said Guin. "How so?"

Honey took another sip of her drink.

"Let's just say I can be very persuasive."

Guin wondered what that meant.

"So I assume you're still here because the police said you couldn't leave."

"Maybe I like it here."

Guin doubted that.

"I have another question."

Honey waited for her to go on.

"What do you know about Mr. Mandelli's relationship with the Victor Group and Hugo Blanchet?"

"They were rivals."

"Friendly rivals or…"

"Definitely not friendly. Hugo couldn't stand Tony."

"So you know Monsieur Blanchet."

"Sure."

"What do you think of him?"

Honey sipped her Cosmo.

"What do you mean?"

"I mean, what's he like?"

"You've never seen him?"

Guin shook her head.

Honey took out her phone, moved her finger around, and then handed the phone to Guin.

"Here."

"Is that Hugo Blanchet?"

"It isn't Prince Charles."

Guin looked at the photo. The man in it was very good-looking with dark hair and eyes that seemed almost violet. He felt familiar, but she was sure she had never seen him before. She would definitely have remembered him if she had. Then she realized who he reminded her of. It was that French actor, Alain Delon. Her mother had been crazy about him. Though Delon was in his eighties now and the man in the photo couldn't have been more than fifty.

"May I have my phone back?" said Honey.

"Sorry," said Guin, handing it back to her.

"So did you know the Victor Group had bid on the San Ybel?"

"Sure."

"And did you know Monsieur Blanchet was here on the island?"

"I may have."

"Did you happen to see him at the holiday lighting?"

"I may have."

"Did you happen to see him in the ballroom?"

"I don't think so."

"Did you speak with him?"

"We may have said hello."

"You're not sure?"

"Why do you care?"

"You said yourself that Monsieur Blanchet and Mr. Mandelli were rivals."

"You don't think Hugo had anything to do with Tony's accident, do you?"

Interesting that Honey called it an accident—and

referred to Blanchet as Hugo.

"I'm just trying to learn what happened that evening and who might have wanted to harm Mr. Mandelli."

"Look, Hugo and Tony may not have been best buds, but I can't see Hugo climbing a ladder and dropping a spotlight on Tony."

"But you said they were rivals, and that Monsieur Blanchet couldn't stand Mr. Mandelli. And Monsieur Blanchet just lost a big deal to him."

"A lot of people didn't like Tony."

"Any of them currently here on Sanibel or Captiva?"

"Maybe. I don't know."

Guin wondered if Honey was being purposely evasive or really didn't know.

"Do you know where I could find Hugo Blanchet? I'd like to speak with him."

"Contact the Victor Group."

"What about Mr. Mandelli's will?"

"What about it?"

"Do you know what was in it?"

"I have no idea. I was his special assistant, not his lawyer."

Guin was about to ask Honey another question when Honey's phone started playing some rap song.

"I need to get this," she informed Guin. "Hey," she said to her caller. "I can't talk right now. I'm with someone. I'll call you later." There was a brief pause. "No, it's a reporter." Another pause. "I will. Bye." She ended the call and put her phone away. Then she looked at Guin. "I need to go."

"Wait," said Guin as Honey got up to leave. Honey paused. "Can I get your number, in case I have more questions?"

"Call the hotel."

Then she turned and headed out of the bar. Guin was tempted to follow her, but she needed to pay for the drinks. She signaled to the bartender and asked him for the bill. She wondered if the paper would reimburse her. Probably not.

She paid for the drinks and went to the front desk. She asked the clerk if Mr. Washburn was available. But when the clerk called his office, she was informed he was not.

"Could I leave a message for him?" Guin asked the clerk.

"You want his voicemail?"

"Please."

The clerk connected her to Washburn's voicemail, and Guin left a message, asking him to call her, saying it was important. She hung up the phone and thanked the clerk. She had only taken a few steps when she spied Washburn walking across the lobby and made a beeline for him.

"Mr. Washburn!"

He immediately stopped and waited for her.

"Ms. Jones," he said. "Is everything all right."

"Yes, fine," she said. "I've been trying to reach you."

"Is this about the other night?"

"It is. But it seems I keep missing you."

"I've been a bit busy."

"I bet. Do you have a few minutes now to talk?"

"I suppose I can spare you a few minutes."

"Thank you. Is there someplace private we can go?"

"Let's go to my office."

Guin followed him up the stairs and down the hall. As they passed Hermione's office, Guin peeked inside, but no one was there.

They entered an office marked General Manager and stepped inside.

"Please, have a seat," said Washburn.

Guin sat.

"I understand the rigging above the stage, where the light was, had been checked before the reception and nothing was found amiss."

"That's correct," said Washburn.

"Yet the police said that the clamp and cable holding up

the spotlight had been loosened. That's why the light fell."

Mr. Washburn looked pained.

"So I understand."

"I spoke to an eyewitness who said she saw a maintenance worker backstage shortly before the light fell. And I understand a maintenance worker named Luis was on duty that evening. He was the one who checked the stage before the event. Is that correct?"

Mr. Washburn continued to look uncomfortable.

"It is."

"Is it possible to speak with Luis? I left a message for him to call me. But he hasn't."

"I'm afraid he's not available."

"You mean he's not available to speak to reporters?"

"No, I mean he's not available."

Guin looked confused.

"I'm afraid Mr. Garcia has disappeared."

"Disappeared?" Hermione hadn't said anything. "When?"

"I'm not sure. He had the day off yesterday. Then he didn't report for work this morning. And no one seems to know where he is."

"Had the police spoken to him?"

"On Saturday, after the incident."

Guin wondered if Luis had run or if something had happened to him.

"And no one's been able to reach him?"

"No, and his wife didn't show up for work today either."

"His wife? Does she also work at the hotel?"

"She's a maid."

"So you think they left town together? Where could they have gone?"

"They're from Nicaragua, but I don't think they'd go there. Maria was waiting to get her green card and was worried about leaving the country."

"Did Luis have a green card?"

"He did. But Maria's was held up for some reason."

Guin recalled Hermione saying that one of the maids Mandelli had molested was waiting for a green card. Could it have been Maria?

"I understand some of the maids had," she searched for the right word, "issues with Mr. Mandelli. That he treated them badly."

Again, Washburn looked pained.

"Had Mandelli accosted Maria?"

"I'm afraid I'm not at liberty to say."

Guin took that as a yes.

"But you knew about the allegations."

Washburn nodded.

"Did you speak with Mr. Mandelli?"

Washburn scowled.

"I did."

"And?"

"He laughed."

"He laughed?"

"He joked about *maid service* being one of the perks of owning a hotel."

"He thought it was okay to fondle the help?"

"I believe his exact words were, You have to show them who's boss."

Guin was appalled. No, she was furious. What gave Mandelli or any man the right to treat employees as their personal property or playthings?

"I hope you said something."

"I informed Mr. Mandelli that the people who worked at the San Ybel were not his personal property or playthings and that I expected him to keep his hands to himself."

Good for Mr. Washburn.

"How did he respond?"

"He winked at me and said he understood."

Which meant he didn't understand and would continue to misbehave. Guin scowled.

She was about to ask Washburn another question when his phone began to ring. It seemed there was a ringing phone conspiracy.

"I should get this," he said.

Guin indicated for him to go ahead.

"Laurence Washburn," he said into the receiver. "I see," he said a few seconds later. "Tell him I'll be right there."

He hung up and looked at Guin.

"I need to go."

"Everything okay?"

"The detective from the Sanibel Police Department is here and wants to speak with me."

"Ah," said Guin. "Could we continue our conversation tomorrow? I had a few more questions I wanted to ask you."

"Call the office in the morning. If I'm not here, my assistant can arrange a time for us to chat. And now…"

Guin took the hint and got up. She followed Washburn down the stairs. Detective O'Loughlin was at the front desk waiting for him.

"Detective," he said.

Guin eyed O'Loughlin, but he ignored her.

"Is there someplace private we can talk?" Detective O'Loughlin asked him.

"We can use my office," Washburn replied.

He gestured for the detective to follow him.

Guin watched as they headed toward the stairs. What did he want to speak with Washburn about? Did he know about Luis and Maria? Guin wanted to follow them and find out, but she knew if the detective caught her eavesdropping she'd be in trouble.

She waited until they had disappeared. Then she reluctantly left.

CHAPTER 17

It was raining when Guin woke up Tuesday morning. So much for a beach walk. Though serious shellers weren't deterred by a few raindrops.

She turned on her phone, hoping for news. She had asked Ginny about the Monteros and Hugo Blanchet the night before, but Ginny hadn't gotten back to her. She'd call her later if she hadn't heard anything. She also hadn't heard from Craig.

She got up and went into the kitchen to make herself some coffee. As it was steeping, she texted Craig.

"Any news?"

She stared at her phone, hoping for a reply. But none came. She sighed. She hated when people didn't get back to her. Though she should be used to it by now, having been a reporter for nearly twenty years.

She stared out the big bay window. The rain was still coming down, and steam or fog was rising off the lake, making it look a bit eerie. She wondered how deep the lake was. It must be pretty deep as alligators lived in it. Good place to dump a body.

She was startled out of her reverie by the sound of her phone vibrating across the counter. She went to get it and saw that Craig had texted her back.

He hadn't heard anything regarding the autopsy.

She had just put her phone down when it started

vibrating again. She picked it up. It was a text from Ginny.

"Sorry I didn't get back to you. We had people over. You want to stop by the office this morning?"

"Sure," Guin wrote back. "When?"

"8:30? And pick me up a cappuccino and some pastries from Jean-Luc's."

Guin rolled her eyes. So that's why Ginny wanted her to come to the office.

"Anything in particular?"

"You pick," Ginny replied.

"Is the paper going to reimburse me?"

Ginny replied with a laughing emoji.

Guin sighed.

"See you soon," she wrote. Then she finished her coffee and got dressed.

Guin arrived at the offices of the *Sanibel-Captiva Sun-Times* at eight-thirty bearing a box of breakfast pastries and a cappuccino from Jean-Luc's. Her hands were full, so she knocked on the door with her foot. Jasmine, the art director, let her in.

"Thanks," said Guin.

"You here to see Ginny?"

Guin nodded and headed back.

The place was humming. It was totally different from summertime when there was practically no one at the office. Guin arrived at Ginny's office, but the door was closed. Guin knocked with her foot.

"Yes?" Ginny called.

"It's Guin. My hands are full. Can you open the door?"

A few seconds later, Ginny opened the door and ushered Guin inside, taking the cappuccino from her.

She took a sip.

"A bit cold but still good."

"You can always heat it up in the microwave."

Ginny took another sip.

"I'll do that." Then she looked at the box. "What did you get?"

"Open it and find out."

Ginny opened the box. Inside was a *pain au chocolat*, an almond croissant, a raisin danish, and a strawberry and ricotta cheese danish.

"I couldn't possibly eat all of that."

"I thought you could share."

"You want one?"

"I had a raisin danish on the way here."

Ginny took out the strawberry and ricotta breakfast pastry and took a bite.

"Sit," she told Guin.

Guin looked at the two spare chairs. As usual, there were papers, folders, magazines, and newspapers on them. She removed one of the piles and sat.

Ginny took another bite of her pastry.

"Mm… So good. That man sure knows how to make a good pastry. If I wasn't married to Joel…"

"Well, technically, you're not," Guin reminded her.

"Still, I could never abandon him." She took another bite of the danish. "Though…"

Guin grinned. She understood. Jean-Luc had a way with dough. He was also French and not bad looking. Not that she was interested.

Ginny took a final bite then put down the danish and looked at Guin.

"So, why did you want to speak with the Monteros?"

"I need them to verify something."

"What?"

"That they spoke with Patrick Finney and Hugo Blanchet at the holiday lighting."

"I'll give Nicole a call right now."

"Isn't it a bit early?"

"I'm sure they're up. They like to play tennis early."

She picked up her phone and dialed a number.

"Nicole? It's Ginny. Yes, I know. I'm afraid we can't make it, but thank you. Look, dear, I have a question for you. I know you were at the holiday lighting Saturday. Do you recall speaking with Patrick Finney and a man named Hugo Blanchet?"

Guin leaned in, but she couldn't hear what Nicole was saying.

"Uh-huh," said Ginny.

"Ask her if she recalls what time it was."

Ginny gave Guin a disapproving look but asked her.

"I see. Well, thank you, dear. And I'll let Joel know you send your best."

She hung up, and Guin immediately asked Ginny what Nicole Montero had said.

"She said she remembered speaking with Blanchet about some art exhibit, but she doesn't remember when."

"Did she mention Patrick Finney?"

"Not specifically. But I assume he was there too from what she said. Why, do you think Patrick or Hugo Blanchet had something to do with that light falling on Tony Mandelli?"

"Maybe. They both disliked him. Speaking of Hugo Blanchet, you wouldn't know how to reach him, would you?"

"I'm afraid not. Did you ask Patrick Finney?"

"I did, but he wouldn't tell me. But I know he bought a place here recently."

"Hm," said Ginny. "If he bought a place here recently…" She began to type on her keyboard. "Aha!" she said.

"What?"

"Come here."

Guin got up and walked around Ginny's desk, so she could see Ginny's monitor.

"There!" said Ginny, indicating the article on her screen. It was in the real estate section. "I bet that's the house."

Guin looked. On the screen was a picture of a mansion on the beach.

"You think that's it?"

"Pretty sure. It was purchased by a company based in France or Switzerland, as I recall. But let me ask Kate."

Kate Landis was the paper's new real estate reporter.

Ginny opened her door and yelled, "Is Kate here?"

"Haven't seen her!" someone yelled back.

"I'll give her a ring," said Ginny.

She picked up her phone and entered Kate's number.

"Kate? It's Ginny. I've a question for you. You know that big house on West Gulf Drive that closed a couple weeks ago? Do you recall the name of the company that purchased it?" There was a pause. "I see. Thank you."

"What did she say?"

"She said it was purchased by a company called the Victor Group."

"That's Blanchet's company. It has to be his house. What's the address?"

"4411 West Gulf Drive. Why? You're not planning on knocking on his door, are you?"

"Maybe, if that's the only way to reach him."

"You could try calling the Victor Group."

"I did. They wouldn't help me."

"The French can be rather secretive. Would you like me to speak with Patrick? I'm sure I could get it out of him."

Guin thought about it but told Ginny that was okay.

"Suit yourself. So any other news on the Mandelli front?"

"I spoke with Hermione Potter and Laurence Washburn at the hotel. They both swear that the stage had been checked that afternoon and no one had reported anything suspicious."

"Hm," said Ginny.

"Though…"

"Yes?"

"Honey said she saw a maintenance worker backstage."

"Honey?"

"The blonde who was sitting on Mandelli's lap, Mandelli's special assistant."

Ginny smirked.

"Special assistant? And her name's Honey? Where did he find her, some beach on Jamaica?"

"I know," said Guin. "Her real name's Henrietta, Henrietta Lamb. Honey's her nickname."

Ginny snorted.

"She goes by Honey Lamb?"

"I know."

"And what else did Ms. Lamb have to say? Did she tell you where she was when the light fell?"

"She claimed she was in the ladies' room."

"Can anyone confirm that?"

"I don't know. But she didn't have a motive to kill him. At least as far as I can tell."

"No motive? Did you not see how he was pawing her?"

"True."

"And what about this maintenance worker she claimed she saw?"

"I've been trying to speak to him. But he seems to have disappeared."

"Oh?"

Guin hesitated, then she told Ginny about Luis and Maria.

"He and his wife didn't show up for work yesterday." Ginny's eyebrows went up. "I think Maria, that's Luis's wife, was one of the maids Mandelli allegedly molested."

"The plot thickens. And the police don't know where they went?"

"I don't know."

"You haven't spoken with O'Loughlin?"

"I've been trying to, but it's like he's avoiding me."

"I'm not entirely surprised."

"What does that mean?"

"Does he know about you and Glen?"

"Yes."

"He's probably jealous."

"Doubtful," said Guin. Though a small part of her liked the idea.

"Well, keep after him."

"I will."

Ginny's phone began to ring. She immediately picked up.

"Ginny Prescott." She listened and asked the caller to hang on. Then she covered the phone with her hand and looked over at Guin. "When are you getting me that review of 400 Rabbits?"

"You'll have it by Friday."

"Good. And keep me posted on the Mandelli story. I need something to run. Can't have Suzy Seashell scooping us."

"I hear you. I'll get you something this week."

"Make it tomorrow."

Guin frowned. She was going to protest but Ginny had begun speaking to whoever was on the phone. So she let herself out.

CHAPTER 18

Guin stood outside the *San-Cap Sun-Times* wondering what she could say about Mandelli or the incident without sounding like one of Suzy Seashell's gossip columns. Everything was conjecture at this point. She needed facts. If only the detective would talk to her, give her something. Hopefully, Craig would hear about the autopsy soon.

She got into her purple Mini Cooper and pulled out of the lot. She was driving down Periwinkle Way, planning to go home, when she made a sudden right turn onto Dunlop Road and pulled into the lot by the police department. She was about to get out when she decided to call instead. No sense going up if the detective wasn't there or was busy. A man picked up, and Guin asked to speak with Detective O'Loughlin. The man told her the detective was unavailable, and Guin asked to be put through to his voicemail. That was assuming he had a voicemail. But the man said he'd put her through.

It was a generic mailbox, but Guin assumed the detective was checking his messages. She left her name and number and asked him to call her as soon as possible, saying it was important. Then she hung up. She sat in her car, wondering if she should call back and ask the man who had answered when the detective would be available. But she changed her mind and turned the key in the ignition instead.

She was driving down West Gulf Drive, glancing at the

large houses that fronted the beach (though you could barely see them through the tall foliage) when she reached the end. She looked at the number on the last mailbox. It was 4355. Blanchet's house was number 4411.

There was a private dirt road that started where the public part of West Gulf Drive ended, with a big No Trespassing sign. Guin had walked down it, or tried to, shortly after she had moved to the area. But one of the people who lived there, a woman, had screamed at her and she had quickly turned around. Did she dare go back down it now? What if someone called the police? Though that was one way of getting the detective's attention. She smiled at the thought.

She stared at the road and made her decision.

She drove slowly, glancing at the large houses and hoping nobody stopped—or took a shot at—her. She had been shot at before and didn't relish being shot at again. She reached the end and stopped the car. There was no mailbox to indicate if this was the right place. All of the mailboxes were at the start of the dirt road. But Guin had seen a photograph of the property on Ginny's monitor, and this looked like the place.

A sign noted that the property was under 24-hour surveillance. However, there wasn't a security gate and Guin didn't see a camera. The camera was probably attached to the house. Or it could have been hidden in a tree. She headed down the driveway, gripping the steering wheel. The property was overgrown. Guin thought it looked like a jungle. She wondered if that was intentional or if the previous owner had let the landscaping go and Blanchet hadn't yet hired anyone to clean it up.

She parked at the end of the driveway and noted that there were no other cars there. Though there could be a car in the garage. Still, the place felt deserted.

She got out and looked around. The house had to be at

least 4,000 square feet. She looked at the flight of stairs. She could still turn around. Instead, she began to climb. She stopped halfway, thinking she should probably text Shelly or Craig, letting them know what she was doing in case something went wrong. But she told herself she was being paranoid.

She finished climbing and rang the doorbell. Immediately, she heard a dog barking. Was it a guard dog? Would it attack her? She thought she heard a man speaking to the dog in what she was pretty sure was French. But she couldn't make out what he was saying. Was he telling it to be quiet or to kill her? Guin hoped it was the former.

The door opened a few seconds later and Guin found herself staring at an enormous bullmastiff. The dog barked, and Guin took a step back.

"*Tais toi*, Victor!" the dog's handler admonished him. The man turned and looked at Guin. "I apologize on behalf of my dog, Mademoiselle. Can I help you?"

Guin looked at the man.

"Hugo Blanchet?" she asked him.

"Yes?"

She glanced down at the bullmastiff, who was drooling, then back up at Blanchet. He really had the most extraordinary eyes, like Elizabeth Taylor's.

"My name's Guinivere Jones. I'm a reporter with the local paper. And I wanted to speak with you about Anthony Mandelli and the San Ybel."

"I see," he said, keeping his hand on the dog's collar.

"And how did you find me, Ms. Jones?"

"I told you, I'm a reporter."

That didn't seem to satisfy him.

"The house was written up in the paper. We publish all the big real estate sales. I knew it had been purchased by the Victor Group, so…"

"I see," he said.

"May I come in? I promise not to take up too much of your time. I just had a few questions."

"About Monsieur Mandelli."

"Yes, and the San Ybel."

Blanchet looked down at his dog.

"What do you say, Victor? Shall we let her in?"

Victor barked loudly, and Blanchet smiled.

"Victor says it is okay. But I only have a few minutes. I have a call at ten."

"That's fine," said Guin. "This shouldn't take long."

Blanchet opened the door wider.

"Please, come in."

Guin stepped over the threshold, keeping an eye on Victor as Blanchet led her into the large living area. There was a wall of windows on the other side with an unobstructed view of the Gulf of Mexico. Guin couldn't help staring.

"It is a nice view, no?"

"Very nice," said Guin, mesmerized. It was a beautiful morning, and the Gulf was aquamarine.

"I fell in love with that view. It is why I bought the house. When I was a boy, I would visit my grandparents who lived near the sea. Though the beaches in France are nothing like your beaches here."

"They're rather rocky, as I recall," said Guin.

"*Oui*," said Blanchet. "But I am being a bad host. Can I get you something to drink? A bottle of Perrier, perhaps?"

"Thank you, but I'm good." However, Guin's mouth felt a bit dry. She had been in large houses before, many of them quite impressive, but she found Blanchet's home, with its big windows and lack of furniture and artwork, intimidating. Or maybe it was just him.

"I know the place is a bit bare," he said, as though reading Guin's mind. "But I just moved in. Would you care to have a seat?" He gestured toward one of the few pieces of furniture in the room, a white sofa.

"Okay," said Guin.

She took a seat on the sofa and Blanchet sat next to her. She immediately scooched back until her back hit the armrest. Blanchet smiled. Victor had sat down next to him and had placed his head in Blanchet's lap. Guin wondered if Blanchet minded the drool.

"So, your dog's name is Victor?"

Blanchet nodded, stroking the dog's head. Victor looked in heaven.

"Did you name your company after him?" Though she realized it was probably the other way around, the Victor Group no doubt being older than the dog.

Blanchet turned to Guin and smiled.

"No. The dog and the group were both named for my grandfather who founded the Victor Group. Is that not right, Victor?"

Victor didn't answer, just drooled. Blanchet smiled, and Guin did too.

"So, you had questions for me?"

"Yes," said Guin. "I understand you had made an offer for the San Ybel Hotel and Resort. Is that correct?"

"That is correct."

"But you were beaten out by the Mandelli Group."

"That is also correct."

"Do you know why your offer was rejected? I understand you offered the Thompsons cash."

"I suppose the Mandelli Group's offer was better."

But Guin sensed he didn't believe that.

"Were you upset about losing the sale?"

"*Bien sur.* We had big plans for the San Ybel."

"What kind of plans?"

"We wanted to turn it into an eco-friendly destination resort."

"An eco-friendly destination resort? Sanibel is already a

popular tourist destination and over two-thirds of the land on the island is under conservation."

Geez, she sounded like a page from a guidebook.

Blanchet smiled.

"Which is why it needs an eco-friendly luxury resort. Have you seen our eco-friendly luxury hotels? We have several, including our latest in L.A."

"No, I'm afraid I haven't."

Guin made a mental note to look at the Victor Group's properties as soon as she got home. She should have done so beforehand and chastised herself.

"They are all unique—designed to fit into the environment with the latest eco-friendly amenities."

"So your properties, they're all green?"

Guin knew that eco-friendly resorts were a big trend.

"Not all of them. At least not yet. But we were planning on making the San Ybel a shining example. We understand the importance of protecting the environment. And what better place than Sanibel to create the first luxury eco-friendly resort in Southwest Florida?"

"That would have been wonderful. What did the Thompsons think of your plan?"

"Mrs. Thompson, she loved it. But her husband…"

Guin guessed that he cared more about dollar signs than the environment. Though she knew the Thompsons were supporters of the Sanibel-Captiva Conservation Foundation, SCCF.

"So, what will you do now?"

"We have not given up on the San Ybel."

"But the Thompsons signed a contract with the Mandelli Group. The deal's supposed to close soon."

"I have it on good authority that the Mandelli Group is having trouble raising the money. And if they cannot…"

Guin tilted her head. Finney had also said something about the Mandelli Group or Mandelli being in trouble.

Though Audra hadn't said anything. Not that she would.

"What happens?"

"If the Mandelli Group does not have the necessary funds to close, the Thompsons can cancel the contract—and keep the deposit."

"I see." *How very interesting.*

"I'm curious, how well did you know Anthony Mandelli?"

"Not very."

"But you had met."

"*Oui.*"

"I understand the two of you were rivals."

"Rivals?"

"You competed for several properties, yes?"

"I suppose we did. However, we did not consider the Mandelli Group serious competition."

"And yet they beat you out for the San Ybel."

Blanchet frowned.

"And I gather you've met Mr. Mandelli's assistant, Ms. Lamb?"

"You mean Honey?"

Guin nodded, and Blanchet smiled.

"I have."

Guin wondered just how well they knew each other.

"Did you see her at the holiday lighting Saturday?"

"She was hard to miss."

"I'm curious, why did you attend when your offer had been rejected?"

"I had been invited, and I did not want to appear the sore loser."

"Did you speak with Anthony Mandelli at the event?"

"Briefly."

"What did you say to him?"

"I congratulated him."

"You did?"

"You seem surprised."

"I am a bit. I heard that Mandelli or someone in his organization had spread nasty rumors about you and the Victor Group and that those rumors could have been why the Thompsons went with the Mandelli Group instead of you."

Blanchet sighed.

"They would not be the first ones to try to discredit me. But I assured the Thompsons that the rumors were false. Though I cannot help being French," he said, smiling at Guin. "However, I think it was the money Mandelli dangled in front of them that won them the deal."

"Why didn't you counter?"

"We do not believe in overspending. We knew how much the resort was worth and how much we needed to put into it."

"So you think Mandelli overpaid?"

"*Absolutement.*"

Interesting, thought Guin. Though she had read that Mandelli was known for overpaying and then losing his shirt.

"And what did Mandelli say when you congratulated him?"

"No hard feelings."

Of course, he'd say something like that.

"Anything else?"

"No."

"And what did you think of him?"

"May I be honest with you?" said Blanchet, leaning forward.

His violet eyes were really quite intense.

"Please," said Guin.

"People like Anthony Mandelli give developers a bad name. The world is better off without people like him."

Was that a confession?

"And where were you when Mandelli was hit?"

"What time was that?"

Guin told him.

"I believe I was in the lobby."

"Did anyone see you?"

"I was there with my broker, Patrick Finney. We were talking to a couple who lived on the island. I believe their last name was Montero. She is French, like me."

Guin was about to ask him a follow-up question, but he stopped her.

"And now, Ms. Jones, I must go prepare for my call."

He got up, dislodging Victor, who had drooled all over Blanchet's pants.

"Of course," said Guin, also getting up. "Thank you for your time. But before you go, could I get your contact information?"

He smiled at her.

"And why do you want it?"

"In case I have more questions. I'd prefer not to have to ring your doorbell again."

There was that sexy smile again.

"I will get you a card." He turned to Victor and told him to stay.

"You're not taking him with you?"

"I will be right back."

Guin looked at the guard dog. He was drooling again and didn't look particularly fierce.

"Just stay there," she said to him.

A minute later, Blanchet returned.

"Here," he said, handing her a card. "My private number is on the back."

Guin took the card and thanked him. Then she reached into her bag.

"Here's my card," she said, handing it to him.

His fingers brushed hers as he took it, and Guin wondered if that was deliberate. He looked down at the card then at Guin.

"It was a pleasure meeting you, Guinivere. I trust you can see yourself out?"

Guin nodded. Then she watched as Hugo and Victor headed down the hall.

Guin had been tempted to take a quick look around while Blanchet was on his call, but she left, not wanting to be caught snooping. She stood at the foot of the stairs, taking a final look at the house. Then she got in her car.

As she drove home, she couldn't help thinking about Blanchet. He had seemed so self-assured without being cocky. So unlike Mandelli. He had corroborated Finney's story. Which Nicole Montero had also corroborated. They couldn't all be lying, could they? Though they may have had the time wrong. She doubted they were looking at their watches or phones. Still, she couldn't picture Blanchet climbing up and loosening the light. But he could have paid someone to do it.

And what was this about the Mandelli Group not having lined up the financing to close the deal? Had that been the case before Mandelli died or was it a result of his death? She wanted to ask Audra, but she doubted she would tell her. From her conservation with the real estate broker, it sounded as though the deal would still go through.

She should speak with the Thompsons. Had Blanchet already approached them?

And was there something going on between Honey and Blanchet?

Guin sighed as she turned onto her street. So many questions and no answers. And she still needed to write something.

She parked in her driveway and went inside. Fauna was waiting for her.

Guin knelt and petted her.

"Did you miss me?" she asked the cat. "Were you lonely?"

Guin could have sworn Fauna nodded.

"Maybe Glen's right and I need to get another cat. Would you like a friend to play with?" she asked the feline.

Fauna purred. Though Guin had a feeling that was because she was stroking her.

Guin got up, and Fauna mewed.

"Sorry, kitty cat. I've got to work."

She headed to her office, Fauna following her.

CHAPTER 19

Guin was feeling frustrated. She didn't know what to write. She had tried several angles but none of them seemed right. Maybe Craig could help her.

He picked up after a few rings.

"What's up?"

"You at home?"

"I am."

"Ginny wants an update on Mandelli, but I don't know what to write. I still have too many questions."

"You speak to O'Loughlin?"

"He's been blowing me off. I was hoping you might have heard something. Any update on the autopsy? Any chance you could get the preliminary results? Not that I'm expecting them to reveal much."

"I'll check again. Why don't you tell me what you know? Maybe we can come up with something in case the results aren't available."

"Okay." Then she told him about her conversations with Audra, Finney, Blanchet, Honey, and Washburn. "As I said, there's a lot there but nothing I'd necessarily want to put in print just yet."

"Hm," said Craig. "I see what you mean."

"Do I say something about the allegations against Mandelli by the maids? But I don't want to get them in trouble. Or do I talk about the battle over the hotel? That could have been a motive. But I don't have proof. And both Blanchet and Finney have alibis."

"What about the assistant?"

"She claims she was in the ladies' room. And I can't go accusing her without proof."

"You could write about the missing maintenance worker."

"I know. But what if he didn't do it?"

"He sounds guilty to me. His wife was assaulted by Mandelli. He had motive and opportunity. And you said Mandelli's assistant saw him backstage."

"She said she saw *a* maintenance worker, not necessarily Luis."

"You don't have to say he did it, just that he's a suspect."

Guin sighed. She knew Craig had a point. But she felt as though she'd be throwing Luis under the bus. Even though she didn't know him, it felt wrong.

"It's possible someone bribed Luis to do it and told him to disappear. But his wife was waiting to get her green card. Why risk it?"

"The person could have offered him a lot of money."

"I suppose."

"You could always try speaking to O'Loughlin again. Tell him what you know. Maybe he'll be more inclined to share when he hears what you already know."

"Maybe. I should speak with the Thompsons. I have a feeling it involves the sale of the hotel."

"Betty plays bridge with Linda. You want her to put in a good word?"

"That would be great. Though if it's at all awkward…"

"Nonsense. Betty would love to help."

Guin thought she heard Betty in the background.

"That was Betty," said Craig. "She wants to know if you're free for dinner tonight."

"Tonight?"

"You free?"

Guin didn't think she had any plans.

"I think so, but…"

"Then it's settled. Be here at six."

"Um, okay. Can I bring anything?"

"Hold on a sec. Betty's yelling something at me. What?" Guin smiled. They were such an old married couple. "She says to bring your friend."

"I assume she means Glen."

"Yeah, him."

"I'll ask, but I'm not sure he's free. So what should I write?"

"I'm afraid you're on your own, kid. But you've got good instincts. I'm sure you'll come up with something."

"Thanks."

They said goodbye and ended the call.

Guin sat back in her chair and frowned. Craig had more confidence in her than she had in herself. At least right now. She looked out the window. She wasn't in the mood to write. Well, not without a plan. But she didn't want to just sit around. She picked up her phone to call the San Ybel, to see if either Thompson was available.

Guin had met Fred and Linda Thompson a few times at various social events. But she didn't really know them. They were in their seventies and had raised their children on Sanibel. Though they were originally from Ohio.

When they purchased the San Ybel, it had been more like an inn. But Fred and Linda had turned it into one of Sanibel's leading hotels, quadrupling the number of rooms and adding tennis courts, an Olympic-size swimming pool, a restaurant, and a spa. But the place had been showing its age recently, and Guin hadn't been too surprised when she heard that the Thompsons had decided to sell. After all, their children were grown and had moved away. And running a resort was a lot of work.

Guin pressed zero to be connected to the operator and asked to speak with the Thompsons.

"Which one?" asked the operator.

"They don't share an office?"

"They do, but they have separate lines," the operator explained.

"How about we try Fred first?"

"One moment, please." Guin waited. "I'm afraid no one's picking up."

"Could you try Linda Thompson?"

"Please hold," said the operator. Again, Guin waited. "I'm sorry, Mrs. Thompson isn't picking up either."

"Could I leave a voicemail?"

"For which one?"

Guin sighed inwardly.

"Mr. Thompson."

"I'll connect you to his voicemail."

At the beep, she left a message.

"Hi, Mr. Thompson. This is Guin Jones with the *San-Cap Sun-Times*. I'd love to speak with you about the San Ybel when you have a minute. You can reach me at…" She left her number and hung up. Hopefully, he would call her back later. Should she call back and leave a message for Mrs. Thompson too? Or was that overkill? She could always ask Betty to reach out to Mrs. Thompson if Mr. Thompson didn't get back to her.

She turned back to her computer. She should probably try to write something, even if it was just random thoughts.

She opened a new document and stared at it. Then she started to type. She filled up half a page and read what she had written. Then she deleted it.

"Let's try this again."

She wrote a few sentences and then stopped and deleted them. It was hopeless.

She looked down at her phone. She kept hearing Craig

in her head, telling her to talk to the detective.

"But what if he won't tell me anything? Screw it," she said a few seconds later and picked up her phone. Even though she had deleted the detective's contact information, she had memorized his cell phone number. She dialed it now—and was surprised when he answered.

"Bill?"

"You were expecting someone else?"

"I was expecting the call to go to voicemail."

"You want me to hang up?"

"No. Stay." She hesitated. "What are you doing for lunch?"

"Lunch?"

"You know, that meal you eat in the middle of the day." She smiled as she said it. It was one of the detective's old lines.

"Very funny," he said.

"So, you free?"

"I may be. What time?"

"Twelve-thirty?"

"Make it one."

"Okay. One it is."

"Where?"

"Jean-Luc's?"

"Fine. See you at one."

Guin couldn't believe the detective had agreed to meet her. Maybe Craig was right. Maybe the detective would give her something if she told him what she already knew. It was worth a shot.

Guin arrived at Jean-Luc's a little before one. The place was busy, which was to be expected. It was a very popular spot. She looked around for the detective, but he wasn't there. She had checked her phone before she left and again when she arrived, thinking the detective might cancel. But she hadn't received a message from him.

At a little after one, he walked in.

"Hey," she said.

He nodded his head.

They waited in line until it was their turn.

Jake smiled at them.

"So, what can we get the two of you today?" he asked them.

"Hm," said Guin, looking up at the menu. "I'll have a ham and cheese galette." A galette was a buckwheat crepe.

"Coming right up. And to drink?"

"A sparkling water, please."

"And for you, Detective?" Jake asked.

"I'll have the mozzarella, tomato, and pesto baguette."

"And to drink?"

"A raspberry sparkling water."

Guin smiled. She knew the detective preferred soda, but Jean-Luc's didn't serve soda.

They stepped aside and waited for their order.

"Here you go!" said Jake a minute later. "You sure you don't want a pastry?"

Guin glanced at the pastry case. Everything looked delicious, as usual.

"I'll take a box of Jo's macarons." She would bring them to Craig and Betty's.

"Which kind?"

They had four different flavors: raspberry, pistachio, coffee, and chocolate. Guin told him she'd take three of each, and Jake carefully placed them in a box.

"They're for Craig and Betty," Guin informed the detective. "I'm having dinner with them later."

Guin insisted on paying for lunch, and for once the detective didn't object. Then they took their meal outside.

They found a place to sit, and Guin cut into her galette.

"Mm," she said, closing her eyes. "It makes you feel like you're in Paris."

"Never been," said the detective.

"Really?"

"Nope. Never had the time. Or, to be honest, the inclination."

"Huh."

Guin couldn't imagine not wanting to go to Paris.

The detective took another bite of his baguette.

"So, any progress on the case?" she asked nonchalantly.

The detective continued to chew. Guin waited for him to finish. Finally, he was done. Well, almost. He took a sip of his sparkling water before replying.

"You know I can't discuss the case."

"What if I told you what I knew and you corrected me or filled me in?"

The detective didn't say anything, just studied her. Guin took that as her cue to spill.

She told him about her conversation with Patrick Finney.

"And I met with Hugo Blanchet this morning. He's the head of the Victor Group and just bought a place here. He and Mandelli were both competing for the San Ybel, but he lost and claims Mandelli didn't play fair. You speak with him?"

The detective didn't say anything. So Guin went on.

"Blanchet claims he was in the lobby with Finney, talking to a couple—Raphael and Nicole Montero—at the time. Ginny and I spoke with Mrs. Montero. She confirmed she spoke with them but couldn't confirm the time. So he could have been in the ballroom."

"He wasn't."

"You know that for sure?"

"No one recalled seeing him in the ballroom at the time, and Mrs. Montero's husband confirmed he was talking with them at the time of the incident."

Guin frowned.

"He could have paid someone to loosen that light."

"He could have."

"What about Finney?"

"Still checking him out. He was seen with Blanchet, but he apparently excused himself around the time of the incident and was unaccounted for for several minutes."

"Huh. So he could have loosened the clamp."

The detective didn't comment.

"I also spoke with Mandelli's assistant, Honey Lamb." Guin couldn't bring herself to call Honey Mandelli's *special* assistant. It sounded a bit tawdry. "She claimed to be in the ladies' room when it happened."

"We're still verifying Ms. Lamb's alibi."

Guin felt she had given him enough information. Now it was his turn to spill.

"What about Mandelli's will?"

"What about it?"

"I assume he left one. Do you know what it said, who the beneficiaries were?"

"No."

"What about the autopsy? I know it was yesterday. Did they find anything?"

"The official report won't be ready for a few days."

"What about unofficially? The medical examiner must at least have told you the cause of death."

Guin assumed it was blunt trauma and was surprised when the detective said Mandelli had suffered a heart attack.

"A heart attack? Not blunt trauma?"

"Heart attack was the official cause."

"Caused by the light falling on him."

"Not necessarily."

"What does that mean? Something else caused the heart attack?" Guin thought quickly. "Was he poisoned?"

"We're waiting for the toxicology report."

"Does that mean you think he was poisoned?"

"I don't think anything."

Guin frowned.

"Look, I know you didn't want to discuss the case, and I appreciate you telling me this much, but Ginny's breathing down my neck to give her something. And while I can tell readers he had a heart attack, I could use a bit more. Surely, there's something you can tell me. Please?"

She gave him a pleading look. She hated herself for sounding desperate, but she hoped an honest plea might sway him.

"All right."

"All right?" Guin immediately perked up. "So you'll give me something I can print?"

"Don't get too excited."

Guin waited.

"They found alcohol and cocaine in his system."

Guin deflated. That was the big revelation? She knew Mandelli had had at least a couple of drinks. And she wasn't surprised that he sniffed cocaine. Though he had seemed more down than up when she had seen him.

"How is that news?"

"You asked me for something you could print."

"How much alcohol and cocaine?"

"Above the legal limit."

"You think he was an alcoholic?" The detective didn't say anything. "An addict?" Again, nothing. "Both? Was it the alcohol and coke that caused the heart attack?"

"Possibly. He apparently had a weak heart. Probably wouldn't have taken much to push it over the edge."

"Huh," said Guin. Well, at least now she had something to write. Though…

"When will the official toxicology report be in?"

"End of the week if they're not too busy."

"Not until the end of the week?"

The detective looked at her.

"This isn't *CSI*. In the real world, toxicology reports can take weeks."

"Weeks?"

The detective didn't say anything.

Guin sighed. Should she wait for the report? Probably not. She could always do a follow-up if the report contained new information.

"Well, will you let me know when you get it?"

The detective was giving her that look of his, the one that said, *what do you think?*

"You arrest anyone?"

"Not yet."

"What about the maintenance worker, the one who disappeared? Any luck finding him?"

"Not yet."

"What about the light?"

"What about it?"

"Any fingerprints on it or the clamp or the rigging?"

"No, everything was clean."

"You think whoever loosened it wore gloves?"

"Probably. There was no trace of cleaning fluid or paper fibers."

More information. However, it didn't really tell her anything. And would Luis have worn gloves? It seemed unlikely.

"Did anyone you spoke with report seeing anyone backstage, other than a maintenance worker?"

"No, only the maintenance worker."

"Did anyone other than Honey reported seeing someone?"

The detective nodded.

"A couple also saw him. Same description."

"Do you have the couple's name?"

"You know I…"

Guin held up her hand.

"I know."

"I need to go," he said, wrapping up the remains of his sandwich. "Thanks for lunch."

"You're welcome," said Guin. "Thanks for the information."

He got up and headed to the parking lot. Guin watched him. She waited until he pulled out, then she got up and headed to her Mini.

CHAPTER 20

As soon as she got home, Guin got to work on her article. And by later that afternoon, she had a first draft. It wasn't long. And it wasn't her best work. But it would do. And if she received new information in the next twenty-four hours, she'd add it.

She saved the document and glanced at the time. It was nearly five o'clock. She would need to head over to Craig and Betty's soon. But she needed to stretch her legs. She went to the kitchen to get a glass of water and glanced outside. Maybe a short walk around the neighborhood.

She headed down the block and saw that the dog walkers were out. Guin quickly caught up with them. They were chatting about some big house that was going up across the way by the beach, another concrete mansion. Sally turned to her.

"So, Guin, any news about what happened Saturday? Suzy Seashell seems to think someone deliberately loosened that light and is demanding that the police find the killer before someone else gets harmed."

Guin didn't know what to say.

"You're covering the story for the paper, aren't you?" said Sally.

"I am."

"You speak with the police?"

"I have."

"And? Do they have any suspects?" asked Greg. He lived around the corner and was the owner of a black lab.

"Probably, but they haven't arrested anyone."

"You were there Saturday," said Sally. "Who do you think did it?"

Everyone stopped and looked at Guin. She could feel their eyes boring into her.

"I can't say."

"Can't or won't?" said Greg.

"I bet Suzy finds out who did it," said Gloria. She was the neighborhood gossip and owned a miniature poodle. "She's got sources everywhere."

Guin felt her nails digging into her palm. Ginny would kill her if Suzy identified the killer before she did.

"I need to go. Nice seeing you all."

"We didn't scare you away, did we?" asked Joan. She had a goldendoodle.

"No, I have a dinner date."

"With that good-looking photographer?" said Gloria.

Was Gloria spying on her?

Guin smiled at the older woman.

"No, with old friends."

Though as she said it, she realized she had forgotten to ask Glen to dinner. Oh, well. The four of them could do dinner another time.

Guin wished her neighbors a good night and headed home to get changed. Not that she needed to dress up to go to Craig and Betty's. They didn't care what she wore. But she felt like putting on something a bit nicer than what she was wearing.

She went into her closet and changed into a sundress. Then she went into the bathroom and examined her hair and face in the mirror. Her strawberry-blonde curls were looking particularly wild thanks to her walk. She attempted to tame them and gave up.

She went into the kitchen and gave Fauna some food. Then she grabbed her bag and her keys, said goodbye to Fauna, and was out the door.

As she headed east, Guin thought about her article. She had researched whether cocaine and alcohol use could weaken one's heart and discovered they could. She had come across a study that said even recreational use of cocaine could damage your heart. And too much alcohol wasn't good for you either. But had the killer known about Mandelli's heart? Had Mandelli?

Guin wanted to ask Honey if she knew. Surely, as Mandelli's assistant—or special assistant—she would know something. She should also talk to Audra. Not that either of them would necessarily reveal anything to her.

She pulled into the Jeffers' driveway but stayed in the car. She was still thinking about Mandelli. She thought about calling over to the San Ybel and asking to speak with Honey, but now was not the time. Instead, she got out of the car and headed to the front door.

"Mm, something smells good," said Guin as she and Craig stood outside the kitchen. "What's Betty making?"

"Pot roast."

"Pot roast?" said Guin. She knew Betty had Craig on a strict low-red-meat, low-carb diet.

"Special occasion."

"Oh?"

"We're going to be grandparents again."

"That's wonderful!" said Guin. "Congratulations. When's the new one due?"

"April."

"Who's pregnant?"

"Sabrina, our youngest."

"Is she the one who lives in Chicago?"

"Yep."

"This is her second, yes?"

"Good memory. It is. They've been struggling to have another, so they waited until they were sure to tell us."

"Will you go up and see them?"

"That's the plan. Betty's already offered to help take care of Noah, so they can focus on the new one." Noah was Sabrina and Rob's little boy, who was three.

"Is the new one a boy or a girl?"

"They don't want to know. Said they don't care as long as it's healthy."

"What are you two whispering about?" asked Betty.

"We weren't whispering," said Craig. "I was just telling Guin about the baby."

Betty smiled.

"You must be very excited," said Guin.

"We are. They've been trying for years to have a little playmate for Noah."

"Well, I'm happy for them and for you," said Guin. And she was. Though a little piece of her heart ached at the news. She and her ex had tried for years to have a child. But it had never happened for them.

"Thank you," said Betty.

"Craig says you're going to go up there just before the baby's due."

Betty nodded.

"Sabrina and Rob have a helper, but I know little Noah will be happier having his Gammy there."

Guin smiled. She didn't know Sabrina and Rob, but she sensed they were doing just fine, and that Betty was using the new baby as an excuse to spend time with her grandson, who she adored.

"But enough about that," said Betty. "Go take a seat at the table. Dinner's almost ready."

"I almost forgot," said Guin. She'd been holding the

pastry box. "This is for you."

Betty took the pastry box.

"What's this?"

"A special treat. I picked them up at Jean-Luc's."

Betty opened the box.

"Are these macarons?"

"They are!"

"They look too pretty to eat."

Craig eyed the treats. He reached a hand in, but Betty slapped it away.

"Not before dinner!"

"I just wanted to have a closer look."

Betty eyed him suspiciously.

"They're very low calorie," said Guin. "And I don't think they have a lot of sugar."

Craig looked hopefully at his wife.

"You can have one after dinner," she replied.

"Just one?"

"Two if you're a good boy and help me."

"Just tell me what to do," said Craig.

"Can I help?" asked Guin.

"No, you're our guest. Go sit. Dinner will be ready in a few."

Guin didn't feel like a guest, more like family. But she knew better than to argue with Betty. A short time later, Betty and Craig stepped out of the kitchen bearing a plate filled with pot roast and another full of roasted vegetables.

"That looks delicious," said Guin.

"Just wait till you taste Betty's pot roast!" said Craig. "Betty could show Julia Child a thing or two."

"Really," said his wife, shaking her head.

"It's true!" said Craig. "Just ask anyone."

Guin smiled

"Did you use Julia Child's pot roast recipe?" she asked Betty.

"No, it's my own."

They each took some pot roast and roasted vegetables and made small talk.

"I heard about what happened at the holiday lighting," said Betty, turning to Guin. "Suzy seems to think it was murder."

Did everyone read Shellapalooza?

"I told you not to pay attention to what that woman prints," said Craig.

"Is she right?" Betty asked Guin, ignoring her husband.

"It wasn't an accident."

Betty gave her husband a smug look.

"Any idea who did it and why?"

"A lot of people were unhappy about Mandelli buying the resort," Guin told Betty.

"But he promised nothing would change."

"Probably said that at the last place he bought too, before he fired everyone," mumbled Craig.

"So any suspects?" Betty asked Guin.

"There are several people who had a motive, but I don't want to name names without more information," Guin said diplomatically.

Betty looked disappointed.

"I supposed I can understand that. Though I heard you talking with Craig. And that Detective O'Loughlin was back. Did you know?" she asked Guin.

"Not until I saw him."

"He didn't tell you he was back on Sanibel? That doesn't seem very nice of him."

"No, it doesn't."

"I don't think Guin wants to discuss the detective," Craig said to his wife.

"I'm sorry," said Betty. "I didn't mean to raise a sore subject."

"It's okay," said Guin. "We actually just had lunch together."

"You and the detective?" said Betty.

Guin smiled.

"Yes. Craig was the one who suggested it."

"I didn't suggest you have lunch, just that you talk with him."

"I thought food might loosen him up. And I took your advice and told him what I knew."

"And?"

"He told me that Mandelli died of a heart attack."

"A heart attack?"

Guin nodded.

"Caused by the light?" asked Craig.

"That may have precipitated it. Though apparently there was a fair amount of alcohol and cocaine in his system."

"Suzy didn't say anything about a heart attack," said Betty. "Or about any drugs."

Guin smiled to herself. *Take that, Suzy.*

"You think he had a drug problem?" asked Craig.

"It wouldn't surprise me. I'm planning on talking to Honey and Audra, to see if they know anything."

"You find out anything else from O'Loughlin?"

"Not really."

Guin helped clear the table.

"Oh, and I tried reaching the Thompsons, but they were both unavailable."

"Did Craig tell you I play bridge with Linda?"

"He did."

"I'd be happy to ask her to call you if you like."

"Thank you. She wouldn't happen to have said anything about the hotel, would she?"

"We don't talk business when we play."

"So you never heard her mention Mandelli or a Frenchman named Hugo Blanchet?"

"Blanchet… I don't think so, though… You say he's French?"

"Yes. He's the head of the Victor Group. They own half

a dozen boutique hotels and other properties and were interested in purchasing the San Ybel."

"He wouldn't happen to look like some famous French actor, would he?"

Guin knew of several famous French actors, but she had a feeling Betty meant Alain Delon.

"Yes, that's the one!" Betty said when Guin mentioned Delon's name. "Linda had lunch with this Mr. Blanchet the other day and said he looked just like that Delon fellow. She even showed us pictures of the two of them. He's very handsome."

Interesting, thought Guin.

"Would you like some coffee or tea?" Betty asked her.

"No, thank you." Betty and Craig drank instant decaf, which Guin couldn't stand.

Craig cleared his throat.

"I think he wants a macaron," Guin said to Betty.

"Two macarons."

Betty signed.

"Let me just get a plate."

She placed the cookies on a plate and brought them out to the table. Craig immediately took two.

"Won't you have one?" she asked Guin. "We can't eat all of them."

"Speak for yourself," said Craig.

Guin smiled and took one, popping it into her mouth.

"These are delicious," said Betty.

"Mm," said Craig, his mouth full.

The Jeffers' phone began to ring.

"I should get that," said Betty. "It could be one of the children."

She went to answer it in the other room and returned a few minutes later.

"You'll never guess who that was."

"Who?" said Craig.

"Linda Thompson."

Well, that certainly was a coincidence.

"What did she want?" asked Craig.

"She was asking if it was okay to change this week's bridge date. Seems they're a bit busy."

"Did you tell her about Guin?"

"I did. She said she'd be happy to speak with her." She turned to Guin. "You should call her office first thing tomorrow. Her assistant will be in at eight-thirty, and she can schedule an appointment."

"That's wonderful!" said Guin. "Thank you."

Betty smiled.

"Now, would the two of you excuse me?"

"She's going to watch *Jeopardy!*" Craig said to Guin in a low voice. Guin smiled.

"Of course," she said. She turned to Craig as soon as Betty had gone into the other room. "I was wondering, do you think Mandelli got the cocaine here or did he bring it with him?"

"It'd be risky traveling with it unless he flew private."

"Good point," said Guin. "Can you make some discreet inquiries, see if he had someone here who supplied him?"

"I can, but…"

"I know. And like I said, I'll ask Honey and Audra. Though I have a feeling that even if they know something they won't tell me. It wouldn't look good for the new owner of the San Ybel to be revealed as a drug addict."

"Definitely not."

"I wonder…" said Guin.

"What?" said Craig.

"Well, if Mandelli had a drug problem, could the Thompsons use it to void the contract?"

"Why would they want to void the contract?"

"What if they got a better offer?"

"You think they got a better offer?"

"I told you what Hugo Blanchet told me."

"Hm."

"And most contracts have a clause stating that if one of the parties was mentally incapacitated or under the influence of drugs or alcohol at the time of signing then the contract could be voided."

"You think Mandelli could have been under the influence when he signed?"

"It's possible. I'd ask Honey and Audra, but I doubt they'd tell me. That's another thing. I did a quick search for *Honey Lamb*, and I couldn't find anything. Well, except for a bunch of lamb recipes. I looked under *Henrietta Lamb* too, but all I found was an obituary for an old woman from Long Island who died back in 2017."

"Maybe Ms. Lamb isn't on social media."

"I guess it's possible. But she doesn't seem the type. I have a feeling she's hiding something."

"Maybe Honey Lamb isn't her real name. You ask me, Honey Lamb is a stripper name."

"I don't think Honey is a stripper. Anyway, I should get going." She got up and headed to the door, Craig following her. "Please thank Betty for dinner and for getting me in to see Linda Thompson."

"I'll tell her."

"And let me know what you find out."

He said he would, and Guin left.

CHAPTER 21

Guin called the San Ybel at eight-thirty the next morning and asked to be connected to Mrs. Thompson's office.

The phone rang, and a woman answered.

"Mrs. Thompson's office."

"Good morning," said Guin. "My name's Guinivere Jones. I'm calling to arrange an appointment to see Mrs. Thompson."

"I'm afraid she's quite busy," said the woman.

"I understand that. But a mutual friend, Betty Jeffers, spoke to Mrs. Thompson last night, and Mrs. Thompson said she'd make time for me today. I'm a reporter with the *San-Cap Sun-Times*."

"Oh, you're that Guinivere Jones!" said the woman. "I just love reading your restaurant reviews!"

"Thank you," said Guin. "So, could you squeeze me in? I only need a few minutes of Mrs. Thompson's time."

"Let me see," said the woman. There was a brief pause. "How soon can you get here?"

"I could be there at nine."

"That should be okay. She has a meeting at nine-thirty, but she's usually here by nine."

"I'll get there as soon as I can," said Guin. "Thank you. I'm sorry, I didn't catch your name."

"It's Marjorie."

"Thank you, Marjorie."

They ended the call and Guin quickly went to her closet to change.

Guin pulled into the San Ybel at five to nine and hurried inside. She stopped at the front desk and asked where she could find Mrs. Thompson's office.

"Do you have an appointment?" said the woman at the front desk.

"I do. Is her office on the second floor?"

"Yes, in the Executive Suite."

"Thank you," said Guin. Then she hurried to the stairs.

Guin passed by Hermione's and Laurence Washburn's offices. The lights were on, but neither was in. Just past them was a door marked Executive Suite. She entered and saw a matronly woman seated at a desk. The woman, no doubt Marjorie, was on the phone. She saw Guin and held up a finger, indicating she'd just be a minute. Guin waited. Finally, Marjorie was off.

"Ms. Jones?"

"That's me. Though please, call me Guin."

"Mrs. Thompson's running a bit late, but she should be here any minute." Marjorie's phone was ringing. She glared at it. "It hasn't stopped ringing since Saturday."

"I'll bet," said Guin. "Please, go ahead and answer it. I'll just wait over there for Mrs. Thompson."

"Thank you," said Marjorie. She answered the phone, and Guin took a seat.

A few minutes later, the door flew open, and Linda Thompson entered.

"You would not believe the morning I've had, Marjorie! I swear, if it's not one thing, it's another."

Marjorie jerked her head towards Guin.

"Is there something wrong with your head?" Mrs. Thompson asked her assistant.

Guin stood up and cleared her throat.

"Oh! I didn't see you there," said Mrs. Thompson, turning around. "You must be Betty's friend. We have a leak in the kitchen and Fred was busy, so I had to wait for the plumber."

"I hope everything is okay."

"I hope so too. Now, what can I do for you, Miss…?"

"Jones."

"Right. Betty said you wanted to talk to me about the sale. Let's go into my office." She turned to Marjorie. "Hold my calls, unless it's important."

Guin followed Mrs. Thompson into her office and watched as she opened drawers as though looking for something.

"Can I help you find something?" Guin asked her.

Mrs. Thompson stopped what she was doing and looked up at Guin.

"Hm?"

"Are you looking for something?"

"I am, but I'll look for it later. Please, have a seat."

Guin sat down in a nearby chair.

"Now, how can I help you?" Guin opened her mouth to speak, but Mrs. Thompson cut her off. "Can I get you something to drink, a coffee, perhaps? I know I could use one. Marjorie!" she bellowed.

Marjorie poked her head in.

"Yes, Mrs. Thompson?"

"Would you be a dear and get me a latte? Ms. Jones?"

"I'm fine," said Guin.

"Come, come. It's no trouble."

"Maybe a glass of water?"

"We have bottles of spring water in the fridge. Still or sparkling?"

"Still is fine."

"Marjorie, can you get Ms. Jones a bottle of water?"

Marjorie nodded and disappeared back into the outer office, returning a few seconds later with a bottle of water, which she handed to Guin.

"Thank you," said Guin.

"Now go fetch me a latte and get something for yourself. And remind them not to add any sugar!"

Marjorie nodded and disappeared once again, closing the door behind her.

"I'd be lost without that woman," said Mrs. Thompson. "Now, where were we?"

"I was about to ask you about the sale of the hotel. I understand you were supposed to close this week. But with the death of Mr. Mandelli, I wondered if that was still going to happen."

Mrs. Thompson sighed.

"It's all rather a mess."

"So is there an issue with the closing?"

Mrs. Thompson eyed her.

"Off the record?"

Guin nodded.

"Off the record."

"There appears to be some issue with the financing. Mr. Mandelli assured us everything was in order, but…"

"It isn't?"

"One of the investors apparently changed his mind at the last minute. And now they're asking us to give them more time."

"I see," said Guin. "And will you give it to them?"

"We're still deciding."

"What do you want to do? Off the record."

Mrs. Thompson studied her.

"Frankly, I was never keen on the Mandelli Group."

"Oh?" said Guin.

"We had received another offer, from the Victor Group. They're French. All cash. It was a good offer. At least I thought so. We were planning on signing a contract with them. Then Audra somehow found out about it and insisted we meet with her client."

"Anthony Mandelli."

Mrs. Thompson nodded.

"I didn't want to, but Fred said, what's the harm?"

"So you met with him."

"We did."

"And he offered you more money."

"He did, but it wasn't a cash offer like the Victor Group's. And there were contingencies."

"But you accepted it anyway."

"We did. Or Fred did. He was adamant about it, and I went along. I regret that now."

"So how much more time does the Mandelli Group want?"

"They want to delay the closing until after the new year."

"So, what, thirty days from now?"

"Approximately."

"And the deal was originally supposed to close this week?"

"On Friday."

"And what happens if they don't come up with the financing?"

"Then they forfeit the deposit and we're free to seek another buyer."

"I see. Do you have to give them the thirty days?"

"Our lawyer says we should, but…"

"But what?"

"We're still off the record, yes?"

"If that's what you want."

"Please. Fred would probably kill me for discussing this with a reporter. But Betty said you wouldn't print anything without my approval."

Betty shouldn't have said that as it technically wasn't true, but Guin told Mrs. Thompson to go on.

"Well, shortly after Mr. Mandelli's demise, I received a call from Hugo Blanchet, the head of the Victor Group. He said he was calling to express his sympathies, which I said was very kind of him, and we wound up chatting."

"What did you chat about?"

"This and that."

"Did he happen to say if he was still interested in acquiring the hotel?"

"He may have mentioned it."

"Did you tell him that the Mandelli Group asked for an extension?"

"I did."

"And what did he say?"

"He said he didn't want to wait until after the new year. That he wanted to close before Christmas."

"Why won't he wait?"

"He's going back to France for the holiday. And he's probably worried the Mandelli Group will raise the money. He even offered us a bonus if we closed in the next couple of weeks."

"How much of a bonus?"

"I'm afraid that's confidential. But enough that Fred is considering it."

"I see."

"The problem is, we're afraid of being sued by the Mandelli Group if we break things off with them before the thirty days are up."

There was a knock on the door.

"Come in!" shouted Mrs. Thompson.

Marjorie poked her head in.

"Don't be shy," said Mrs. Thompson. "You have my latte?"

Marjorie nodded and brought it over. Mrs. Thompson grabbed it and took a sip.

"It's warm."

"Sorry," said Marjorie.

"That's all right. Thank you for fetching it."

"Is there something else I can get you?"

"Ms. Jones?"

"I'm good."

"You may go, Marjorie."

Marjorie left.

"Now, where were we?"

"We were just discussing the Victor Group's revised bid."

"Right."

"When do you have to let them know?"

"He's given us until Monday to decide. So you can see why we're at sixes and sevens."

"Well, I hope you sort it out."

"Me too, dear. Me too."

"I had another question, it's about the incident on Saturday."

"Dreadful that," said Mrs. Thompson.

"I assume you've spoken with the police."

"Several times now."

Just then there was another knock on the door, and Marjorie poked her head inside.

"What is it now?" said Mrs. Thompson.

"It's Mr. Thompson. He says it's urgent."

Mrs. Thompson sighed.

"Put him through."

"Should I go?" asked Guin.

"This will only be a minute… I hope." She picked up her desk phone. "What is it now, Fred?" There was a pause. "Well, if he says the pipe needs to be replaced, have him replace the pipe." Guin felt Mrs. Thompson's annoyance. "Look, you're there, I'm not. I just don't want to come home to find the kitchen flooded. I'm in the middle of a meeting. Just handle it."

She hung up and turned to Guin.

"You would think after running a hotel for three decades, he could deal with a leaky pipe."

Guin suppressed a smile.

A cell phone began to ring. Guin knew it wasn't hers.

"Do you need to get that?" she asked Mrs. Thompson.

"If it's important, they'll leave a message or call the office."

Mrs. Thompson's cell phone stopped ringing. But a few seconds later, her desk phone started. She sighed.

"It never ends. I should probably get this." She picked up the phone. "Yes?" She looked annoyed. "I'm in a meeting." She frowned. "Very well. Just give me a few minutes." She replaced the handset and turned to Guin. "I'm afraid I need to go."

"Is everything all right?"

"No. But such is life when you own a resort. Would you excuse me?"

"Of course," said Guin. They both stood. "I still had a few questions I wanted to ask you."

"Talk to Marjorie. She'll arrange something."

They walked to the outer office.

"Duty calls," Mrs. Thompson told Marjorie. Then she left.

Guin stayed behind.

"I had a few more questions I wanted to ask Mrs. Thompson. Can I arrange another interview?"

"You could always email her."

"Is she good about answering email?"

"Not really."

"Can I arrange an appointment now?"

The phone was ringing, and Marjorie answered it.

"Mrs. Thompson's office."

"I'll call you," Guin mouthed. "Thanks for the water."

Marjorie nodded, and Guin left.

CHAPTER 22

As soon as she got back to the lobby, Guin checked her phone for messages. There was nothing important. She looked at the time. It was nearly nine-thirty. As she was at the San Ybel, she may as well see if Honey was around.

She found a house phone and asked to be connected to Honey's room. The phone rang several times and then went to voicemail. Guin frowned and left a message. Then she took out her phone and called Audra Linwood's office.

"Linwood Real Estate," said a male voice.

It sounded like Fletcher.

"Is this Fletcher?" said Guin.

"It is. Can I help you?"

"Fletcher, it's Guin Jones with the *San-Cap Sun-Times*. We met the other day. Is Ms. Linwood available?"

"I'm afraid she's rather busy this morning."

"Any chance she could squeeze me in later? It's important that I speak with her."

"Let me check her schedule. Can you hold?"

"I can."

Guin waited as the music on hold played. A minute later, Fletcher was back.

"She has appointments all day, but I could possibly squeeze you in for a few minutes at noon."

"Put me down."

"Can I tell her what this is about?"

"It's about the Mandelli Group's purchase of the San Ybel. You wouldn't happen to know anything about that, would you?"

"I'm afraid I don't," he replied. Though would he say anything if he did? Guin knew Audra valued discretion.

"Okay, well thanks for getting me in to see Audra later."

She ended the call and glanced around the lobby. The hotel was bustling. Apparently, even a murder couldn't keep people away during Christmas season.

Guin wondered how Hermione was faring. She didn't have any place to be until noon, so she went back up the stairs to see if Hermione was in. The light was on in her office, and the door was ajar. Guin peered inside. Hermione was on the phone. Guin waited for her to finish. As soon as Hermione hung up, Guin knocked on the door. Hermione looked up.

"Okay if I come in?"

"I'm a bit busy," said Hermione. She looked tired, Guin thought, and there was an edge to her voice.

"This'll only take a minute."

Guin stepped inside.

"Yes?" said Hermione.

Now that Guin was closer, she saw dark circles under Hermione's eyes, and she wondered if Hermione had gotten much sleep since Saturday. Probably not.

"I wanted to know if this weekend's events were still going off as planned." There was the hotel's popular Meet Santa! event on Sunday, which took place in the ballroom.

"They are."

"Really?"

"It's Christmastime, our busiest season."

"But…"

Hermione looked annoyed, or maybe it was just fatigue. "What's the old saying, the show must go on?"

"But… Did the police say it was okay to reopen the ballroom?"

"They did, after we swore we'd have the place triple-checked before we let any children inside."

"I'm sorry, did I do something to annoy you?"

Hermione sighed.

"Sorry. I've just been under a lot of pressure."

"They didn't threaten to fire you because of what happened, did they?"

"No. But this is high season for us, and we can't afford to scare away our customers, especially with the sale pending. And as the person in charge of special events…"

"I understand," said Guin. Hermione's job was on the line.

The phone on Hermione's desk began to ring. She frowned.

"Do you need to get that?" asked Guin.

"Probably." But she let it ring.

"Do you know if Luis and Maria Garcia have been found?" Guin asked her.

"Not as far as I know."

The phone began to ring again. Hermione sighed.

"I should get this."

"Take care of yourself," said Guin.

Hermione picked up the phone.

"Special Events. Hermione Potter speaking."

Guin quietly let herself out.

So, the holiday events were to go off as scheduled. Guin wondered if that was wise. But Hermione had said that everything would be triple-checked before they let any children inside the ballroom. Though the thought of Santa—the real Santa, the one the hotel hired to portray him—sitting in that chair with a child on his lap gave Guin the chills.

She peaked in Laurence Washburn's office, which was

next to Hermione's. But he wasn't there. She would reach out to him later to see if they had tracked down Luis and Maria.

Guin thought briefly about going to the SPD, but she suspected she wouldn't get anything more out of the detective. So she drove home. When she arrived, she found a message from Ginny, asking her where her article was. Guin rolled her eyes and told Ginny she'd send it to her later. Then she sent a message to Craig, asking if he had heard anything from his sources.

At eleven-forty-five, she left for Audra Linwood's office. Fletcher was on the phone. So Guin waited. Finally, he was off. She smiled at him.

"Hi, Fletcher. Is Ms. Linwood available?"

"She's out with a client, but she should be back soon," he informed her.

"Okay," said Guin. She took a seat on the overstuffed sofa and began flipping through one of the shelter magazines.

A few minutes later, Audra came through the door. She was talking on her cell phone.

"Look, Sid. I need to know now: Are you in or are you out? A deal like the San Ybel only comes around once in a lifetime."

Guin suspected Audra hadn't seen her as she kept on talking.

Fletcher tried to signal to her, but Audra wasn't paying attention. All of her attention was focused on Sid, whoever he was.

Guin watched as Audra headed to her office.

"Sorry," said Fletcher. "I'll let her know you're here."

"Thank you," said Guin.

Fletcher got up and headed back to Audra's office. He

was gone for several minutes. He was probably waiting for her to finish with Sid. Finally, he returned.

"Sorry about that," he said. "Ms. Linwood's rather busy. She asked me to reschedule your interview."

Guin frowned.

"I only need a minute."

"Sorry, but…"

"Tell her I have news that could affect the sale of the San Ybel."

That got his attention.

"Let me go speak with her again."

"Thank you."

He disappeared and returned a minute later.

"She said to give her five minutes. But she only has a minute."

"That's fine," said Guin, smiling to herself.

Fifteen minutes went by. Was Audra blowing her off? Guin was about to leave when Audra appeared. She didn't look pleased to see Guin. No doubt she had been hoping Guin would leave.

"You're still here."

"I am."

"Very well. I can give you five minutes, no more."

"I'll take it," said Guin. "Shall we go back to your office?"

"Fletcher said you had news regarding the sale of the San Ybel."

"I do."

Audra waited.

"I received information from the medical examiner's office, regarding Mr. Mandelli. The autopsy revealed a high level of alcohol as well as cocaine." Guin looked at Audra. She seemed neither surprised nor upset.

"So?"

"That doesn't surprise you?"

"So, he had a few drinks. Is that a crime?"

"What about the cocaine?"

"It must be a mistake."

"I don't think so."

"Did he have a habit?"

"Don't be ridiculous."

"So you never saw him use or suspect?"

"No."

Guin couldn't decide whether to believe her or not.

"What about that evening? Did he seem at all high to you?"

"High on life maybe."

Guin suppressed a snort.

"What does this have to do with the sale of the San Ybel?"

"Well, if it can be proven that Mr. Mandelli had an alcohol or drug problem and was intoxicated or on drugs when he signed the contract, the Thompsons could void the contract."

"I was there when he signed, and Tony was in complete control of his faculties."

"Can you prove that?"

Audra scowled.

"I don't see what bearing the autopsy—which was done, when? On Monday?—has on the contract, which was signed weeks ago."

"Yes, but if the Thompson's lawyer can prove Mr. Mandelli had a history of drug abuse…"

"Drug abuse? You're accusing Tony of being an addict? Really, Ms. Jones. You know I could sue the paper for libel if you print that."

"I wasn't going to print that." *At least not yet.* "I was just letting you know what the medical examiner found."

Audra continued to look annoyed.

"Another thing. I heard you asked for an extension. Some problem with financing."

"Where'd you hear that?"

"Is it true?"

"Of course it's not true. The deal is going to close."

"This week, as scheduled?"

Audra hesitated.

"No, we asked for an extension as a courtesy, to allow everyone to mourn."

Guin had to suppress another snort. She was about to ask another question when there was a knock on the door. Why were her interviews constantly being interrupted?

"Yes?" said Audra.

Fletcher poked his head in.

"I'm sorry to disturb you, Ms. Linwood, but I have Mr. Cantor on the line."

"Thank you, Fletcher. Tell him I'll be right with him."

Fletcher nodded and left.

"I need to take this," said Audra. "I trust you can see yourself out?"

Guin nodded.

"Thank you for your time."

Guin hovered by the door, where Audra couldn't see her.

"Sid! I knew you'd want in," she heard Audra say to her caller. "I'm telling you, you won't regret it. The San Ybel is a once-in-a-lifetime investment opportunity."

Guin wanted to continue to eavesdrop, but someone was coming down the hall. So she headed back to the reception area.

She went over to Fletcher's desk.

"Yes?" he said.

"I heard Audra speaking with Sid Cantor earlier. Is he a client?"

"He is. Do you know him?"

"Oh, yeah," said Guin. Though she didn't. "Sid and I go

way back. So, Audra's trying to convince old Sid to invest in the San Ybel with her?"

"That's right."

Guin was about to ask him about Sid when a couple walked in.

"Can I help you?" Fletcher asked them.

The couple looked over at Guin.

"I was just leaving," she told them.

She headed to the door, stopping briefly to watch the exchange. The couple looked to be in their late fifties or early sixties. They told Fletcher they were interested in purchasing a home on Sanibel.

Fletcher gave them a red carpet-worthy smile.

"Well, you've come to the right place," he told them. "I'd be happy to help you."

Guin smiled and left.

Guin pulled out her phone as soon as she stepped outside. There was nothing from Craig or Honey. She frowned. Then she heard a rumbling noise. She looked down. It was her stomach. It was nearly one o'clock. There it was again. She should probably get some food. She drove over to the Sanibel Deli and ordered a turkey club on whole wheat bread, which she ate outside. She had been reading the news on her phone when she received a message from Ginny, again asking where her article was. Guin groaned. The woman was relentless.

"I'll send it to you later," she informed Ginny. Then she finished eating her sandwich.

CHAPTER 23

Before she drove home, Guin phoned Craig on the off chance he had news. She listened as Craig's phone rang and was preparing to leave a message when he picked up.

"I was about to call you," he said.

"Oh?" said Guin. "You hear something?"

"I did, about your Mr. Blanchet."

"What did you hear?"

"The man has quite a reputation."

"What kind of reputation?"

"A reputation for getting what he wants."

"Well, he didn't get the San Ybel."

"You sure about that?"

"What do you mean?"

"In at least two cases where the Victor Group bid on a property and lost, something happened to the winning bidder and the Victor Group wound up securing the deal, often on better terms."

"What do you mean *something happened to the winning bidder*? Like what?"

"They had a sudden change of heart or encountered financial difficulties and had to withdraw."

"Huh. And this happened more than once?"

"At least twice."

And now possibly a third time, thought Guin.

"You think Blanchet had something to do with that light

falling on Mandelli?"

"I don't know. Just be careful. Blanchet is clearly a man who doesn't like to lose. He's also known for suing papers that paint unflattering portraits of him."

"Good thing I'm not a portrait painter."

"You know what I mean, Guin. Be careful what you say about him."

"Did the threat of a libel suit ever stop you from writing articles about notorious people?"

"No, but…"

"I just want to find out the truth, Craig. I'm not Suzy Seashell. I don't deal in conjecture or gossip."

"I know you don't. I'm just saying to be careful."

Guin sighed.

"You hear anything else from your contacts?"

"Word on the street is the Mandelli Group's in trouble."

"What kind of trouble?"

"The usual: money trouble. Mandelli was heavily in debt. And now that he's dead, his creditors and investors are worried they won't be able to collect. Several are already demanding their money back or canceling commitments."

"That explains why Audra was so anxious to line up new investors for the San Ybel."

"Speaking of the San Ybel, one of the people who reportedly canceled their commitment to the Mandelli Group is a celebrity chef by the name of Fabrizio Bellini."

The name sounded familiar.

"Was he going to open a restaurant at the hotel once Mandelli took it over?"

"That was the plan. Here's the interesting part: He just signed a multi-restaurant deal with the Victor Group."

"He did? When?"

"It was just announced."

"Well, that doesn't sound at all suspicious."

"I know. And there's more. The announcement said they

planned on opening a place in Southwest Florida."

"That could mean anywhere, like Naples."

"Maybe."

"You think I should go speak with Bellini, see what he knows?"

"It couldn't hurt."

"Where is he?"

"He has a place in Palm Beach. May as well start there."

"Do you know the name of his restaurant?"

"I believe it's called Bellini."

"Well, that should make it easy. I'll give them a call when I get home. Anything else?"

"That's it for now."

"Okay. Thanks, Craig. And I promise I'll be careful."

They ended the call and Guin got in her car and drove home. As soon as she got in, she went to her office, opened her laptop, and did a search for *Fabrizio Bellini Palm Beach*.

"Bingo!" she said.

She entered the number for the restaurant. The phone rang several times, then a woman answered.

"Bellini."

"Good afternoon," said Guin. "I'm looking for Fabrizio Bellini. Is he available?"

"He is busy at the moment," said the woman, who spoke with an Italian accent. "Who is calling?"

Guin had already planned her cover story.

"I'm calling from the *Sanibel-Captiva Sun-Times*. We're doing a piece on Palm Beach, things to do and places to dine. And I was hoping to include Bellini as it's one of the top places to dine on the island and interview Mr. Bellini."

"I see," said the woman. She sounded a bit suspicious. "I have never heard of this *Sanibel-Captiva Sun-Times*."

"It's a newspaper serving the islands of Sanibel and Captiva on the West Coast of Florida, just across the peninsula from Palm Beach. Every month, we do a feature on day trips, and Palm Beach is next."

"Give me your name and number. I will see if Signore Bellini is interested."

Guin had a feeling she wouldn't be hearing from Signore Bellini, but she gave the woman her name and number anyway.

"If you could let him know soon, I'd appreciate it. We have the trip scheduled for later this week."

"I will tell him you called," replied the woman. Then she ended the call.

Guin frowned. If Bellini didn't call her back within twenty-four hours, she'd call the restaurant again. At least it sounded like he was there.

She pulled up the article she had written for Ginny on Mandelli and read it through one last time. Then she sent it off to Ginny.

While she was at it, she opened the review she had started of 400 Rabbits. True, she had one more visit—tonight. But she pretty much knew what she was going to say. When she was done typing, she got up and stretched. Their dinner reservation was at seven, and it was just past five. She had just enough time for a beach walk.

It was an eight-minute walk to the beach. The sun would be setting soon, and the temperature had cooled slightly. The perfect time for a beach walk. Guin headed west. As she walked, she passed by several people waiting for the sun to set. Some of them had elaborate setups complete with wine and cheese. She smiled and said hello to a couple enjoying a pre-sunset repast, and they raised a glass to her.

When she first moved to Sanibel, Guin would drive to the beach several nights a week to watch the sunset. However, now that she lived less than ten minutes from the Gulf, she rarely came out to watch it. Funny that.

She meandered along the shoreline, gazing down in hopes of finding shells. But her thoughts kept returning to what Craig had told her. Had Hugo Blanchet tried to destroy the Mandelli Group? It certainly sounded like it. But she couldn't reconcile the charming man with the violet eyes and drooling dog with the ruthless businessman Craig had described. Though she knew looks could be deceiving.

But would Blanchet stoop to killing to get what he wanted? Was the San Ybel that important? Or was something else going on?

She was lost in thought when she heard someone shout, "Look! A dolphin!" Guin looked out into the Gulf and saw not one but several dolphins making their way east. She immediately reached for her phone to take a picture only to realize she had left it back at the house. She sighed. Oh well.

The sun was nearly touching the horizon now. Guin watched as the sun disappeared. Then she headed home. The sky now had an orange glow and the clouds looked like cotton candy. It was like she was in a painting. She sighed contentedly, feeling grateful to live in such a beautiful place.

A little before seven, the doorbell rang.

"Coming!" Guin called.

She opened the door to find Glen standing there.

"You look very nice," he said.

Guin made a face.

"What?" he said. "Did I say something wrong?"

"No. It's just, you always say that."

"Because it's true."

Guin doubted that but gave him a kiss and told him to come in.

Immediately, Fauna came over and started rubbing herself against Glen's legs. He knelt to pet her.

"You miss me, girl?"

Fauna purred loudly.

"You give any more thought to getting her a friend?" he asked Guin.

"I've been busy. And what if she doesn't want a friend? You know, cats can be very territorial. What if I adopted another cat and Fauna hated it?"

"I doubt that would happen. You'd never be mean to another kitty, would you, Fauna?" Glen said to the cat.

"You never saw Fauna and Flora fight."

"Maybe they were just playing."

"Uh-huh. Come on," she said. "We should go. Steve and Shelly are probably there already."

They arrived at the restaurant to find Steve and Shelly at the bar having a drink. Jimbo and Sally were also there. Indeed, it felt as though their whole neighborhood was there. Not a surprise as the restaurant was only a couple of miles away. And who didn't like Mexican food, especially washed down with some tequila?

Guin tapped Shelly on the shoulder.

"Oh, hey!" she said. "Steve and I were just having a drink with Jimbo and Sally."

Guin smiled. That was rather obvious. She said hello to her neighbors and then asked Shelly what she was drinking. It was purple.

"This?" said Shelly. Guin nodded. "It's called a Purple Haze."

Guin looked over at Steve.

"And what are you having?"

"Hare of the Dog."

"What's in it?"

"Tequila, agave, lime juice, and lychee purée."

"Mine has blackberry purée," said Shelly. "That's what makes it purple."

"You mind if I take a picture?"

"Go right ahead," said Shelly. "Should we hold them up?"

"Sure," said Guin, "if you don't mind being in the picture."

They held up their drinks and Guin took a couple of pictures.

"You want to have a seat?" asked Steve. Though there was only one free seat at the bar.

"That's okay," said Guin. "We should probably grab our table. Bring your drinks with you."

They said goodbye to Sally and Jimbo and headed over to the hostess stand.

CHAPTER 24

Guin had wanted a margarita, but she was technically working. Then again, what kind of reviewer would she be if she didn't have one of the restaurant's famous margaritas? So she ordered one on the rocks. Glen ordered a beer.

They looked at their menus after ordering drinks and decided to get an order of the hand-crafted guacamole along with two orders of the empanadas for the table to share.

"What are you going to order for your main course?" Glen asked Guin.

"I was thinking about getting the grouper tacos again."

"Oh, those sound good!" said Shelly. "Maybe I'll get them too."

"Why don't you get something else?" Guin said, giving Shelly a look.

"Oh, right. I'll get the coconut shrimp tacos instead."

"If you want the grouper tacos, you should get them," said Steve.

"Guin's writing a review," said Shelly, loud enough for others to hear here. "So we all need to order something different."

Guin winced.

"Oops! Sorry!" said Shelly. "It's supposed to be a secret," she told her husband.

Guin shook her head. Hopefully, none of the staff had heard her.

"Well, I'm going to have the steak fajitas," said Steve. "That is, if that's all right with you, Guin."

"Perfectly fine. Glen?"

"I was thinking of ordering the al pastor burrito. That okay, Guin?"

Guin gave him a dirty look.

"Sorry," mouthed Shelly.

Their server came over with their drinks and they ordered dinner. A few minutes later, the guacamole and empanadas arrived, and they dug in.

"Ooh, I love these empanadas!" said Shelly.

"They are good," said Guin.

"And the guacamole's not bad," said Steve, scooping another helping with a tortilla chip.

Guin held her phone under the table and typed.

When they were finished, a busboy cleared away their plates. Not long after, their entrees arrived.

Guin took a picture of everyone's food. Then she took a bite of one of her tacos. She chewed it thoughtfully and then began typing under the table again.

"How's everyone's food?" she asked when she was done.

"You want to try my fajitas?" Steve asked her.

"Sure," she said.

He placed a helping of steak, onions, and peppers on her plate. Guin took a bite.

"Mm," she said. "It's good."

"You want a bite of my burrito?" Glen asked her.

She nodded.

He cut off a piece and held the fork near her mouth.

"Open wide."

"Just put it on my plate."

He shook his head, clearly enjoying himself. Guin reluctantly opened her mouth.

"What do you think?" he asked her after she had swallowed.

"It's good," she said, taking a sip of her margarita, which was almost gone. "Just a little dry."

"You want a bite of mine?" asked Shelly.

"Sure," said Guin.

Shelly cut off a piece of her taco.

"Here comes the airplane!" she said, waving her fork around.

"Cut it out, Shelly. Just put it on my plate."

Shelly sulked.

"You let Glen do it."

Guin gave her a look, and Shelly put the piece of taco on her plate.

"Spoilsport."

"Thank you," said Guin.

She picked up the piece of coconut shrimp taco and popped it into her mouth.

"Whatcha think?" asked Shelly.

"It's good!"

"Can I have a bite of your grouper taco?"

Guin cut off a piece and gave it to Shelly.

"It's good, but I like my taco better."

Guin began typing on her phone again. The busboy came over and cleared away their dishes. A couple of minutes later, their server reappeared.

"You guys have room for dessert?" she asked them.

Everyone looked at Guin.

"Why is everyone looking at me?" She turned to their server. "Can you give us a minute?"

"Just signal when you're ready." Then she turned and left. As she did, Guin noticed the back of her t-shirt. It read, *If you're going to be salty, bring the tequila.* She smiled.

"So, we ordering dessert?" asked Shelly. "We probably should for your you-know-what."

Guin sighed.

"Sure."

They studied the dessert menu.

"I vote for key lime pie," said Glen.

"I love key lime pie!" said Shelly.

"I vote for the cookie skillet," said Steve.

"What are you going to get, Guin?" asked Shelly.

"That's probably more than enough," she replied.

"Come on, that's like barely half the dessert menu. Don't you want your readers to be informed?"

Guin scowled.

"What do you suggest?"

"I think we should get the warm churros."

"Fine."

Shelly signaled to the server, who came right over.

"We're ready!" she said, clearly enjoying herself. Then she gave the server their dessert order.

"Why did I eat so much?" Shelly groaned as they stood outside. She turned and hit her husband.

"Hey! What was that for?" he asked her.

"Why did you let me eat all that dessert?! You know I'm trying to diet."

Steve rubbed his arm.

"Why are you blaming me? You're the one who ordered them."

"It's all Guin's fault."

"My fault?" said Guin. "Why am I to blame?"

"You're the one who encouraged us to get dessert."

"As I recall, you were the one who insisted on ordering the warm churros—*and* having a bite of everyone's dessert." She didn't mention the second drink Shelly ordered, which had clearly gone to her head. Steve had ordered a beer after his cocktail, but he looked fine. Still, Guin was concerned. "You okay to drive?" she asked him. "We can give you a lift."

"I'm good," said Steve. "Thanks for dinner."

"My pleasure," said Guin. She had insisted on paying as the paper would reimburse her.

They said goodnight, and she and Glen walked to his car.

"Are you okay to drive?" she asked him as they were about to get in.

"Perfectly fine. I only had that one beer—and I'm pretty sure all that food more than compensated."

"Okay."

They got in the car and Glen looked over at Guin.

"Is everything okay?" he asked her. "You seemed a bit preoccupied at dinner."

"Sorry. I was making notes."

"Okay," he said and put the car in gear.

They were quiet as they drove back to Guin's.

Glen pulled into the driveway and turned off the engine.

"You going to invite me in?"

"I was planning on working."

"You sure everything's okay?"

"Everything's fine. I just have a lot to do. Ginny's been keeping me busy. "

"You want me to talk to her?"

Glen had a way with their boss.

"No, it's fine. Things will hopefully slow down a bit after Christmas."

"I'd be happy to keep you company, maybe even give you a back rub to help relax you."

Guin was sorely tempted. She'd been feeling rather tense. And Glen gave a mean back rub.

"Fine. You're on."

Guin unlocked the front door. Fauna was there to greet them and instantly began to meow. Glen knelt to pet her.

"Did you miss us, girl? Were you lonely?"

Guin rolled her eyes and ignored him.

"You want some decaf?"

"Sure."

She took out her old coffee pot and put ground decaf into the filter. Then she added water and hit the brew button. A few minutes later, it was ready.

As they sipped their coffee, Guin told Glen about her conversation with Craig.

"What if Bellini doesn't call me back?"

"You could always just go to his restaurant," he said.

"That's not a bad idea. Let's go tomorrow!"

"Whoa. Wait a second. You want me to go with you?"

"It would look better if I had a photographer. I told them I was doing a day-tripper column on Palm Beach."

"You did?"

Guin nodded.

"Come on. You have something better to do?"

"Actually…"

"Please?"

"Palm Beach is three hours from here."

"So? We'll leave before ten and be back in time for dinner."

"What if he isn't there or won't talk to you?"

"I'm willing to take my chances."

"You can't just talk to him over the phone?"

"You know I prefer to meet with people in person whenever possible."

"There's always Zoom."

"I hate video calls."

"Fine," said Glen.

"Does that mean you'll go with me?"

"I'll go. But I'm driving."

"Deal."

They finished their coffee.

"Well, if we're going to Palm Beach tomorrow, I should head home."

"What about my back rub?"

"Sorry, you'll have to take a raincheck."

"Okay. So, what time should I be at your place? And don't say you'll pick me up. That's ridiculous."

"Be there at nine-thirty."

Guin said she would and walked him to the door. He was about to leave when Guin told him he was forgetting something.

"What?" he said.

Guin smiled and got up on her toes to give him a kiss.

"Maybe I should stay," he said a few minutes later.

"You should probably go. I have work to do. And you probably do too."

She gave him another kiss and then sent him on his way. Then she walked back to her office. She wasn't in the mood to work. But if she was going to Palm Beach in the morning, she should finish her review of 400 Rabbits.

The next morning Guin got up early, fixed herself a mug of coffee, took it to her office, and read through her review of 400 Rabbits. Not bad, she said to herself. She made a couple of tweaks, then she sent it off to Ginny, feeling proud of herself, and went to take a shower.

She was out the door before nine o'clock, having given Fauna extra food and water in case they didn't get back until late. As she drove to the Causeway, Guin rehearsed what she would say to Fabrizio Bellini. She didn't want to bring up Mandelli right away. First, she would ask him about his restaurants and his plans for Southwest Florida. Then she'd ask him about why he had changed horses, so to speak.

She arrived at Glen's a little before nine-thirty. He let her in and said he needed a few minutes. While she was waiting, she looked at the photos on his walls. Some were Glen's, the others by photographers she didn't know.

Ten minutes later, they were in Glen's convertible, heading to Palm Beach.

CHAPTER 25

Guin called the restaurant from the road. A man answered this time, and she told him she was a reporter doing a piece on Palm Beach and would be there with a photographer around one. Would Signore Bellini be there?

The man seemed delighted that she would be dining with them and said that although Signore Bellini was very busy, he was sure he would make time for her. Then he asked for her name and the name of her publication.

Guin told him, and he said he would reserve a table for her. Guin thanked him and ended the call.

"Well, that was different," she said to Glen.

"Different how?" he replied.

"Yesterday, the woman I spoke with seemed uninterested. But this man seemed thrilled to have us there. Said he'd reserve us a table and have Signore Bellini come out and chat with us."

"That's what you wanted, wasn't it?"

It was, but Guin felt unsettled for some reason.

They arrived in Palm Beach a little before one. Guin hadn't been on the island in years, but it looked the same. They found a place to park near the restaurant, Glen's silver BMW convertible looking right at home on Worth Avenue. Then they got out and looked around a bit before going inside. Worth Avenue reminded Guin of 5th Avenue South in Naples, though it was older.

"You should take some pictures," Guin told Glen.

Glen had brought his camera bag with him and removed his Nikon.

He took half a dozen shots of the avenue and the exterior of the restaurant and then asked if they could go in. He was hungry.

"I'm hungry too," said Guin.

She had seen pictures of the restaurant online, but it was nicer in person. If she had to describe it, and she probably would (assuming Ginny agreed to publish a column on Palm Beach), she'd say it had a Mediterranean vibe. Outside, there was a dining area set around a stone fountain. Inside, the walls were painted white, with one of the walls covered in natural stone, and the tables were covered with white tablecloths. She went over to the host and introduced herself and Glen.

"Ah, Ms. Jones," he said, smiling at her. It was the man she had spoken to on the phone. "Thank you for coming all this way. Fabrizio is excited to have you try his food."

"He is?"

"*Sì.* You are the restaurant reviewer from Sanibel, no?"

"I am, but I'm here to do an article on Palm Beach." Though that wasn't technically true. Still, it was her cover story.

"But surely you picked Bellini because Fabrizio is opening a restaurant there, no?"

"No, I... Signore Bellini's opening a restaurant on Sanibel?"

The host looked confused.

"You did not know?"

"I heard he was opening a new place in Southwest Florida, but..."

"*Sì,* on Sanibel. That's why when he heard the restaurant reviewer from Sanibel was coming here, he was very excited."

"Excuse my ignorance, Mr…."

"Conte. But please, call me Sergio."

"When is this new restaurant opening and where?"

"We have not finalized the date. Hopefully, in the spring. And it is to be located at the famous San Ybel Resort and Spa," he said, smiling at her.

"I see," said Guin.

"Of course, you will be invited to the opening. Now, please, let me show you to your table. Since it is such a lovely day, I thought you would like to sit in the courtyard, by the fountain."

"That's fine," said Guin.

He led them to a table outside. Sergio pulled out a chair for Guin, then he placed two menus on the table.

"A server will be right over. I hope you both will enjoy your meal. If you have any questions, please ask."

"Actually," said Guin. Sergio waited. "When can we speak with Signore Bellini?"

"After the lunch rush is over." A woman—the other host?—was signaling to Sergio. "Now if you will excuse me?"

"Of course."

Sergio headed back inside, and Guin turned to Glen.

"So, Bellini is planning on opening a restaurant at the San Ybel. Which is interesting as the hotel is being sold to the Mandelli Group and Bellini no longer works with them. What do you make of that?"

"I don't know. It does sound odd."

"I know. Unless…"

She was interrupted by a busboy who wanted to know what kind of water they wanted. They decided to get a bottle of sparkling water. A few seconds later, another server, carrying a tray of bread, came over. There was focaccia, whole grain bread, and ciabatta. Which kind would they like? They took one of each. Then Guin thanked him.

"Well, I give the service here high marks," said Guin.

"You were about to say something about Bellini," said Glen.

"Right. I was going to say, it doesn't sound odd if the hotel was being sold to the Victor Group."

The busboy returned with their sparkling water and poured. Guin thanked him and drank.

Glen looked down at his menu.

"What are you thinking of getting?" Guin asked him a minute later. "If I'm supposed to be writing a review, we should probably get appetizers and a main course."

"Fine by me," said Glen. "I was thinking of getting the tuna tartare with avocado relish and the Bellini burger with fries."

"Sounds yummy."

"What about you?"

"I'm going to get the Caprese salad and the chicken paillard. Will you let me have a bite of yours?"

"Of course!"

Their server came over to take their order and then departed.

Glen took a bite of focaccia.

"Mm," he said. "Much better than my focaccia."

"You made focaccia?"

He nodded.

"I've made it a couple of times. But it wasn't as good as this," he said, taking another bite.

Their appetizers arrived a few minutes later. They both took pictures before eating them. Both the tuna tartare and the Caprese salad were delicious.

"If the food is as good at his new place on Sanibel, I'll be eating there often," said Guin.

Their main courses arrived a few minutes later and were just as good as the appetizers.

When they were done, Sergio appeared.

"So, did you enjoy your meal?" he asked.

"Very much," said Guin. "Everything was delicious."

"Good, good," said Sergio. "I hope you saved room for dessert."

"Of course!" said Guin, although she was feeling full.

Sergio grinned.

"Everything here is homemade."

"What do you have?" asked Glen.

"I personally recommend the lemon ricotta cheesecake. Our pastry chef is from Italy, and everyone says her ricotta cheesecake is the best. But we also have tiramisu, gelato, and biscotti."

Guin looked over at Glen.

"What do you say?"

"I say we try the lemon ricotta cheesecake."

Sergio beamed.

"An excellent choice!" He turned to Guin. "Anything for you?"

"We'll share the cheesecake."

"Do you have cappuccino?" asked Glen.

Sergio looked offended.

"Of course!"

"I'll have a cappuccino," said Glen.

"And I'll have an espresso," said Guin.

"Very good," said Sergio. "And perhaps a little limoncello, on the house?"

"I'm good," said Guin. "But thank you."

He looked over at Glen.

"Thanks, but…"

"Come! A little limoncello never hurt anyone. I will bring you a glass."

He disappeared before Guin could ask him when they could speak with Signore Bellini.

A few minutes later, Sergio returned with a slice of lemon ricotta cheesecake and a glass of limoncello. He placed them on the table and waited for Guin and Glen to try the cheesecake.

They picked up their forks and took a bite as Sergio looked on.

"Mm," said Guin. "It's delicious."

Glen nodded.

"Did I not tell you Carlotta's cheesecake was the best?"

"Will Signore Bellini be available to chat with us soon?" asked Guin.

"*Sì, sì,*" said Sergio. "He is just finishing up in the kitchen."

The server came over with their coffees, and Sergio excused himself.

Guin and Glen polished off the lemon ricotta cheesecake, scraping the plate. Guin leaned back in her chair.

"That was good, but I couldn't eat another bite. Let's go for a walk after we speak with Bellini."

"Good idea," said Glen.

Finally, Bellini appeared. Guin knew it was him from the photos she had seen of him online. He was wearing chef's whites, and Guin wondered if he had been working in the kitchen. Most chef-owners she knew of had executive chefs.

Bellini smiled as he came toward them.

"Thank you for coming to my restaurant," he said. "I hope you enjoyed your food."

"Very much," said Guin. Glen nodded in agreement.

"*Bene.* So, Sergio tells me you are from Sanibel."

"*Sì*, I mean, yes," said Guin. "I understand you will be opening a restaurant there."

"That is right."

"Please, won't you sit?" said Guin.

Bellini pulled over a chair and joined them.

"When we're done chatting, would it be okay if Glen took a few pictures of you?"

Bellini glanced at Glen.

"Of course."

"Thank you. So, I had a few questions."

"Please," said Bellini.

"I know you have several restaurants," Guin began. "All of them very successful."

"I am most fortunate," Bellini said.

Guin smiled. He seemed modest.

"Why open a place on Sanibel?"

"Why not?"

"Well, it's not as upscale or as busy as Naples."

"That is why I chose Sanibel. Well, part of the reason. My wife, she loves your island."

"Oh? She's been there?"

"Many times. She collects your seashells."

"Ah," said Guin. "Though Palm Beach has seashells."

"Not as many or as nice as the ones she finds there."

"Sergio said you were planning on opening a place at the San Ybel Resort."

"Yes, in the spring, God willing."

"I'm a bit confused though. The San Ybel is in the process of being sold to the Mandelli Group. But I recently read that you signed a deal with the Victor Group."

"Ah," said Bellini.

"Could you explain? I'm curious to know why you decided to no longer do business with the Mandelli Group. They financed your first restaurant, no?"

"*Sì*. And my second one too."

"So why not continue to do business with them?"

Bellini's face took on a pained expression.

"Things changed."

"Is that why you signed a deal with the Victor Group?"

Bellini nodded.

"They made me a very generous offer."

"Did you know that the Victor Group and the Mandelli Group were rivals?"

There was that pained expression again.

Guin continued. "What I don't understand is, if you're no longer working with the Mandelli Group, why are you opening a restaurant at one of their hotels?"

Bellini looked distinctly uncomfortable now.

"I…" He was about to say something then seemed to change his mind. "I should get back to the kitchen. I need to start preparing for dinner."

"You don't have an executive chef?"

He smiled at her.

"I do, but I like to be in the kitchen when I am here."

He started to get up, but Guin stopped him.

"Before you go, could Glen take a photograph or two of you, for my article?" Though she wasn't sure there would be an article.

"Very well," said Bellini. "Where would you like to take it?"

"I was thinking we could take a few here and then a few in the kitchen," Glen said. "If that's all right with you."

"That is fine."

Glen posed Bellini by the fountain. Then, when he was done taking photos there, they headed inside.

"I just had one more question," Guin said to Bellini as she followed them inside.

"Yes?" he said.

"Did you ever invest any money with the Mandelli Group?"

"No. Why do you ask?"

"So you didn't give them any money for the San Ybel deal?"

"No. Signore Mandelli asked me if I was interested in investing, but I told him I was only interested in opening a restaurant there, not in being an owner."

So Bellini wasn't the mysterious investor who decided to pull out at the last minute. Though he could be lying.

"Now I have a question for you," said Bellini.

"Yes?" said Guin.

"Would you send me a link to your article when it is published?"

"Of course! What's your email address?"

"Talk to Sergio. And now, I must go. A pleasure meeting you both."

"You said Glen could take a picture of you in the kitchen."

"Of course," said Bellini. "Come," he told Glen.

Guin waited in the courtyard.

"You get some good pictures?" she asked Glen when he came out.

"I think so. But I felt a bit disingenuous. What if Ginny doesn't want the article?"

"Oh, she'll want it. She's always desperate for content. And the day-tripper columns always do well. Though we should probably do a bit of sightseeing, so I have something more than lunch to write about."

"Okay. Though it's getting late."

"Not that late. We still have a few hours of daylight. Let's check out some more of Worth Avenue and then drive along South Ocean Boulevard and go see the Breakers and the Flagler Museum."

"You're in charge."

Guin smiled, and they began to walk, Glen stopping every few feet to take photos. Then they got into Glen's convertible and headed to South Ocean Boulevard.

"So did Bellini say anything to you about the San Ybel?" Guin asked Glen as they drove.

"He asked me if he thought his restaurant would do well there."

"What did you tell him?"

"That I thought it'd do very well. Sanibel doesn't have a lot of Italian places."

"Though that new one is about to open."

"True, but Italian food is very popular."

Guin gazed out the window then turned back to Glen.

"I'm still confused though. I mean, Bellini must have known that the Mandelli Group was purchasing the San Ybel when he signed that agreement with the Victor Group. Yet he plans on opening a restaurant there."

"He could have signed a deal with the Mandelli Group to open a restaurant there before he defected."

"True, but…"

Guin looked out the window again. They were approaching Mar-a-Lago.

"Let's turn around and go to the Breakers."

They turned around and arrived at the famous hotel a short time later. They left the car with the valet and went inside. As at the San Ybel, the lobby of the Breakers was decorated for Christmas.

"Have you ever been here before?" Guin asked Glen.

"Once. What about you?"

"A few times but not in a while. This is my first time since moving to Sanibel."

Guin wandered over to a plaque about the history of the hotel and began to read.

"The Breakers was originally built by industrialist Henry Flagler back in 1896. The original hotel burned down in 1903. It was rebuilt but burned down again in 1925. The version of the hotel that we see today, modeled after the Villa Medici in Rome, opened in 1926." She paused. "Did you know that they commissioned seventy-five artisans from Italy to decorate the place?"

"I believe it," said Glen.

They wandered around, Glen taking photos here and there.

"Let's go down to the beach."

They headed outside. The beach by the Breakers was

quite different from the beaches on Sanibel. It was far more manicured. And the Atlantic Ocean was considerably rougher than the Gulf of Mexico.

They walked along the water's edge, Guin looking for shells.

"We should probably head to the Flagler Museum," she said, looking down at her watch.

They headed back to the Breakers, rinsing their feet off by the pool. Then they walked back through the ornate lobby and out to the valet stand, Glen having had to valet park his car. He handed the valet his ticket, and they waited for his car to be brought around.

The Henry Morrison Flagler Museum was just a short drive away. Housed in a 100,000-square-foot Gilded Age mansion near the Intracoastal, it had 75 ornate rooms and spectacular views of the water. Neither Guin nor Glen had been there before, and they gawked at the over-the-top decoration, with rooms inspired by the Italian Renaissance and France's Louis XIV, XV, and XVI.

"They don't make houses like this anymore," said Glen.

"No, they do not," said Guin. "Then again, who knows? Some billionaire could have a place just like this somewhere."

"True," said Glen.

They finished the self-guided tour and headed outside.

"Time to head back to Sanibel," she said.

CHAPTER 26

They arrived back at Glen's a little after seven-thirty.

"Shall I fix us some dinner? I have pasta and…"

"Thanks," said Guin. "But I'm still full from lunch. And I should get going. I told Fauna I'd be back by dinnertime, and she's probably wondering where I am."

"Your cat can tell time?"

Guin made a face.

"No, but she knows when dinner is."

"You could always ask Sadie to feed her."

Sadie was Guin's next-door neighbor who adored Fauna.

"I don't know if she's home." Though Sadie and her husband Sam were in their seventies and rarely went out at night.

"You could call her."

"I could, but…"

"Is everything all right, between us, that is?"

Guin looked at him. This was not the first time he had asked her if things were all right between them.

"I told you, everything's fine. I've just been busy and have a lot on my mind."

"I know that. It just seems that…" He breathed in, slowly letting the air back out. "Since Detective O'Loughlin reappeared, you've seemed a little… distant."

Guin took a few steps toward him.

"Do I seem distant now?"

"No, but…"

She got up on her toes and wrapped her arms around his neck.

"What about now?"

Glen started to say something. But no sooner had he opened his mouth than Guin kissed him. He was startled at first, then he kissed her back.

"Let's go to the bedroom," he whispered in her ear a few minutes later.

Guin pulled away.

"What?" said Glen, a frown creasing his face.

"I should go."

"What? No! Why?"

"I told you, I need to tend to Fauna. And I have work to do."

Guin knew they probably sounded like poor excuses, but she meant them.

"Can't Fauna and work wait?"

Guin gently laid a hand on Glen's face.

"I'm going to see you tomorrow at the soft opening."

"Yes, but…"

"Why don't you plan on staying over?"

"I have a wedding to photograph Saturday."

"When?"

"At five."

"So, you can leave in the morning. That gives you plenty of time."

Glen mulled it over.

"I guess that would work." He pulled her back in. "But I don't see why you can't just stay tonight."

Guin looked up at him.

"I told you why. Now let me go."

"What if I don't want to?"

"You can hold me all you like tomorrow night."

Glen sighed.

"All right," he said, letting her go.

"Thank you. Frankly, I'm surprised you're not sick of me."

"Sick of you?"

"We had dinner together last night and just spent all day together."

"I could never be sick of you."

Guin gave him a look that said she found that hard to believe.

"Thanks for going to Palm Beach with me."

"You're welcome."

"Send me your pictures when you've edited them."

"You really think Ginny's going to give you the okay?"

"I think there's a good chance."

She said goodbye, giving him a quick kiss on the cheek, and then left before she changed her mind.

It was nearly eight-thirty when Guin walked through her door. Fauna was there waiting for her and immediately began to complain.

"I know! I know!" said Guin. "I said I'd be home by dinnertime, and I'm late."

Fauna let out another angry meow.

"Would you feel better if I gave you some tuna fish juice?"

Fauna cocked her head. She loved the "juice" from the bottom of tuna fish cans.

"Come on," said Guin.

She headed to the kitchen, Fauna trotting next to her. As soon as Guin opened the cabinet and reached for a can of tuna fish, Fauna began to meow again.

"Hold on!" said Guin.

She opened the can and squeezed the juice into a little bowl. Then she placed the bowl on the floor. Fauna lunged.

"I should probably eat something too."

She looked at the can of tuna fish. She wasn't really in the mood for tuna fish, but she didn't want to waste it. So she made herself a tuna salad sandwich. As she sat at the counter eating it, she sent Ginny a text, telling her she had a fabulous idea for a day-tripper column: Palm Beach.

She hit "send" and finished eating her sandwich. When she was done, she washed her plate and put it in the drying rack. She was heading to her office when she changed her mind and went into the living room to watch TV. Why bother to type up her notes if Ginny wasn't interested in a piece on Palm Beach?

She had just turned on the TV when she received a reply from Ginny and immediately turned it off.

Ginny thought doing a day-tripper column on Palm Beach was a great idea. When could Guin do it?

Guin smiled.

"Actually," she wrote. "Glen and I were there today, and I can have it to you early next week."

"Excellent," Ginny replied. "What about Tutti Pazzi?"

"You'll have that early next week too."

Ginny sent her a thumbs-up emoji.

"And don't forget the Santa meet-and-greet at the San Ybel on Sunday."

Guin had almost forgotten.

"I'll be there. Who are you sending to photograph it?"

"Take a guess."

That meant Glen. But he hadn't mentioned it.

"Did you remind him?"

"I'll do it now."

"OK," typed Guin. "Anything else?"

"Nope. Enjoy your weekend."

"You too," wrote Guin.

She opened the browser on her phone and went to the San Ybel's website, clicking on the Events page. There it was: "Meet Santa this Sunday between 3 and 5 p.m. in the San Ybel Ballroom! There will be food, drink, and treats for kids young and old."

Guin wondered if Laurence Washburn would be there. She hadn't heard anything about the missing maintenance worker and his wife and wanted to know if they had turned up. Though she could always call and ask him.

She was looking at pictures from last year's Meet Santa! event when she spied a photo of Santa with a little blonde girl on his lap. Immediately, Guin thought of Mandelli and Honey. Honey still hadn't gotten back to her. She opened her browser and typed *Honey Lamb*. She still couldn't believe Honey had no online presence.

The screen began to populate with lamb recipes. Guin frowned. Who knew there were so many recipes for lamb that involved honey? Next, she typed *Henrietta Lamb*. That led her to a cartoon sheep and an obituary, just as before. She then searched LinkedIn, Facebook, and Instagram. Nothing for either a Honey or a Henrietta Lamb. Or nothing for *her* Henrietta Lamb.

How was it possible for someone in her twenties (or early thirties) to not be on the internet? Unless Henrietta Lamb wasn't her real name. But why lie? Guin let out a yawn. It wasn't that late, but she was suddenly tired. It had been a long day.

She thought about going to her office and typing up her notes from Palm Beach, but that could wait until the morning. Instead, she turned the TV back on.

She had started to nod off when her phone rang. She looked at the caller ID. It was her brother. She immediately picked up.

"Hey," she said. "Everything okay?"

"Everything's fine. I just hadn't heard from you in a few days. You okay?"

"I'm fine. I've just been busy. I was in Palm Beach today."

"Ooh, Palm Beach! What were you doing there?"

"Interviewing a chef."

"What chef?"

"Fabrizio Bellini. You know him?"

"Not personally, but I've dined at his restaurant here several times."

Lance and his husband Owen, who ran a gallery in Chelsea, loved to dine out.

"What were you interviewing him for? You run out of restaurants to review on Sanibel?"

Guin made a face. Though it was true that there were only so many restaurants to review on Sanibel and Captiva.

"No, it was for the paper's day-tripper column."

"You go there alone?"

"No, I took Glen."

"And how is my favorite photographer?"

"Very good, thank you."

"Glad to hear it. So, anything else going on? What's been keeping you so busy?"

"It's Christmas season, Lance. The island's hopping. And you probably heard about Anthony Mandelli."

"I did hear about that."

"What are they saying up there?"

"To be honest, I haven't paid that much attention. Real estate development's not really my thing. I just saw that he died."

"Could you do me a favor and keep your ears open for any gossip?"

"You're suddenly interested in gossip?"

"If it concerns Anthony Mandelli I am."

"Do tell. Anything in particular I should be on the lookout for?"

"See if there's anything about drugs or being in financial trouble."

"Now that you mention it…"

"Yes?"

"I think I did hear something about the Mandelli Group being in some sort of financial trouble."

"Where?"

"I don't recall."

"Can you try to remember? And if you do, send me the link."

"I will."

"So nothing about drugs?"

"What kind of drugs are we talking about?"

"Cocaine."

"That's so eighties."

Guin rolled her eyes.

"Why do you care if the guy did coke or not?"

"I don't. Except it could have been what killed him."

"I thought a light fell on him."

"I thought you hadn't paid attention."

"Okay, maybe I paid a little attention because it happened on Sanibel. So it wasn't the light?"

"You sound disappointed."

"Maybe a little bit. A light falling is just so much more interesting than someone ODing."

"We don't know for sure if he OD'd."

"We?"

"You know what I mean."

"So, you covering his death for the paper?"

"I am."

"What's your theory? Who do you think dropped that light on him?"

Guin then told him about Honey, the missing maintenance worker, Patrick Finney, and Hugo Blanchet.

He whistled when she was done.

"Sounds like an episode of *Murder, She Wrote*. Though I can't imagine Hugo climbing up and loosening a spotlight."

"Hugo? Do you know him?"

"Uh, hello? I worked with him in Paris."

"You did?"

"You don't remember? I'm sure I told you about him."

Guin remembered that Lance had established a partnership with a French advertising agency and had gone to Paris a couple of times. But she didn't remember who his clients there were or remember him mentioning a Hugo Blanchet.

"Sorry."

Lance sighed.

"It was during that big ad campaign we did, Where to Be Gay in Paris. It was for the Victor Group, for their hotel there."

"Right. Of course." Guin had forgotten. "So you worked with him on the campaign?"

"I did."

"What did you think of him?"

"Very commanding and very good-looking. And those eyes! I think Owen was a bit jealous of all the time we spent together."

"Is Blanchet gay?"

"Hugo? Sadly, no."

"Married?"

"Why, are you interested in him? I thought you said things were good with the photographer."

"I'm not and they are. I was just curious."

"Well, I'm pretty sure he's single. Or else he has a mistress. We had dinner with him and a rather attractive blonde who I'm pretty sure wasn't his wife."

"Do you recall her name?"

"Sorry. I wasn't really interested in her. Why?"

"I was wondering if it could have been Honey, the blonde who worked for Mandelli."

"What does she look like? Do you have a picture?"

"No, but Glen might."

"She's not on social media?"

"That's the weird thing. I did a search for her online and nothing came up. Just a bunch of recipes for lamb, an old woman's obituary, and a cartoon sheep."

"That is odd. And you checked social media?"

"I did. Nothing. Nada. Zip."

"Huh. How very mysterious. Though I wonder…"

"What?"

"Well, she could be a porn star."

"What makes you say that?"

"You don't really think *Honey Lamb* is her real name, do you?"

"I thought of that, but if *Honey Lamb* was her porn name, wouldn't it still show up?"

"True. And you say she's good-looking?"

"Very, if you like that type."

"Hm. Well, send me a picture of her. You never know. I might recognize her."

"Okay. As I said, I don't have one, but Glen might."

She let out a yawn.

"Sorry."

"That's all right. I know it's nearly your bedtime."

"That's okay. I'm glad you called."

"I'm glad I called too. I should get going."

"Where are you going?" It was nearly ten o'clock.

"Not everyone goes to bed at ten, Guin. It's New York, not Sanibel. Owen and I are meeting some people."

Guin shook her head. She couldn't imagine heading out at ten p.m.

"Well, have fun."

"You talk to Mom?"

"No. And before you say anything, I'll call her this weekend."

"Do that. And send me that picture. I'm dying to see this Honey Lamb of yours."

They said goodnight and ended the call. Then Guin texted Glen.

"Do you happen to have a picture of Honey?"

"Why?" he wrote back.

"I want to send it to my brother."

"Why does he want it?"

"He may know her."

"Why would he know her?"

"Can you just send me a pic?"

"I'll go look."

"Thank you. I'm going to bed. See you tomorrow." She added a kiss emoji followed by the sleepy emoji. Then she headed into her bedroom, too tired to work.

CHAPTER 27

Guin woke up the next morning to find an email from Glen. Attached to it were two photos of Honey. Guin wondered how he got them. She thanked him for the pictures and forwarded his email to her brother. She doubted Honey was the blonde he had seen with Blanchet in Paris, but you never knew.

She went into the kitchen to make herself some coffee. As she waited for it to brew, she filled Fauna's bowl with dry food. Then she gazed out the window. Yet another nice day. She thought about going for a beach walk, but she had too much work to do.

As soon as the coffee was ready, she poured it into a mug and inhaled. Was there anything better than the smell of freshly brewed coffee? She took a sip. It was strong and slightly bitter, just the way she liked it. She took the mug to her office and sat at her desk, determined to crank out the first draft of her Palm Beach day-tripper article if it killed her.

It took her all morning, but she did it.

"Not bad, if I do say so myself." Though she would need to review it later.

She sent the draft to Glen, asking him what he thought and if he had started editing his Palm Beach photos. He replied a minute later, saying he'd take a look and not yet. But now that he had her draft, he'd start going through them. Guin thanked him and then checked her messages. There was one from her brother and another from Craig. She opened Lance's first. He had written to let her know that he had received her email and would be in touch. Next, she opened the message from Craig. He wanted her to call him. She immediately speed-dialed his number.

"What's up?"

"The results from the toxicology tests are in."

"And?"

"And in addition to coke and alcohol, they found zolpidem in his system."

"Zolpidem? Isn't that what's in Ambien and those other sleeping pills?"

"Correct."

"So? That's not that unusual, is it? Many people take sleeping pills."

"Yeah, but not enough to possibly kill them."

Guin stared.

"You think he was trying to kill himself? But that doesn't make sense."

"Suicide rarely does."

Guin frowned. Not that long ago people thought a local attorney had killed himself when it turned out he was murdered.* And she didn't think Mandelli had killed himself either.

"I'm not buying it. I think someone was out to get him. That light didn't fall on its own. Maybe someone spiked his drink, wanting to make him too sleepy to move."

"It's possible." But it sounded like Craig was dubious.

"What does the medical examiner think? Is he still ruling it a heart attack?"

"That's the cause of death listed on the autopsy report."

"What do the police have to say?"

* Read Book 8, *For Whom the Shell Tolls.*

"You should talk to O'Loughlin. You did well the last time."

Guin frowned again. She doubted the detective would tell her much, but she could try.

"You didn't hear anything? No updates? No arrests?"

"Nothing new."

"And nothing about the missing maintenance worker?"

"Nope."

"Well, will you let me know if or when you do hear something?"

"You know I will."

"Okay, thanks."

They said goodbye, and Guin sent the detective a text. Then she went to take a shower. When she was done, she quickly got dressed. Then she checked her phone. Nothing from the detective.

She called over to the San Ybel and asked to be connected to Laurence Washburn's office.

A woman picked up.

"General manager's office."

The voice sounded familiar.

"Marjorie?"

"Yes?"

"It's Guinivere Jones. We met the other day."

"Oh, hi, Ms. Jones!"

"Is Mr. Washburn available?"

"I'm sorry, he's not. Would you like to leave a message?"

"Actually, maybe you can help me. Do you know if Luis Garcia and his wife Maria have turned up?"

"I haven't heard anything. I just hope they're okay."

"So no one there has any idea where they could be?"

Marjorie didn't say anything.

"Marjorie? Are you still there?"

"Sorry. I was distracted. Been a bit busy."

"I can imagine."

"What were you saying?"

"I asked if anyone had any idea where Luis and Maria could be."

"Are you writing about them for the paper?"

"Possibly."

"It's just… I don't like spreading gossip."

"So you did hear something."

"Yes, but…"

"You can tell me off the record."

"Okay, I guess that's all right. Though I don't know if what I heard is true."

"What did you hear?"

"I heard one of the maids saying that she thought they went to Miami."

"Miami?"

"She said Maria has a sister there."

"Do you know if the maid told the police?"

"I don't."

"You wouldn't happen to have overheard the sister's name, would you?"

"No, sorry."

"That's okay. Any news about the sale?"

"Actually…"

"Yes?"

"I probably shouldn't say anything."

Guin was dying to know what Marjorie had been about to say.

"We're still off the record."

She waited, hoping that would get Marjorie to spill.

"I guess that's okay then. So you won't print anything I tell you?"

"I promise," said Guin. Though she hated to do so.

"Well, the other day I overheard Mr. and Mrs. T. arguing. Mrs. T. thinks they should take the Victor Group's offer, but Mr. T.'s worried about them being sued."

"I see. So you think they'll stick with the Mandelli Group?"

"I think Mrs. T convinced Mr. T. they made a mistake, but that Ms. Linwood's been kicking up quite a fuss. And Mr. T. doesn't want a lawsuit. And now Mrs. T says Mr. T's ruined Christmas for her."

"Oh, dear."

Guin thought she heard someone speaking to or calling Marjorie.

"I need to go," said Marjorie. "Should I tell Mr. Washburn that you called?"

"Please," said Guin.

Guin put down her phone and sat back in her chair. She wondered if Mrs. Thompson would prevail. Had Blanchet been working on her? Guin wouldn't put it past him. She reached into the drawer in her desk and pulled out his card. He had written his private number on the back. She entered it into her phone and waited as his phone rang.

"Hello?" he said. (Though it sounded like *Allo.*)

"Monsieur Blanchet?"

"*Oui.*"

"This is Guinivere Jones. I had a few questions I wanted to ask you about the Victor Group. It's for an article I'm working on. By any chance, are you free later this afternoon? I'd be happy to meet you somewhere."

"Have you eaten?"

"Excuse me?"

"I asked if you had eaten yet."

"You mean lunch?"

Guin looked at the clock on her monitor. It was just past twelve-thirty.

"*Oui.*"

"No, but…"

"I have not eaten either and was about to go into town. Would you care to join me?"

"Join you?"

"Unless you have already eaten."

"I haven't."

"Then join me for lunch."

"Okay," said Guin, a bit stunned. She wasn't expecting Hugo Blanchet to invite her to have lunch with him. "Where were you planning on going?"

"I had not decided. You write about restaurants. Where do you suggest we go?"

Guin immediately thought of Jean-Luc's. Though would Blanchet want French food? He must eat plenty of it at home. But she was craving one of Jean-Luc's sandwiches.

"I don't know if you'd want French food, but there's a very good French bakery on the island that makes delicious sandwiches and galettes. It's on Periwinkle Way near Tarpon."

"I love French food. What is it called?"

"Jean-Luc's."

"Shall we meet there at one?"

"That's fine," said Guin.

"*Bon!*" said Blanchet. "*À bientôt.*"

The call ended. Guin looked down at what she was wearing and frowned. She knew the French paid attention to fashion. And that Blanchet would probably look down on her showing up for lunch in a pair of capris and a t-shirt. So she went to change.

She picked out a dress—nothing too fancy—and went into the bathroom to do something with her hair. She twirled it into something resembling a French twist. Then she applied a little makeup.

"*Pas mal,*" she said to her reflection.

She gave Fauna some food. Then she grabbed her bag and her keys.

The parking lot by Jean-Luc's was nearly full. Good thing the Mini didn't take up much space. She went inside the bakery but didn't see Blanchet. She waited several minutes. Then she went back outside. A few minutes later, he arrived.

"Sorry to be late," he said. "I had to take an urgent call."

"No worries," Guin said. "Shall we go in?"

He nodded, and they entered the bakery.

Jake and Jo were behind the counter helping customers. Guin and Blanchet joined the line and waited for their turn. Fortunately, the line wasn't long.

"Everything here is excellent," Guin told Blanchet as they waited. "Jean-Luc's from France."

"Hm," he said, glancing up at the menu.

Finally, it was their turn.

"Is Jean-Luc around?" Guin asked Jake. "I have a fellow countryman with me."

Jake eyed Blanchet then looked back at Guin.

"He's in the back."

"Could you get him? I'm sure he'd like to meet Monsieur Blanchet. He recently bought a place here."

She smiled at Jake, and he said he'd see if Jean-Luc could spare a minute.

They had just placed their order with Jo when Jean-Luc appeared.

The baker looked at Blanchet.

"Hugo?"

Blanchet smiled.

"Jean-Luc!"

Immediately, Jean-Luc went over to Blanchet, putting his hands on Blanchet's arms.

"Is it really you? What are you doing here?"

"I could ask you the same!"

The two men then began speaking in rapid French. Guin had studied French in school but couldn't understand what the two men were saying. They were speaking too fast. But they seemed happy to see each other. Finally, they stopped talking. However, they were still smiling.

"I take it you two know each other," said Guin.

They turned to her, continuing to smile.

"Jean-Luc used to work for me," said Blanchet.

"A long time ago," said Jean-Luc.

"Though it feels like only yesterday," said Blanchet.

"What did he do for you?"

"Cook, of course."

"I spent several years working as a private chef," Jean-Luc explained. "So, what can I make for you?"

"We already ordered," said Guin.

"Cancel the order," Jean-Luc told Jo. "I will make them my special galette."

Jo shrugged, and Jean-Luc began gathering ingredients, humming as he did. He poured the mixture for the galette onto the hot crepe plate and swirled it around. Then he added the ingredients—ham and cheese and tomato and spinach.

"*Et voilà!*" he said a few minutes later, presenting a galette each to Blanchet and Guin.

"Wow," said Guin. "It looks delicious." Jean-Luc looked pleased. "How much do we owe you?"

"It is on the house."

Blanchet said something to Jean-Luc in French, and Jean-Luc frowned. Guin suspected Blanchet was trying to pay Jean-Luc for their meal. But Jean-Luc wouldn't hear of it.

"Go eat, before it gets cold. Then come find me, my friend. We have much catching up to do."

Blanchet said that he would, and he and Guin headed outside to eat.

They found an empty table and sat down. Guin cut into her galette. She had wanted one of Jean-Luc's sandwiches, but she wasn't complaining. The galette was delicious.

She watched as Blanchet took a bite of his.

"Do you like it?"

He nodded.

"What is there not to like?"

He had a point.

"So, you had questions for me about the Victor Group?"

Guin nodded.

"I understand you recently partnered with Fabrizio Bellini."

"That is true."

"Why?"

"Why what?"

"Why did the Victor Group partner with him?"

"Because he is a very good chef."

"Yes, but he had a deal with the Mandelli Group."

"So? We offered him a better deal."

"Why?"

"As I told you, he is a very good chef."

"Surely, there's more to it."

"He is interested in opening several new restaurants and…"

"Including one at the San Ybel," Guin said, interrupting him.

"Where did you hear that?"

"From Bellini. I met with him while I was in Palm Beach."

Blanchet's eyebrows rose.

"What were you doing in Palm Beach?"

"I was working on an article and had lunch at his restaurant."

"Interesting that you chose his restaurant."

"Not really. It's a very popular spot."

"And you say he told you he was planning on opening a restaurant at the San Ybel?" Blanchet said as he cut off a piece of his galette.

Guin nodded.

"In the spring. Which I found curious as the Mandelli Group is buying the hotel, but Bellini is no longer affiliated with them. He's affiliated with you."

Blanchet regarded her.

"What is your point, Ms. Jones?"

"Did you lure Fabrizio Bellini to the Victor Group to get back at the Mandelli Group?"

He laughed.

"We did not have to *lure* Fabrizio. He came willingly."

"And why was that?"

"Fabrizio wants to open several new restaurants. The Mandelli Group did not have the money to help him do so. We did."

"I've been hearing about the Mandelli Group's financial troubles a lot recently. The Victor Group wouldn't have anything to do with that, would it?"

"It is not our fault that Mr. Mandelli made several bad deals, is it?"

"So you had nothing to do with one or more of his investors pulling out?"

"They have been losing investors?" he asked innocently.

Guin sensed that he knew very well that the Mandelli Group had been losing investors.

"Though I am not surprised," he added.

"And if they haven't secured the necessary financing, they won't be able to close on the San Ybel."

"A shame," said Blanchet.

"I'm not so sure about that. Not everyone was excited about the Mandelli Group purchasing the hotel."

Blanchet ate another bite of his galette.

"I understand you renewed your offer on the hotel." Blanchet didn't say anything. "But you're insisting on closing before Christmas. Why can't you wait until after the new year? If the Mandelli Group is truly in trouble…"

"I do not like to wait."

"Yes, but the Thompsons could be sued by the Mandelli Group if they don't give them thirty days."

"That is not my problem. And I do not think it will come to that."

"Oh? How come?"

Just then Blanchet's phone began to ring. He immediately answered it, speaking in French to the caller. Guin had no idea what he was saying.

Blanchet put a hand over the phone.

"I must take this. Please give Jean-Luc my regrets and tell him I will be in touch."

"I…"

But Blanchet had already gotten up and was heading to the parking lot.

CHAPTER 28

Guin took a bite of her galette, but it was now cold. She picked up her plate and the one Blanchet had left and brought them inside, telling Jo to tell Jean-Luc that Monsieur Blanchet had to run. Then she headed back outside to her Mini. She was about to get in when she decided to check her phone. There was a voicemail. She checked her call history and saw that it must be from her brother. She called her mailbox and listened. He apparently had news. She immediately hit the number to call him back.

"What's up?"

"I know who Honey Lamb really is."

"You do? Was she the blonde you saw with Blanchet in Paris?"

"No."

"Then how do you know who she is?"

"Because I recognized her. And frankly, I'm surprised you didn't."

"What do you mean? I never saw her before."

"Really?"

"Why? Is she famous?" *Or infamous*, thought Guin.

"In a manner of speaking."

"What does that mean?"

"You don't watch *The Bachelor*?"

"You know I'm not a fan of reality TV."

"You watched *American Idol*."

"That's different. *American Idol*'s a talent show. So she was on *The Bachelor*?"

"Oh, yeah. Made quite an impression too."

"When was she on?"

"A few years ago. She was one of the finalists that season."

"So she's a reality TV star."

"She is. Pretty sure she was on that show about worst cooks too and some other stuff."

"And I take it her name isn't Honey Lamb."

"Nope, it's Henny Lambert."

"But why tell everyone here her name was Honey Lamb?" Guin wondered if Mandelli knew her real name. Probably. But why the charade?

"Don't know. Maybe she was practicing for a role and didn't want anyone to know she was an actress."

Guin found that unlikely.

"I found something else."

"What?"

"Guess who I found pictures of her with?"

"Is it a man?"

"Yes."

"Do I know him?"

"Yes."

"Is he famous?"

"In a manner of speaking."

"Another reality TV star?"

"No."

"An actor?"

"No."

"A famous musician?"

"No."

"Just tell me already!"

"You're no fun. I found pictures of her with Hugo. She wasn't the blonde I saw him with in Paris. Though they could be sisters or cousins. He must have a type."

"Hugo as in Hugo Blanchet, the CEO of the Victor Group?"

"The same."

"Where were the pictures taken?"

"At various parties and events."

"Anything to suggest they were a couple?"

"They did look rather chummy. But they could have just been playing it up for the paparazzi."

"Were the photos taken recently?"

"You want me to send you links? Though you can just Google *Henny Lambert*."

"I'll do that."

"So, you never watched *The Bachelor*?"

"I may have turned it on once or twice, but I couldn't get into it. I can't believe you watch."

"Not regularly. Anyway, I've got to run."

"Thanks for your help."

"No prob. And remember to call Mom."

Guin rolled her eyes.

"Bye."

Guin leaned against the Mini. So Honey's real name was Henny Lambert. Guin immediately did a search. This time there were hundreds—make that thousands—of results. Honey, or rather Henny, even had an IMDb page. Guin clicked on it. Yup, that was definitely Honey. She clicked on a few more links. Then she did a search for *Henny Lambert and Hugo Blanchet*.

She found a photo of Henny/Honey with Blanchet taken at some event in New York celebrating French cinema. And another of the two of them at some gala. There were several more. And in each of them, Hugo had his arm around her, and she was smiling. But that didn't mean they were dating. Still it made Guin wonder.

And another thing: If Honey, or Henny, was famous,

why was she working for Anthony Mandelli? Did he know who she was? He must have. Then she had another thought. Could Mandelli have hired her to play a role? Though she wasn't sure what that role would be. Was he paying her to sit in his lap? She wouldn't put it past him. However, she couldn't imagine Honey being that desperate.

She went back to Honey's IMDb page. She had a number of credits to her name. Though nothing Guin had seen or what anyone would consider A-list. Still, this was big news. And she wanted to share it with the detective. She was about to phone the police department when she decided she would just drive over there.

Sue was seated behind the window.

"They have you chained to the chair?" Guin teased.

"Feels that way sometimes," Sue replied. "Let me guess, you're here to see a certain detective?"

"Is he in?"

"He is, but I think he's on the phone."

"Can you let him know I'm here and that it's urgent?"

Sue gave her a look, one that said, *Is it really urgent?*

"I have information regarding the Mandelli case that I think he'll want to hear."

"I'll let him know, but I can't promise."

"I know."

Sue got up and disappeared into the back. A minute later, she reappeared.

"He said to give him a few minutes."

"He's not going to blow me off again, is he?"

"I told him it was important."

"Okay. I'll just be outside."

A few minutes later, Sue poked her head out.

"He'll see you now."

"Great!" said Guin.

She hurried back inside.

Sue buzzed her back, and Guin held open the door.

"Is he using his old office?" Now Detective Brown's office.

"He is."

Even though she hadn't been there in a while, Guin knew the way. She stood in front of the door, which was ajar, and hesitated. Then she raised her hand and knocked.

"Come in," he called.

Guin opened the door. The detective was seated at his old desk. But the room looked entirely different. Gone were all of the posters of New England sports teams and all of the New England sports paraphernalia. Instead, there were a few art posters on the walls. The place seemed bare in comparison.

"Yes?" said the detective. "Sue said you had something urgent to tell me."

Guin remained standing.

"I do. It's about Honey Lamb. She's really an actress by the name of Henny Lambert."

"I know."

"You know?" Guin couldn't believe it.

"You want to have a seat?"

Guin didn't but she sat anyway.

"How did you know about Honey? When?"

"I recognized her."

"You recognized her? How?"

"From that show she was on."

"You mean *The Bachelor*?"

"That's the one."

"You watch *The Bachelor*?" Guin couldn't believe it.

"Maggie did."

Maggie was the woman the detective had dated before Guin. Though they hadn't dated for very long.

"You recognized her from a reality TV show she was on a couple of years ago?"

"And from that cooking show she did."

"You mean *Worst Cooks*?"

"I forget what it was called."

Guin knew she was staring but couldn't help it.

"She looked a bit different, but I thought it was her."

"Did you ask her if she was on *The Bachelor*?"

"I did."

"And she admitted it?"

"She did."

Guin didn't know what to say. She hadn't been expecting this.

"But she lied! About her name, about…"

"She didn't lie about her name."

"What? Don't tell me Honey Lamb is her real name. I searched for her online. There was nothing there, other than a bunch of lamb recipes."

"Her real name's Henrietta."

"I did a search for Henrietta Lamb too. Unless she's a cartoon sheep or an old lady who died, she lied to you."

"I don't know about the sheep, but the other Henrietta was her grandmother. She was named after her."

"What about Honey?"

"A nickname."

"I still don't see…"

"She legally changed her name to Henny Lambert when she was a teenager and started modeling."

"Oh. Did you know she was cozy with Hugo Blanchet?"

"What do you mean by *cozy*?"

"I'll show you," Guin said. She pulled up one of the photos she had bookmarked on her phone and showed it to the detective. "And there are more." She quickly showed him.

The detective didn't say anything. Guin put her phone away.

"Did she tell you why she went to work for Mandelli?"

The detective didn't say anything for several seconds. Then he spoke.

"She said he made her an offer she couldn't refuse."

"Did he threaten her?"

"No, he wanted to use her acting talent to help land new investors and close deals. And said he'd give her a cut of any deal she helped close."

"Huh. Still, I can't imagine her giving up acting to go work for him, unless she wasn't getting any acting gigs. But why go by a different name?"

"She didn't want directors or producers finding out what she was doing."

That was understandable.

"You think she was sleeping with him? Mandelli, that is."

"Don't know."

"You didn't ask her?"

"She said they had a business arrangement."

"Did she mention Blanchet?"

"I didn't ask."

"But you will now."

The detective didn't say anything.

"I heard the toxicology report was out."

The detective didn't comment.

"Heard there was zolpidem in his system, enough to make him very sleepy."

Again, the detective didn't say anything.

"No comment?"

"No comment."

"You know what I think? I think someone gave him the zolpidem without him knowing, so he'd be too tired to move when the light fell."

Again, the detective didn't say anything. Guin grew frustrated.

"Come on, Bill. You don't really think he was trying to kill himself, do you? What about the light?"

"What about it?"

"Someone was trying to kill him!"

"That may be, but…"

"You find out who loosened it?"

"Not yet."

"What about the missing maintenance worker, Luis Garcia? You find him?"

The detective didn't answer.

This was infuriating. Guin wanted to grab him by the collar and demand that he give her some answers. Though he'd probably arrest her for aggravated assault if she did.

The phone started to ring, and he picked up.

"O'Loughlin." Guin watched as he listened and nodded his head. "I'll be right there." He hung up and turned to Guin. "I need to go."

"Did that call have anything to do with the Mandelli case?"

He didn't reply, just got up and headed to the door.

"You coming?"

"You're inviting me to go with you?"

"No. You just can't stay here."

Right.

Guin followed him out the door.

"Where are you off to?"

He didn't answer.

"You know I could follow you."

"Don't."

Guin followed him out of the police department and down the stairs.

"I'm telling you, Guin…"

"Just give me something and I'll stop."

They stared at each other. The detective ran a hand over his face.

"Fine. If I give you something, you'll leave me alone?"

"For now."

He looked like he was weighing it over.

"We just located Garcia."

"What about his wife? Are they okay?"

He didn't answer.

"Where were they?"

"In Miami."

"You bringing them in for questioning? You going to arrest them?"

Again, he didn't answer.

"You think they were involved?"

"I need to go."

"But you'll tell me if you arrest them?"

"You'll be the first to know."

Guin knew sarcasm when she heard it.

They had reached the detective's car. He unlocked it and got in, not sparing her a look.

Guin watched him back out. She was tempted to follow him. But she knew he wouldn't be amused. Well, she had better things to do, like have a talk with Henny Lambert, aka Honey Lamb.

CHAPTER 29

Guin thought about calling over to the hotel and asking to speak with Honey. But Honey had a habit of not answering her phone. Well, she would just go over there and find her.

She unlocked the Mini and got in, arriving at the San Ybel a short time later. She immediately headed to the front desk.

"May I help you?" asked the front desk clerk.

"Yes, I'm looking for Honey Lamb. Could you please tell me what room she's in?"

"I'm afraid I can't do that."

Right. Guin knew it was a long shot.

"Can you call her then?"

"Who should I say is calling?"

Guin hesitated. She thought about giving a fake name, but that was silly.

"Tell her Guinivere Jones, and that it's urgent."

The clerk picked up a phone. It appeared Honey wasn't answering.

"I'm sorry, Ms. Jones. She doesn't appear to be in. Would you like to leave a message?"

"Can you try her again? Maybe she was in the bathroom."

The clerk looked dubious but rang Honey's room a second time.

"I'm sorry, Ms. Jones."

"Do you know if Mr. Washburn is in his office?"

"I can check."

"Please."

Guin waited as the front desk clerk called Washburn's office.

"I see," said the clerk, after he asked if Mr. Washburn was available. "Thank you."

"Yes?" said Guin.

"I'm sorry. He's in a meeting."

"Any idea when he'll be out?"

"Sorry, no."

Guin saw that a line had formed behind her and felt a bit guilty.

"Thank you for your help," she said to the clerk and stepped aside.

Where could Honey be? Maybe by one of the pools? Guin could picture her lying poolside. She decided to check and had taken a few steps when she nearly collided with Marjorie, who was looking down at her phone.

She immediately looked up and apologized.

"That's okay," said Guin. "Is everything all right?"

"Just busy."

"I heard they found Luis and Maria."

"They did? Are they okay?"

"I don't know."

"Did the police arrest them?"

"I don't know."

Marjorie's phone was ringing. She immediately answered.

"I'm coming!" she said to her caller. Then she turned to Guin. "Sorry, I have to go."

Guin watched as Marjorie hurried across the lobby and saw two familiar figures arguing a short distance away. It was Audra Linwood and Patrick Finney. They were shooting daggers at each other. Figuratively, not literally. Though Guin suspected that if a dagger had been around, one of them would have plunged it into the other.

"Don't make me sic my lawyer on you, Patrick," said Audra.

"Go ahead," said Patrick. "You don't have a leg to stand on."

"Go away. You lost."

"You raise the money?"

Audra scowled. Then she turned and headed toward the stairs. But she stopped when she saw Guin.

"You!" she said.

"Oh, hello, Audra," said Guin, trying to sound casual.

"I know what you've been up to."

Guin tried to look innocent.

"You've been sticking your nose where it doesn't belong."

This wasn't the first time Guin had heard that.

"Fletcher told me you had been eavesdropping on my conversation with Sid Cantor."

"You weren't trying to get old Sid to invest in the Mandelli Group, were you?" It was Patrick. "Really, Audra."

Audra scowled at him.

"It's none of your business, Patrick."

"I think it is. Sid's a client."

"Was a client, you mean. He's my client now. And he's very interested."

"In what, losing money?"

Audra scowled.

"I'm going."

"Wait!" said Guin.

"I'm rather busy, Ms. Jones."

"I'll make it quick, but I need to ask you a question about Mr. Mandelli."

Audra waited.

"Go on, spit it out. I'm in a hurry."

"Did he take sleeping pills?"

Audra looked at her.

"*That's* what you needed to ask me?"

"Do you know?"

"How should I know? Probably. Doesn't everyone?"

"So he had a prescription?"

"Do I look like his doctor or pharmacist?"

"I just thought…"

"I'm going," said Audra.

"I'm going with you," said Finney.

Guin had forgotten about him.

"Go away, Patrick," said his ex-wife. But he followed her to the stairs.

Guin watched them go. Should she follow them? She thought about it for a few seconds then headed outside in search of Honey.

The San Ybel had several pools. There was the big main pool, a kiddie pool, and an adults-only pool. Guin ruled out the kiddie pool. That left the main pool and the more private adults-only pool. She tried to think like a reality TV star and headed to the adults-only pool.

She walked along the path to the private pool, which paralleled the Gulf, arriving there a couple of minutes later. The pool was ringed with private cabanas. She paused at the entrance. What exactly would she say to Honey, assuming she found her?

Guin let herself in through the gate and scanned the pool area. Several couples were lounging there as well as some singles. Then she saw her. At least, she thought it was Honey. The woman she was looking at was wearing a large straw hat and sunglasses that obscured her face. But the hair and body resembled Honey's.

Guin went over. Was Honey asleep? Maybe she was just resting her eyes. She moved closer.

"Honey?" she said softly.

The woman didn't move.

She said Honey's name again, a little louder this time.

Again, no response.

Was she dead? Guin chided herself. She could see Honey's chest moving up and down.

Guin cleared her throat.

"Excuse me, Ms. Lambert? Could I get an autograph?"

That got Honey's attention.

"Hm?" she said, rising slightly. However, when she realized it was Guin, she frowned.

"Oh, it's you. What do you want?"

"A word. I've been trying to reach you, but you haven't been returning my calls."

"I'm rather busy."

"Oh?" She didn't look busy. "Doing what?"

"I'm rehearsing."

"Rehearsing?"

"I have an audition coming up, and I need to memorize my lines."

"So you admit you're an actress."

Honey lowered her glasses and looked at Guin.

"You didn't know?"

Guin shook her head.

"I guess Tony was right."

"About?"

"He didn't think anyone here would recognize me."

"Detective O'Loughlin recognized you."

"Yes, and I was a bit surprised by that. Apparently, his lady friend watched the show."

"I don't understand, though. Why say you were Mandelli's special assistant and use a fake name?"

"It was Tony's idea. And the name wasn't fake. I just hadn't used it in a while."

"So Tony, I mean Mr. Mandelli, knew you were an actress."

Honey looked at Guin as though she was feeble-minded.

"Of course. That's why he offered me the job."

"To be his assistant."

"*Special* assistant."

"Excuse me. And what exactly did he hire you to do?"

"He wanted me to butter up potential investors and help close deals."

Which is what the detective had said she had told him.

"You mean to flirt with them."

Honey shrugged.

"And you were okay with that? What about your acting career?"

"Do you know what it's like being a reality TV star, Ms. Jones?"

"I have no idea."

"Let me tell you then. You get your fifteen minutes or whatever of fame, and then that's all people see you as, a reality TV star. I thought that going on *The Bachelor* would help my acting career, but it hurt me instead. Sure, it landed me a few guest appearances and commercials. But not the TV roles I craved. Everyone wanted me to play the character I played on *The Bachelor*, the vixen."

"And you didn't want to play the vixen?"

"I mean, sure, it was fun on *The Bachelor*. But playing the vixen gets old. And I didn't want to get typecast."

"So how did you meet Mandelli?"

"At a party. A mutual friend introduced us. Tony said he saw me on *The Bachelor* and thought that I should have gotten the final rose. But I doubt that he ever watched the show. Still, I was flattered."

"And then he what, offered you a job?"

"Not right away. He was more interested in getting me into bed at first."

"So he did want to sleep with you. Did you?"

"No. I made it very clear to him that I wasn't interested."

"And he accepted that?"

"I told him I had a black belt in taekwondo."

Guin smiled. She wished she had a black belt in taekwondo.

"So you said you wouldn't sleep with him and he, what, offered you a job instead?"

Honey nodded.

"He noticed the way men looked at me and invited me to attend a meeting with him. Said he was trying to land this big fish and that he'd give me a piece of the action if I could reel him in."

"So you agreed?"

"I thought it might be fun."

"And were you able to convince the big fish to invest?"

Honey grinned.

"Hook, line, and sinker."

"So you what, gave up your acting career to go work for Mandelli?"

"I wouldn't say I gave it up. Just put it on hold. And I was still playing a part."

"But why use a fake name?"

"As I told you, it wasn't fake."

Right. The detective had told her Honey Lamb was her real name.

"But why not pick a different name?"

"Because Tony loved the name Honey Lamb."

That came as no surprise to Guin.

"Why did Mandelli bring you here? Did he want you to help him with the San Ybel deal?

"Who do you think convinced Freddie to sign with Mandelli?"

Freddie?

"You mean Mr. Thompson?"

Honey nodded.

"You didn't sleep with him, did you?"

"I didn't have to. I just had to let him think I might."

Guin was appalled.

"Don't look so shocked. I'd never sleep with a married man. Well, almost never."

"But you flirted with him."

"More like he flirted with me, and I let him."

"I see. If you don't mind my asking, what exactly did you do?"

"I may have given him the impression that I'd be grateful if he signed with us."

Honey gave her a sly look.

So that's why Fred Thompson was eager to do business with Mandelli.

"What about Mrs. Thompson?"

"What about her?"

"How did she feel about you and her husband flirting with each other? I can't imagine she was pleased."

"No, but I got the sense she was used to his boorish behavior."

"I understand she didn't want to sell to the Mandelli Group."

"She didn't. She was hot to sell to Hugo."

"Speaking of Monsieur Blanchet, I saw pictures of the two of you online looking very cozy."

"Have you been cyberstalking me, Ms. Jones?"

"I thought you barely knew him."

Honey sighed.

"We ran into each other at a few parties and events, and we had our picture taken together. Big deal."

"He's very handsome and rich."

"So? I know lots of handsome, rich men. Most of them are boors. But if you find him so attractive, maybe you should make a play for him. He's very fond of redheads."

Guin was going to correct Honey and tell her she was a strawberry blonde, but she suspected Honey wouldn't care.

"He's not my type."

"He's everyone's type."

"I'm seeing someone."

"I'm happy for you. Now if you don't mind…"

"I just had a couple more questions."

Honey sighed dramatically.

"Make it quick."

"Did Mandelli have a cocaine habit?"

"A cocaine habit?"

Guin waited.

"He may have done the occasional snort. But I wouldn't say he had a habit."

"Did you ever…?"

"Take cocaine? Once. Felt high as a kite. Then felt like hell the next morning. Once was enough."

"So that was it? One and done?"

"You don't believe me?"

Guin didn't answer her.

"What about sleeping pills?"

"What about them?"

"Did Mandelli take them?"

"I don't know. Probably. Doesn't everyone?"

That's what Audra had said. And, come to think of it, Guin had a bottle of sleeping pills in her medicine cabinet. Though they were old.

"Do you know if he took any sleeping pills or did any cocaine the evening of the holiday lighting event?"

"No, why?"

"Just curious."

Honey gave her a suspicious look.

"And where were you again when the spotlight fell?"

"In the ladies' room, as I told you. And now, Ms. Jones, I must ask you to leave so I can finish memorizing my lines."

"What about your work for the Mandelli Group?"

"I worked for Tony. And he's gone. Now good day."

Honey had put her sunglasses back on and had leaned back on her chaise longue. That was Guin's cue to leave.

CHAPTER 30

Guin was standing in the lobby, checking her phone for messages. There was a reminder about the Tutti Pazzi soft opening. She had forgotten about that. Cocktails began a little over an hour from now. She looked down at what she was wearing. At least she didn't have to change.

Should she go home or camp out at the hotel? She glanced around. The lobby was pretty busy. Better to go home and get a little work done.

She headed outside and unlocked the Mini.

As Guin headed home she reviewed what she had learned that afternoon. Not that much, to be honest. So Honey was a reality TV star who Mandelli had hired to play a role. Had she killed him? She could have easily slipped him some sleeping pills. But why? Had he not paid her? Or maybe he had tried to take advantage of her. She had seen how he had pawed her at the holiday lighting event. But Honey had said she had a black belt in taekwondo. She could easily have put him in his place.

No, as much as she may have wanted to believe Honey was responsible, she couldn't see her doing him in. Unless… She thought of the pictures she had seen of Honey and Hugo Blanchet. Could they have been working together? Had Blanchet told her to slip Mandelli some sleeping pills and then bribed someone—Luis?—to have the light fall on him?

Guin pulled into her driveway and parked her car in front. She had a little over half an hour before she had to turn around and head to Tutti Pazzi. She went inside and headed straight to her office.

She pulled up her Palm Beach article to review it and immediately started to tweak it. She had lost track of time and didn't realize it was nearly five-thirty until she happened to glance at the clock on her monitor. She reached for her phone only to realize she had left it in her bag. She quickly went to retrieve it, to let Glen know that she would be late.

Sure enough, there was a message from him, letting her know he was at the restaurant. She wrote him back saying she was about to leave and would be there soon.

She saved the document, went to the bathroom to apply a fresh coat of lip gloss, and then left.

When she got to Tutti Pazzi, the parking lot was nearly full. And it was a large lot. How many people had the owners invited to this shindig? She chastised herself for getting carried away and not arriving earlier. Then she managed to squeeze the Mini into a spot in the back. That done, she hurried to the restaurant, climbing the flight of stairs. There was music coming out of a pair of speakers. The kind of Italian music she imagined was popular in the 1950s. She went inside to look for Glen.

The restaurant was packed. There were people everywhere, talking and drinking. Guin frowned. She didn't like crowds. But there was nothing she could do.

She looked for Glen, but she couldn't see him. Well, he was there somewhere. She wondered if he was able to get any good pictures with all the people there.

"Excuse me," she said to a passing server. "Where can I find the owners?"

The young man pointed to the other side of the bar, and Guin saw them, chatting with some guests. She began to head that way then thought she saw Glen. She made a beeline for him. Then she saw Patrick Finney. He was speaking with an older couple. She detoured over to him.

Finney was telling the couple to give him a call when they were ready to sell and handed the husband his card. Guin wondered if the couple was planning on moving to Shell Point, the local retirement community.

"Patrick," she said as the older couple moved away.

Finney turned. He didn't look happy to see her.

"What do you want?"

"I just thought I'd say hello."

He looked at her suspiciously.

"Any news about the sale?"

"No."

"I imagine the San Ybel deal would be quite the feather in your cap and net you a sizeable commission."

"What are you getting at?"

"Nothing."

"I told you, I had nothing to do with that light falling."

"But you didn't like Mandelli. He had stolen your wife and ruined the deal you had arranged with the Thompsons."

"It's no secret that I didn't like the guy. But as I told you, I wasn't near the ballroom when it happened."

"You could have paid someone to loosen the light."

"I'd be taking a big risk."

"Maybe you were desperate."

"I may be a lot of things, Ms. Jones, but desperate isn't one of them. Now if you would excuse me?"

"Just one more question." Finney waited. "How did Mandelli appear to you that evening?"

"What do you mean?"

"Did he seem at all… different?"

"Different how?"

"Did he seem high?"

"High?"

"Or tired?"

Finney looked thoughtful.

"Now that you mention it, he did seem a bit glassy-eyed, like he had had too much to drink."

"There you are!" It was Glen.

Guin turned to look at him and Finney slinked away. Guin frowned.

"Is everything all right?" Glen asked her.

"Yeah, I just got carried away with work and lost track of time."

"No, I meant between you and Finney."

"I was asking him about the hotel."

"And?"

"He said nothing had changed."

"You look disappointed."

"Let's change the subject. Seems like a good crowd. You able to get any pictures?"

"Not really. Just people shots. I'm going to come back tomorrow."

"Will you have time before the wedding?"

"If I don't leave your place too late."

"You meet the owners?"

"Not yet. They've been kind of busy."

"Let's go find them."

They made their way through the crowd over to the bar where the owners, the Giacomettis, were still chatting with guests. Guin waited for a break in the conversation. Then she cut in.

"Excuse me. I don't mean to interrupt, but I wanted to introduce myself. I'm Guinivere Jones from the *San-Cap Sun-Times* and this is Glen Anderson. He's a photographer."

Mr. Giacometti gently slapped his wife on the arm.

"I told you the paper would send someone!" He turned

back to Guin. "Gianna didn't believe me."

"Well, we're here!" said Guin. "And it looks like you have a good crowd."

Mr. Giacometti looked around.

"To be honest, I wasn't expecting so many people to show up. But I guess the lure of free food…" He smiled at Guin. "I'm Salvatore, by the way," he said, extending a hand. "Though everyone calls me Sal."

"Nice to meet you, Sal."

Sal frowned.

"You don't have a drink." He signaled for the bartender to come over. "What'll you have?"

"I'm working," said Guin.

"You can surely have a little something? Joe! Get the lady a glass of white wine."

Guin was going to say that wasn't necessary, but she thanked him instead.

"What about you?" he said to Glen.

"I'll have a beer. What do you have on tap?"

Joe brought over a glass of white wine and gave it to Guin. She thanked him. Then he reeled off the beers they had on tap. Glen picked a local beer.

"So, what can I tell you about the place?" said Sal.

"I read your About page," said Guin. "So, you were an accountant?"

"That's right. An accountant with dreams of opening a restaurant one day."

"And now you have."

"With a little help from our friends."

"You mean the Carusos."

Sal nodded. Guin had read about the Carusos. They were Sal and Gianna's silent partners.

"Would you excuse me?" said Gianna.

"Could you wait a minute? I had a few questions I wanted to ask you."

"I'm sure Sal can answer them."

"Maybe just a quick picture of the two of you?" said Glen.

"Come on, Gi. Let the man take a quick picture. Then you can check on the food."

"All right," said Gianna.

Glen smiled at them.

"Get close," he said. "That's good. Now smile."

He took several pictures. Then Gianna said that she needed to check on the food and headed to the kitchen.

"Is everything all right?" Guin asked Sal.

"My wife's a bit of a perfectionist. This is a big night for us."

"I'm sure it'll be a success."

"I hope so. Have you tried any of the food?"

"Not yet," said Guin.

"Well, what are you waiting for?!"

He signaled to a passing server, who came over. Sal took two bite-sized meatballs off of the tray.

"Here. Try these," he said, handing Guin and Glen each a meatball.

"Mm," said Guin, taking a bite. "It's good."

Sal looked pleased.

"What do you think?" he asked Glen.

"Very good," Glen replied.

"You should try our fried calamari. It's outta this world."

"We'll do that," said Guin. "Now if I could just ask you a few questions…"

"Fire away," said Sal.

"I'm going to go take some more pictures," said Glen, excusing himself.

"I'm glad that's over with," said Guin as she and Glen stood in the parking lot.

"It was a bit crowded," said Glen. "But the food was good."

"It was. I bet they'll do well. Did you ask Sal if you could come back in the morning?"

"I did."

"And?"

"He said no problem. It just means cutting our morning short."

"I'll live."

"You're not disappointed?"

"It's not like I haven't seen you all week. And I'll see you Sunday afternoon at the Santa thing."

"I know, but…"

"Fine. I'm devastated that you have to leave early tomorrow. Feel better now?"

"Much," he said, grinning at her. "So, you get what you need? You could always come back with me in the morning."

"I'm good. Sal talked my ear off. And I'm stuffed. I couldn't eat another bite."

"I'm still hungry."

"How is that possible?"

"I was busy taking pictures."

"Well, you can eat something at my place."

He grinned.

"What?"

"Nothing," he said. "Shall I follow you?"

"You know the way."

CHAPTER 31

"You're really going to work?"

They had arrived back at Guin's, and Guin had announced that she needed to do a little work before they hung out.

"I need to type up my notes while everything's still fresh."

"It can't wait until tomorrow?"

"No, but I won't be long. I just need to get my thoughts down. I'm not going to actually write the article. Go watch TV. I'll be there in a few minutes."

"Fine," he said.

Guin went to her office, opened her laptop, and quickly got down her impressions of the restaurant. She had taken a photo of the menu, so she could describe what she had eaten. But she would save the real writing for tomorrow after Glen had left. That done, she went to the living room.

Glen was sitting on the couch, Fauna asleep in his lap. Guin couldn't help smiling at the scene.

A commercial was playing, and Guin asked him what he was watching.

"*Diners, Drive-Ins and Dives.*"

"Anything good?"

"Yeah. This Jamaican place Guy visited in Miami looks great. We should go."

"I'm game."

Guin sat next to him on the couch and leaned her head

on his shoulder. He put his arm around her, and Guin snuggled closer.

"How's the article going?"

"It's not an article yet. I was just getting my thoughts down. I'll start writing the article tomorrow."

The episode of *Diners, Drive-Ins and Dives* ended, and Guin let out a yawn.

"You tired?"

"A little."

Glen looked up at the clock. It was nine-thirty. But he knew that Guin went to bed early.

"You want to go to bed?"

"Not just yet," she said, though her eyes were closed.

Another episode of *Diners, Drive-Ins and Dives* began playing, and Guin nodded off. Glen smiled.

Fauna climbed into Guin's lap and began kneading her stomach. Guin immediately woke up.

"Did I miss anything?"

"Just some barbecue place in Austin. You sure you don't want to go to bed?"

Guin looked up at the clock.

"It's only nine-forty-five. Let's wait until this episode is over."

"Okay," said Glen. "I can change the channel if this is putting you to sleep."

"Maybe we should watch something with a plot?"

"Any suggestions?"

"There's always Netflix."

Glen started scrolling, but they couldn't find anything they both wanted to watch.

"I just remembered. There's a new documentary about the Go-Go's. You game?"

"Sure," said Glen. "Is it on Netflix? I didn't see it."

"I think it's on Showtime."

"You get Showtime?"

"No, but we can do the free trial."

Guin picked up the remote, clicked on the Showtime icon, and entered her information.

"Guin," said Glen, gently nudging her.

"Hm?" she said.

"You fell asleep again."

"I did?"

"I stopped the documentary. Let's go to bed."

Guin looked at the clock. It was ten-thirty.

"How long was I asleep for?"

"Not that long. Maybe ten minutes."

"Ten minutes?! Why didn't you wake me?"

"You looked so peaceful."

"But I could have missed something important!"

"We can rewind it. Come, let's go to bed."

He got up and led her into the bedroom, but they didn't go to sleep right away.

Guin felt something or someone tickling her arm. Was it Fauna? No, it was Glen. She glanced over at her clock. It was six-forty-five.

"What are you doing up?" she asked him. *And why do you always look so damn good in the morning?*

"I've been up for a while."

She knew Glen was an early riser, but they had been rather busy last night. So she thought he'd sleep in. Guess she'd been wrong.

"What've you been doing?"

"Watching you sleep."

"That must have been very exciting."

"I also fed Fauna and made coffee."

"Thank you."

"I can think of another way you can thank me," he said, grinning at her.

"Let me go to the bathroom first."

Guin quickly got up, returning to bed a few minutes later.

"You were saying?" she said.

"Come over here," he commanded.

Guin moved across the bed so that their bodies were touching.

"Better?"

"Much. Now give me a kiss."

"So bossy," she said. Then she gave him a kiss. He kissed her back, and they wound up staying in bed another half hour.

"Let's go for a beach walk," Glen suggested as they sipped their coffee.

"Don't you need to head over to Tutti Pazzi and then prepare for the wedding shoot?"

"I have some time. And I feel as though I haven't been to the beach in ages."

"You sure it's okay?"

"You don't want to go?"

Guin was always up for a beach walk.

"I'll be ready in five minutes."

She got dressed and they were out the door ten minutes later.

It was a beautiful morning, with the temperature in the upper sixties and barely a cloud in the sky. They had missed the sunrise, but the sky was still that lovely shade of early morning blue.

"Which way?" asked Glen as they reached the end of the beach access.

"Hm," said Guin. "Let's go east."

They began walking towards Beach Access #1. Guin had

her head down, searching for shells; Glen had brought his camera and was taking pictures.

They had been walking for around ten minutes when Guin heard a familiar voice calling her name. She turned around to see Lenny hurrying toward them.

"Lenny!" she said, beaming. "Glen, this is my friend, Leonard Isaacs. Lenny, this is Glen."

"I've heard a lot about you," said Glen.

"I could say the same."

Lenny was eyeing him. Then he turned to Guin.

"You're late."

Guin felt herself blushing.

"I was a bit busy this morning."

"Mm," said Lenny. "Well, you didn't miss much. Not a lot of shells this morning."

"What time did you get out here?"

"Around six-thirty. I was just heading back."

"Well, I'm glad we ran into you."

"You take good care of her, you hear?" Lenny said to Glen.

"I will," said Glen. "Though Guin's pretty good at taking care of herself."

Guin smiled at that.

"Yes, well, she could still use some looking after." He eyed Glen again. "You planning on making an honest woman out of her?"

"Lenny! You can't ask a question like that! Glen and I've only been dating a few months."

"So? I knew my wife was the one as soon as I met her."

Lenny was a widower and rarely talked about his wife. It hurt too much.

Glen looked at Lenny.

"I know what you mean. I felt the same way when I met Guin."

Guin felt herself blushing again. Glen had told her how

he felt about her when they were in Italy. But she still found it hard to believe that he knew she was special from the first time he saw her.

"Oh, you did, did you?" said Lenny. "So, what took you so long to ask her out?"

Guin was mortified. But Glen didn't seem to mind the question.

"We were both seeing other people at the time."

"Hm," said Lenny. "Well, don't take too long. Life's too short. Take it from me."

Guin looked at him.

"Is everything okay? You're not sick, are you?"

"I'm fit as a fiddle, but you never know. I never thought I would lose Ina so soon."

Ina was Lenny's wife.

"Well, I should go."

"It was nice meeting you," said Glen.

Lenny grunted then headed away.

"You have to forgive Lenny," said Guin. "He's a bit of a curmudgeon and old-fashioned. And Ina was the love of his life."

"I understand. My grandfather was the same way. He was from Brooklyn too."

"Oh? I thought your family was from Florida."

"Only part of it. My mother's father was from Brooklyn and not that different from Lenny. And Lenny was right about one thing."

"What's that?"

"Life's too short not to spend it with the person you love."

He was looking right at her, and Guin felt her heart start to race. She was terrified Glen was about to propose. She cared about him, probably even loved him. But she wasn't ready to get married again. Though… would it be the worst thing to be married to Glen? He had been a good friend as well as a good lover. And he listened to her and made her laugh. Which was more than she could say about certain other people.

She felt relieved when Glen didn't get down on one knee.

"You want to walk some more, or do you want to turn around?" she asked him.

"Let's walk a little further. Then we should turn around."

They continued their walk, Glen reaching out his hand to take Guin's.

CHAPTER 32

"I should get going," said Glen.

They were back at Guin's place.

"You want something to eat before you go? You can't shoot a wedding on an empty stomach."

Glen smiled.

"The wedding's not until five, and I'll grab a bite before I go. But thank you for being concerned about my welfare."

"I could make us pancakes."

Glen paused.

"Pancakes, eh?"

Guin smiled.

"I have bananas and chocolate chips."

"Hm… Well, I'm not one to turn down banana-chocolate-chip pancakes. But I really should leave after that. I need to stop at Tutti Pazzi."

"Right. Well, the pancakes shouldn't take too long to make."

Glen took a seat, and Guin moved around the kitchen, taking out flour, baking powder, sugar, and salt. She mixed them together in a bowl. Then she added two eggs, milk, a drop of vanilla, a tablespoon of canola oil, and a splash of seltzer. When the ingredients were thoroughly mixed, she added the bananas and chocolate chips. She heated some butter in a pan. Then she ladled in the batter.

A few minutes later, the first batch of pancakes was

ready. She flipped them onto a plate and presented them to Glen.

"Very impressive!"

"There should be some maple syrup in the fridge."

Glen got up, retrieved the maple syrup, and poured some on his pancakes while Guin made the next batch.

"How are the pancakes?" she asked him.

"Very good. Won't you join me?"

"In a minute. I need to make the rest of the pancakes."

"I can wait."

"Don't. I don't want your pancakes to get cold."

However, by the time Guin removed the last pancake from the pan, Glen was done. And he said he needed to go.

"Do you want me to clean up?"

"No, that's okay," said Guin. "Go."

"You sure?"

"Yes."

He went over and kissed her.

"You're the best."

"You're only saying that because I made you pancakes."

"That's not the only reason," he whispered in her ear.

Guin felt her face grow warm.

He said goodbye to Fauna and then left.

Guin sat at the island and ate two pancakes. Then she cleaned up and went to take a shower. As she showered, she thought about Glen. He hadn't asked her to marry him or to live with him, but she thought he might soon. Call it a feeling. They had been spending so much time together lately, and she had gotten used to him. He was easy to be around and respected her space. Would it be the worst thing for the two of them to live together? But where would they live? She didn't want to live in Fort Myers. And she worried her place wasn't big enough for the two of them and all of his camera equipment. Though they could always buy a place together.

Guin shook her head. What was she thinking? They hadn't even talked about living together. She quickly toweled off and then went to get dressed.

Guin had stashed her phone, with the ringer off, in her desk drawer so she wouldn't be disturbed as she worked. She had finished editing her Palm Beach article and had sent it off to Ginny, letting Glen know he should send Ginny his pics. And she had begun working on her Tutti Pazzi piece.

It was after one. Time to take a break and stretch. She took her phone out and checked her messages. There was a text from Shelly asking if she wanted to meet for brunch tomorrow.

"Sure," Guin wrote back. "When and where?"

"Rosie's at 10?" Shelly replied.

"Sounds good!"

Rosie's Café & Grill was a family-owned restaurant over on Palm Ridge Road that served breakfast and lunch and was popular with both locals and visitors. Guin had only been there a couple of times, the restaurant having been sold shortly after she had moved to Sanibel and then repurchased by the original owners. But the food had always been good.

There was also a text from her brother, asking Guin if she had called their mother yet. Clearly, their mother must have called him to complain. Guin groaned. She knew she should call, but she didn't want to.

"May as well get it over with," she said aloud. "Maybe she's not home."

She speed-dialed her mother, hoping to get her voicemail. But, of course, she picked up.

"Guin, is that you?"

"Yes, it's me, Mom." *Obviously.* Like her mother didn't have caller ID. "How are you?"

She heard her mother sigh.

"I'm fine."

Which meant that she wasn't.

"What's up?"

"Nothing you need to concern yourself with."

Which meant that Guin was expected to ask her what was wrong.

"Please, tell me. Is it anything I can help with?"

"Well, if you *really* want to know…"

Guin already regretted asking. But too late now.

"I wouldn't have asked if I didn't."

"Well, you know the Petersons, yes?"

"Your friends who live in the building who you have dinner with occasionally?"

"Yes, them. Well, they're having this big Christmas party next Saturday, and your stepfather and I weren't invited."

"Why didn't they invite you?"

"I haven't a clue. We had dinner with them just before Thanksgiving, and I thought everything was fine. Then Antoinette, who lives in the apartment just below the Petersons, said she was dreading all of those people bouncing on her ceiling next Saturday. And I had no idea what she was talking about. And when I asked her, she told me the Petersons' Christmas party, of course. Weren't Philip and I going? She had assumed we'd been invited. I'm telling you, Guin, I was mortified."

"Did you say something to Mrs. Peterson? Maybe your invitation got lost."

"And what exactly was I supposed to say? Hi, Paula, I heard you're having a big party next Saturday. Did our invitation get lost, because we didn't receive anything, and I thought we were friends?"

Well, when she put it that way.

"Do you really care if you weren't invited, Mom? I know you're friendly with the Petersons, but it's not like you're bosom buddies."

"I know. But it seems we're always inviting them to do things, and they never reciprocate."

"Maybe it's time to stop inviting them."

"That's what your stepfather said. But we always have a good time when we're with them."

"Look, Mom, I don't know the Petersons, but it seems you have two choices: either say something to them about the party or let it go."

"I know, dear. It's just a bit hurtful. I thought we were friends."

"So say something."

"I can't."

Guin sighed.

"So, what are you and Philip doing for Christmas?"

"Actually, we're going to Bath."

"Bath?" They had just been to Bath in July. "Is Lavinia okay?"

Lavinia was her stepfather's sister, who had celebrated her eightieth birthday that summer, which Guin and the family had attended.

"She's fine. Just a bit lonely."

"Where are Harry and Vicky and the grandkids?"

Harry and Vicky were Lavinia's children, who were around the same age as Lance and Guin.

"They're around, just busy with their own families. And poor Lavinia's friends are either in nursing homes or dead."

That was not technically true. Guin had met two of Lavinia's friends that summer and they seemed hale and hearty.

"And it's not like we have grandchildren to share Christmas with."

There it was. The not-so-subtle dig. It wasn't as though Guin hadn't tried to give her mother grandchildren. It just hadn't happened. And Lance and Owen seemed perfectly content not to have kids.

"What about Lance and Owen? Won't they miss spending Christmas with you?"

"They're going away."

"Oh?" said Guin. Lance hadn't said anything.

"One of Owen's artsy friends invited them to spend Christmas at his place somewhere in the Caribbean."

"So, when are you two flying off to England?"

"On the twenty-second."

"How long will you be gone?"

"Just a week. We have plans for New Year's in the City."

"Well, I'm sure you'll have a wonderful time with Lavinia and the family."

"Mm," said her mother. "You know, you're more than welcome to join us. Lavinia says you made quite an impression on Harry's friend David."

David was a friend of Harry's from university, who Lavinia and her mother had tried to fix Guin up with that summer. Guin had found David funny and charming but had not been interested in him that way. And she was pretty sure that David, who was recently divorced, had felt the same way about her.

"Thanks for the invite, but Glen and I are planning on spending Christmas here." Though they'd be spending part of the day with Glen's parents.

"Glen…" said her mother, as if she didn't remember who he was. "He's your latest photographer."

Guin rolled her eyes. She knew her mother hadn't forgiven her for blowing off her wedding to Birdy McMurtry, the famous wildlife photographer. Though, to be fair, the wedding had been a ruse to flush out people who were after Birdy, not a real wedding. But that's another story.*

"I should go," said Guin. "I have work to do."

---

* Read Book 7, *A Perilous Proposal.*

"On a Saturday?"

"It's the busy season here on Sanibel, lots of holiday events to write about."

"Doesn't that paper employ other writers?"

"They do, but several of them are away right now."

"No doubt spending the holiday season with their families."

Guin groaned inwardly. She had just spent Thanksgiving with her family. However, her mother seemed to have conveniently forgotten that.

"Anyway, I love you. And I hope you and Philip have a great time in Bath."

"You make it sound like we won't talk before Christmas."

If only.

"You know you can call me anytime, Mom. And you can always visit." Though she bit her tongue as soon as she said it.

"Actually," said her mother. "Philip and I were thinking about renting a place in Naples."

"Oh? When?"

"February or March."

"This February or March?"

"What did you think I meant? Anyway, Philip and I are tired of the cold, and he's taken up pickleball."

"He has?"

"It's all the rage here. And one of his friends told him there's some kind of pickleball league and tournament in Naples. So now he's insisting we find a place."

"He wants to join a pickleball league? In Naples?"

"That's the plan."

"But isn't it a bit late to find a place? Most places around here are booked a year ahead of time."

"Well, Harriet's son Alfred—you remember Alfred, don't you? His wife is a real estate broker in Naples. And Harriet says that if anyone can find us a rental, Alicia can. In fact, she sent us a couple of places just yesterday."

"In Naples?"

"Yes, in Naples. Weren't you listening?"

"Sorry, I meant where in Naples?"

"On Fifth Avenue South."

"So they're condos."

"I know. Philip and I would have preferred a house, but…"

"You going to rent one of them?"

"We're thinking about it."

"Well, I wouldn't wait too long. If they're halfway decent, they'll be gone in a flash."

"Now, Guin, you know I don't like to rush these things."

"Just saying. Well, good luck. Let me know what you decide."

"Of course."

"I need to go."

Her mother sighed.

"So you said. They really should hire more writers," she mumbled.

Guin ignored her.

"Love you."

"If you change your mind about Bath, we have points…"

"I won't, but thank you."

She said goodbye to her mother and ended the call.

Fauna was looking up at her.

"What?" said Guin.

Fauna rubbed against Guin's legs and started purring. Guin knelt and petted the feline, feeling some of her tension melt away.

"Thank you, Fauna," she said to the cat. "Now I need to get back to work."

CHAPTER 33

Guin entered the restaurant and saw Shelly waving at her.

"Sorry, I'm late."

"I just got here a few minutes ago," said Shelly. "Take a load off. Were you at the farmers' market?"

"No. I was working."

"What on?"

"A piece about Tutti Pazzi. I needed to go over it one more time before sending it off to Ginny."

"That the new Italian place?"

"It is."

"Did it open?"

"Not yet. There was a soft opening Friday."

"So, what did you think?"

"Everything I had was good, and the place looked nice. But hard to tell how it will do from a publicity event."

"Steve and I'll definitely go there when it opens. You think you'll review it when it does?"

"Probably."

"Well, let me know if you need a taster."

"You'll be the first person I call."

A server came over and asked Guin if she wanted coffee. Guin had already had a mug at home but said sure.

"You ready to order or do you need a few minutes?"

"Give us a few minutes," said Guin.

The server nodded and left, and Guin picked up a menu.

"Hm," she said, staring at it.

"What are you thinking?" asked Shelly.

"I would normally order pancakes, but I made Glen banana-chocolate-chip pancakes for breakfast yesterday."

"Oh ho! Do tell."

"Nothing to tell," said Guin.

"Oh, come on. I don't believe that. So, he stayed over Friday?"

Guin nodded.

"After the soft opening."

"And?"

"And what?"

"You get any sleep?" Shelly had a goofy expression on her face.

"Some."

Shelly's grin widened.

"You have a dirty mind, Shelly Silverman."

"Oh, come on. It's not like I asked you how many times you did it or what positions."

"Shelly!"

"What?"

But Guin just shook her head and held up her menu.

"Fine," said Shelly. "So, you know what you're going to have?"

"I think so."

Shelly signaled to the server, who indicated she'd be there in a minute.

"So, things serious between the two of you?"

"Define serious."

"You know. You two talk about moving in together or…"

"We've only been dating a few months, Shell." Though Guin had been thinking about the two of them living together for the past twenty-four hours.

"But you're together all the time. And you're not getting any younger."

"Thanks."

"You know what I mean."

"I do. Actually…"

"Yes?"

"Never mind."

"Tell me."

Guin sighed.

"Glen and I were walking on the beach yesterday morning and we ran into Lenny."

"How is he? I feel as though I haven't seen him in ages."

"Fine. Anyway, he was hinting that Glen should make an honest woman out of me."

"As in?"

"Yes."

"And what did Glen have to say?"

"He hinted that that was his intention."

"He did? He told Lenny he wanted to marry you?"

"Not in so many words, but… I have a feeling he'd ask me if he thought I'd say yes."

"You wouldn't say yes if he asked you?"

"I don't know. I…"

The server arrived to take their order. Shelly ordered the pineapple upside-down pancakes, and Guin ordered the Florentine omelet with whole wheat toast.

"So getting back to our conversation," said Shelly as soon as the server left. "If Glen asked you to marry him, you'd turn him down?"

"I didn't say I'd say no. I'd just have to think about it."

"What's there to think about? You're perfect together."

"You thought Ris and I were perfect together too. And the detective."

"Ris, maybe. But I never thought you and the detective were perfect."

"Whatever. You just want me to get married."

"Only because I love weddings. And I think you and Glen belong together."

"Yes, well. But I've grown used to living on my own."

"Is that the only reason? I'm sure you'd get used to having him around. He doesn't seem the clingy type."

"He isn't. But what if he wants me to live with him at his place?"

"Tell him he should move in with you."

"My place is too small for the two of us and all of his equipment."

Shelly shook her head.

"What?"

"You're being unreasonable."

"I'm being perfectly reasonable. Now, could we please change the subject?"

"Just tell me the real reason why you wouldn't say yes if Glen asked you to marry him."

Guin looked at her friend. Should she tell her the real reason, that she was terrified he'd grow bored with her or restless and cheat on her or leave? Glen's wife Margaux had cheated on him. So she liked to think that Glen would never cheat. Then again, she had never expected Art to cheat on her.

"I'm waiting," said Shelly.

"Can we please change the subject?"

"Just answer the question."

Guin knew what Shelly was like when she had a bone between her teeth.

"Fine," she said and told her.

"Oh, Guin," said Shelly, taking Guin's hand in hers. "Glen would never cheat on you."

"I know that. Or I want to believe that. But Art…"

"Art was a jerk and didn't deserve you."

"Look, can we please talk about something else? I don't want to talk about Glen or Art."

"Fine. Did you see Suzy's latest?"

"No. What or who did she write about this time?"

"The San Ybel. You should really read Shellapalooza, Guin."

"Whatever. What did she have to say?"

"Well," said Shelly, glancing around to make sure no one was listening. Though if it was in Shellapalooza, it wasn't exactly a secret. "Suzy heard that the Thompsons were trying to back out of their deal with the Mandelli Group and sell the resort to the Victor Group."

Guin frowned. How did Suzy know that? It had to be Audra.

"Is it true?" asked Shelly.

"It's true," said Guin.

"Can the Thompsons do that?"

"They can. But they risk being sued."

"You think the Mandelli Group will sue them?"

"Audra threatened to if the Thompsons didn't give them thirty days."

"Thirty days?"

"The Mandelli Group asked for an extension in light of Mandelli's death."

"I guess that's reasonable."

"But rumor has it they're having trouble raising the money, and the Victor Group doesn't want to wait thirty days."

"How exciting!" said Shelly.

"Not for the Thompsons. I think it's caused a rift in their marriage. Mrs. Thompson wanted to go with the Victor Group from the beginning, but Mr. Thompson insisted on going with the Mandelli Group."

Guin didn't know why she was telling Shelly all of this. She must have drunk too much coffee.

"Well, I'm rooting for the Victor Group," said Shelly.

"How come?"

"You don't really want the Mandelli Group taking over the resort, do you?"

"Mandelli's no longer running it."

"Still, I think the Victor Group should buy the hotel."

"Why? It wouldn't have anything to do with their CEO, would it?"

"You know I can't resist a French accent, Guin! And he is quite a dish. I read that he's not married."

"You planning on making a play for him?"

"I'm a happily married woman! Though…" she said with a grin.

Guin smiled back at her and shook her head. Shelly was incorrigible.

"And did you see their hotels? Their one in the South of France is to die for. Just think what they could do with the San Ybel!"

Guin had looked at pictures of the Victor Group's hotels. They were exquisite, like something out of a high-end travel magazine.

"Okay, I'll admit that their properties are nice-looking. But we know nothing about their management style."

"Can't be worse than Mandelli's. No one who's worked for him has nice things to say."

True.

"Speaking of the late Mr. Mandelli, any news?"

"Actually…"

Shelly leaned forward.

"Don't get too excited. I assume you saw what I wrote in the paper."

"That it was a heart attack. No doubt brought on by the light falling."

Their food arrived, and they thanked the server.

"So, any suspects? What does the detective have to say? I assume you've talked to him."

"I have, though I was the one doing most of the talking. As usual, he wouldn't say much."

"Have they arrested anyone?"

"No. At least as far as I know. But they found the maintenance worker who was on duty that evening and had supposedly checked the rigging beforehand."

"And? Do you think he's the one who loosened the light?"

"I don't know. His wife is one of the maids Mandelli allegedly molested."

"Sounds like a good motive to me!"

"I know, but… I wish I could talk to them."

"Any other suspects?"

"Well, there's Hugo Blanchet. Though he has an alibi."

"You think he killed Mandelli so he could buy the hotel?"

"It's possible."

"Huh. Anyone else? What about Honey?"

"Actually…"

"Yes?" said Shelly.

"About Honey…"

Shelly waited for Guin to go on.

"The reason she looked familiar to you is because she was on *The Bachelor*."

"She was?" Shelly scrunched up her face. Then her eyes went wide. "Oh my God! She's the vixen from Season 23, Henny Lambert! I can't believe I didn't figure that out. Though her hair's different. It's her, isn't it?"

"It is."

"But why was she working for Mandelli?"

"She was playing a role."

"What kind of role?"

"Helping to convince Fred Thompson to sell the hotel to Mandelli."

"Whoa. So she really is a vixen. But why the fake name?"

"Honey Lamb's actually her real name. Or was. She changed it to Henny Lambert when she started modeling."

"Huh."

They picked at their food, neither saying anything for several minutes.

"You think Henny—I mean Honey—had something to do with Mandelli's death?"

"I don't know. She claimed she was in the ladies' room. But the medical examiner found zolpidem in his system. You know, sleeping pills, and it's possible that…"

"You think she could have drugged him, so he'd be too tired to move when that light fell? I could see Henny doing something like that. She was vicious on *The Bachelor*."

"That was a TV show, Shelly. It wasn't real."

"Then why do they call it reality TV?"

Guin didn't have a good answer.

"Anyway, there were other people there who weren't fans of Mandelli."

"Like?"

"Patrick Finney for one. He had a lot to gain from the hotel being sold to the Victor Group. And he didn't like his ex-wife being involved with Mandelli."

"Good point. So you think he loosened the light?"

"Maybe."

"Or…" said Shelly.

Guin waited.

"Or what?"

"Maybe they worked together."

"What do you mean?"

"You know, like in that movie we rented, *Murder on the Orient Express*."

Guin stared at her.

"What?" said Shelly.

"I didn't think about that."

"So, you think I'm right?"

"I don't know. I assumed it had been one person. But the more I learn… You may be onto something."

Shelly looked pleased.

"Maybe I should write mystery novels. I bet I'd be good at it."

"Trust me," said Guin. "You're better off making jewelry."

They finished brunch, and Shelly said she needed to get back to her workroom. She was swamped with jewelry orders for Christmas and was racing to fill them.

"Glad to hear business is booming," said Guin.

"Oh yeah," said Shelly. "Steve's even been talking about me taking on a partner. Says it's too much work for one person. But I'm a bit nervous about hiring someone."

"You must know somebody on the island who could help you out, though, yes?"

"I know a few people, but…"

"But?"

"I couldn't pay them much. And you know how picky I can be."

"I know. But there must be someone out there who could help you, at least part-time. You could always ask at BIG ARTS."

"True. Anyway, got to run. Good luck with your articles."

"Thanks. You have time for a beach walk later this week?"

"Is that a trick question? Just text me."

Guin read through her Tutti Pazzi article one more time before sending it off to Ginny. Then she pulled up her notes on the Mandelli case and the San Ybel. She really wanted to speak with Luis and Maria. Were they back at the hotel, or had the police arrested them? She thought about calling the detective, but he was probably out fishing or else working. Besides, she'd be at the San Ybel that afternoon and could find out then.

She also thought about what Shelly had said. Could Blanchet, Finney, and Honey have been working together?

Or could she have missed someone? Was it possible a former associate of Mandelli's or a former girlfriend had been at the hotel, undetected? Who would know? Both Audra and Honey had said Mandelli had enemies. But neither recalled nor mentioned seeing any of them on the island, at least to her.

Guin picked up her phone and entered Craig's number. Of course, he could be out fishing too. In which case, she'd leave him a message. But he picked up.

"What's up?" he said.

"Could you ask your source at the SPD if any of Mandelli's former business associates or girlfriends happened to be on Sanibel at the time of the incident and were at the holiday lighting?"

"Why don't you just ask O'Loughlin?"

"Because I doubt he'd tell me. Can't you just ask?"

"I can ask, but I can't guarantee an answer."

"Understood. Also, I heard that they located the maintenance worker and his wife, but I don't know if they arrested them. You hear anything?"

"Nope."

"Oh, and I found out why I couldn't find anything about Honey Lamb online."

"Why?"

"Her real name, or her legal name, is Henny Lambert. And get this: She's a reality TV star."

"A reality TV star, eh? What was she doing working for Mandelli?"

"He hired her to butter up prospective investors and help him close deals."

"So he pimped her."

"Something like that."

Guin heard someone talking to Craig, and Craig tell him just a minute.

"You out fishing?"

"Yup."

"I won't keep you then. You catch anything?"

"A couple of snook."

"Well, have fun."

CHAPTER 34

Guin met up with Glen at the San Ybel a little before three, and the two of them headed to the ballroom, where the Santa meet-and-greet was taking place. There was a line of children with their parents waiting to go in.

Guin stopped to chat with a mother and son as Glen took a photo. Then the doors opened and the parents and children filed inside.

The ballroom was decorated to look like Santa's workshop. And there was the toy train. Up on the stage, just as before, was a big chair, which now contained the real Santa (or someone dressed as Santa), looking very jolly. Guin was surprised that they had kept the chair on the stage after what had happened. Though it was the obvious place to put it. And Hermione had said that the rigging would be triple-checked before a single child was allowed in. Still.

Speaking of Hermione, Guin found her standing off to the side, watching the proceedings. Guin went over to her.

"You didn't move Santa's chair."

"No. Laurence said it would be safe there."

"Oh, did he now?"

"Yes. He said he personally checked the rigging and that it was fine."

Guin looked at her.

"Laurence Washburn, the hotel's general manager, personally checked the rigging?"

Hermione was looking up at the stage, where an elf was escorting a child to meet Santa.

"He used to be a rigger in the circus."

"He worked at a circus?"

Hermione turned to her.

"You didn't know?"

Guin shook her head.

"I'm surprised. He loves telling people how he ran away from home as a teen and joined the circus, and how he worked his way up from helping put up the big top to running the show."

"So he went from managing a circus to managing a hotel?"

"He did. But I believe there was a stop or two in between. Though as Laurence likes to say, there's not much difference between managing a circus and managing a hotel."

"Ha!" said Guin. She looked up at the stage. A little boy was sitting on Santa's lap. The boy was saying something to Santa. Santa smiled back and said ho-ho-ho. "Who's the Santa? He's very good."

Hermione smiled.

"You don't recognize him?"

The boy was being escorted off the stage and now a little girl was approaching Santa. Guin looked closer at him.

"No. Should I?"

"It's Laurence."

Guin turned to Hermione.

"It is?"

Hermione nodded.

"The Santa we hired had a family emergency and was unable to make it."

"Something happen to Mrs. Claus?"

Hermione smiled.

"Something like that. When Laurence heard, he

immediately volunteered. Said he played Santa at that resort he used to work at in the Hamptons."

"A circus rigger, hotelier, *and* Santa impersonator. Mr. Washburn certainly has an interesting resume."

"Indeed," said Hermione. "You should hear some of his stories, especially the ones from when he was the GM at the Mecox."

"The Mecox?"

"The resort he worked at in the Hamptons. Sounded very chichi. Well, until it went south."

Why did that name, the Mecox, sound familiar?

"It was his first turn as GM," continued Hermione. "And I think he was a bit terrified at first. Many of the guests who stayed there were famous or titans of industry with very high standards. But he grew to love it."

"If he loved it, why did he leave? Did something happen?" Hermione had said the resort had gone south.

"The owners sold the hotel to some investment group. And the new owners refused to spend money on repairs or upgrades. Laurence warned them the place was an accident waiting to happen, but they didn't care. Just ignored him. Then, of course, one did."

"What happened?"

"Some lawyer tripped and broke his leg and sued the hotel."

"But that wasn't Laurence's fault, was it?"

"No, but he was the GM."

"So, what, the new owners fired him?"

"They needed a scapegoat. Claimed they had no idea the hotel needed work."

"Sounds rather unfair."

"Indeed."

"So is that how he wound up here?"

"He worked at a resort in South Carolina first."

Guin looked up at the stage again. Washburn as Santa

was now chatting with a little red-headed boy who looked very intent. Guin couldn't help smiling. She turned to Hermione again.

"I should go interview people. Though, care to give me a quote for the paper?"

"Well, as you know, the Meet Santa! event has been a tradition at the San Ybel for years. People come from all over the island and from far away to attend. Some families have been coming to the hotel for the event for years and now bring their grandchildren. Christmas is a very special time here at the hotel."

"Thank you," said Guin. "So, do you think the new owners will keep the tradition alive?"

"I hope so."

"Me, too."

Guin excused herself and went in search of families to interview.

Guin was seated in a quiet part of the lobby with Glen. They had ducked out of the ballroom, having gotten what they needed.

"You get some good pictures?" she asked Glen.

"I think so."

"What did you think of the Santa?"

"He was very good. If I didn't know Santa was still at the North Pole, I'd say he was the real deal."

"You don't still believe in Santa, do you?"

Glen looked shocked.

"You mean you don't?"

Guin couldn't tell if Glen was pulling her leg.

"I gave up believing in Santa when I was four and Lance told me Mom was the one putting the presents under the tree."

"That was rather cruel of him."

"I don't think he was trying to be cruel. He was just telling me what he saw."

"Did you ever think he had it wrong and maybe your mother was just helping Santa?"

Guin looked at him.

"What?" said Glen. "Look, *you* may not believe in Santa, but I do. Maybe not that there's some old white guy with a beard and a pack of elves making toys up at the North Pole. But I believe in the idea of Santa, which is the spirit of giving."

Guin softened. This was why she loved Glen, he was an optimist who truly looked for the good in things and in people too.

"Well, I'd like to have a word with Santa. The Santa in the ballroom, that is."

"You could always go sit on his lap," Glen said with a grin.

"That would be inappropriate. I'll wait until the meet-and-greet is over."

"Okay. Though if you change your mind about sitting in his lap… I'd love to get a picture."

Guin scowled, and Glen laughed.

They went back into the ballroom a little after five. Washburn was still seated in Santa's chair, talking to one of the elves, when Guin climbed the stairs and approached him.

"Ho-ho-ho!" he said. "And what would *you* like for Christmas, young lady?"

To find a big red true tulip shell, Guin immediately thought. But she didn't say it out loud. Instead, she smiled at him.

"You make an excellent Santa, Mr. Washburn."

"You found me out," he replied, a twinkle in his eye.

"Actually, Hermione told me. I had no idea."

He continued to smile.

"It's been years since I played Santa. Good to know I've still got it."

"The children looked very happy. I just hope they're not disappointed."

"Well, we tell their parents what they wanted. So hopefully not too many will be. And every child who visits with Santa gets a toy."

Hermione had mentioned that.

"That's very generous of the hotel."

"It's a tradition. One I'd hate to see go away. So, what can I do for you, Ms. Jones?"

"You weren't at all nervous about sitting here after what happened? What if another light fell and a child got hurt?"

"I would never allow that to happen. That's why I personally inspected the rigging this afternoon."

"Hermione said you had worked in a circus."

Washburn smiled.

"It was a long time ago. But I can still climb a ladder."

"She said you were a rigger. Does that mean you helped put up the tent?"

"Big top. And while I helped with that at first, a rigger helps with the aerial gear. I always wanted to be the daring young man on the flying trapeze. But I wound up putting up the trapeze equipment instead."

Guin couldn't picture Washburn flying through the air. But she didn't comment.

"I heard that the police found Luis Garcia and his wife. Do you know if they arrested them?"

"Not as far as I know."

"So, will they be coming back to the San Ybel then?"

"I hope so. Luis is invaluable, a regular Mr. Fix-It."

"Do you know how I could get in touch with Luis?"

"I," he began. But he was interrupted by one of the elves, who said she needed to speak with him. "Would you excuse me?" he said to Guin.

"Of course," said Guin.

As she stood on the stage, she looked up at the rigging. Had the spotlight been replaced? She couldn't tell. She felt a bit exposed standing there and quickly got off the stage. Glen was speaking with another elf. She went over to them. The elf stopped talking as soon as she saw Guin.

"Am I interrupting something?" asked Guin.

"Not at all," said Glen. "Lucy here was just asking me if I ever took senior pictures."

"Senior pictures?"

"You know for the yearbook and stuff," said Lucy. "The deadline's in a few weeks, and I thought maybe…"

Glen smiled at the young woman.

"I'd be happy to take your senior picture, Lucy."

"You would? That's great!" she said. Then she paused. "How much do you charge?"

"For you, nothing."

Lucy looked suspicious.

"What's the catch?"

"No catch. Just permit me to use some of the photos in my portfolio. You never know who else might need a senior photo."

"Oh, lots of people," said Lucy. "And they'd be happy to pay for good ones."

"Then we have a deal. We'll do a photo shoot. And if you like the photos, be sure to tell your friends."

"Deal!" said Lucy.

Glen smiled at her and reached into his pocket for a business card.

"Here's my card. Let me know when you want to meet."

Lucy looked at his card as though it was the winning lottery ticket.

"I'll do that. Thank you."

"That was very nice of you," said Guin after Lucy had left.

"Just playing Santa in my own way. And right now this Santa could use a beer. Care to join me?"

Guin had been planning on going home and working, but the article could wait.

"Sure," she said.

CHAPTER 35

They were almost to the bar when Guin put out a hand to stop Glen.

"What?" he said.

"Over there," Guin pointed. Glen looked over at the bar. "Who's that man with Honey?"

"I don't know."

"I feel like I've seen him before."

Guin watched as Honey and the man chatted. What were they discussing?

"We could always just go over and say hello to them." Guin hesitated. "Come on," he said.

Glen headed over to where Honey and the man were seated, and Guin followed.

"Fancy running into you here!" he said, smiling down at Honey. "I thought you'd have gone back to New York."

"Yes, well," said Honey.

"Did the police say you could leave?" asked Guin.

Honey frowned.

"Hi, I'm Guin Jones," Guin said to Honey's companion. "Have we met? You look familiar."

The man was about to reply when Honey stopped him.

"Better be careful, Tim. She's a reporter."

"I've got nothing to hide," he told Honey. "Timothy Sadler. Who do you write for?"

"The *Sanibel-Captiva Sun-Times*."

"That's probably why I look familiar. My picture's been in your paper. In fact, one of your colleagues just did an article about a fundraising event my wife and I hosted."

"Oh? Who for?"

"CROW." Which stood for the Clinic for the Rehabilitation of Wildlife. "My wife and I are big supporters of the wildlife here. We also give money to SCCF, F.I.S.H., and CHR."

F.I.S.H. was the local food pantry; CHR stood for Community Housing Resources; and SCCF stood for the Sanibel-Captiva Conservation Foundation.

"How very generous of you."

"We do what we can."

"So, do you live here full-time?"

"No, we're seasonal. We also have a place in the Hamptons. Had one in Kentucky too, but we just sold it."

"And how do you two know each other?" Guin asked, looking from Sadler to Honey.

Honey was giving her drinking companion a warning look, but he ignored it.

"We met through Anthony Mandelli."

"I see," said Guin. "Are you one of his investors?"

"I was going to be."

"You changed your mind?"

"I did."

"How come?"

"I," he began. Then Guin saw Honey shaking her head, albeit subtly.

"I had my reasons."

Guin heard a phone ringing. It was Sadler's.

"I need to take this," he said. "Would you all excuse me?"

"Of course," said Guin. "Nice meeting you."

He nodded, got up, and stepped away from the bar.

"So," Guin said to Honey. "What were you and Mr. Sadler talking about?"

"None of your business."

"I thought your job was to convince people to invest in the Mandelli Group not warn them off."

"I told you, I'm not working for them anymore."

"Were you asking Mr. Sadler for a job?"

Though Guin had no idea what Timothy Sadler did for a living. She would Google him later. And Honey had said she was auditioning for a role, assumedly on TV.

"It's not any of your business. Now, if you would excuse me? I have things to do."

"It was nice seeing you," said Glen.

Honey gave him a quick nod and then left the bar.

"I wonder what that was about," said Guin.

"I got a feeling Honey didn't want you talking to her friend."

"Ya think?"

Then she realized, she hadn't told Glen who Honey really was. But maybe he had heard. Word traveled fast on Sanibel.

"By the way, Honey isn't her real name."

"I know, it's a nickname."

"No, I mean… Her real name's Henny Lambert. She's a reality TV star Mandelli hired to help him close deals."

Glen stared at her.

"How do you know that?"

"I meant to tell you. Lance recognized her. She was on *The Bachelor*. She played a vixen."

"You're serious."

"I am."

"Wow. Let's find a seat. I could use a drink."

They found two seats at the bar and Glen ordered a beer. Guin ordered a glass of white wine. Though she was tempted to order a margarita.

"I wonder if Sadler's the investor who pulled out," she mused.

The bartender brought over their drinks. Guin took a sip

of her white wine and then turned to Glen.

"How was the wedding?"

"It was fine."

"Just fine?"

"It was a beautiful evening and it looked like everyone was having a good time."

"Nice bride?"

"Nice enough."

"And the groom?"

"He seemed all right."

Guin sensed he didn't want to talk about the wedding. Just as well. She didn't really want to talk about it either. She was just being polite.

They sipped their drinks, neither saying anything for several seconds.

"Did you know Laurence Washburn used to be in the circus?" Guin asked him.

"He was?"

"Yup, he started as a rigger and went on to manage it."

"Huh," said Glen.

They finished their drinks. Glen insisted on paying. But Guin insisted on leaving the tip. Then they made their way out of the hotel to the parking lot.

"My car's just over there," Glen said, pointing.

"And I'm over there," said Guin, pointing in the other direction. "You going to edit your photos tonight or wait until morning?"

"Probably tonight. Got a lot to do."

"Like the wedding photos?"

"I told the couple I wouldn't have proofs for them to see for at least a couple of weeks. For now, the paper takes priority."

"Lucky Ginny. Were they annoyed when you told them?"

"Nah, it's standard practice."

Guin tried to recall how long it took after her wedding

to Art for them to receive proofs of their wedding photos. It had probably been a couple of weeks, now that she thought about it. Possibly longer.

"Shall I walk you to your car?"

"You don't have to," said Guin.

"Maybe I want to."

Guin smiled.

"All right."

They walked to the Mini.

"Well, goodnight," she said.

"Goodnight," said Glen. He leaned down and kissed her. "I'll check in with you tomorrow."

As soon as Guin got home, she searched for Timothy Sadler online. She immediately found several pictures of him and his wife, Tori, taken at various charity events.

She wondered what he did. Then she came across an article with the headline "Leading Maker of Saddles and Equestrian Equipment Rides off into the Sunset."

"Well, what do you know?"

It turned out that Timothy Sadler and his wife were in fact saddlers, makers or purveyors of bespoke saddles, bridles, harnesses, and other equestrian equipment used by Olympians, top equestrians, polo players, and the horsey set.

"I wonder what brought them to Sanibel?" Guin said aloud, Sanibel not exactly being known as a horseback rider's paradise. In fact, she doubted there was a stable within 50 miles of the island. "I would have thought they'd have retired to Palm Beach or someplace horsey." She would have to ask Mr. Sadler about it, along with a few other things. But how to find him?

She typed *Timothy Sadler Sanibel* into the search box and found an address for him. But she couldn't just show up on his doorstep as she'd done with Hugo Blanchet, could she?

She searched for an email or a phone number for him, but she only found the website for his now-former business. Frustrated, she sat back. Then she had an idea.

"Ginny must know how to get in touch with him."

She picked up her phone and texted her boss.

"You know how I can reach Timothy Sadler or his wife Tori?"

A few minutes later, Ginny got back to her.

"Why?"

"It's for an article."

"What article?"

"Can I call you?"

Ginny gave her a thumbs-up, and Guin entered her number. Ginny answered right away.

"So what do you want with the Sadlers?"

"Sadler was going to invest with the Mandelli Group but suddenly changed his mind. I want to find out why."

No reply.

"You still there?"

"I am," said Ginny.

"So will you give me his number or his email?"

"I'll give you his email, which you probably could have found on your own."

"I looked, but…"

"Just don't tell him I gave it to you."

"I won't."

Ginny told her the email address, and Guin jotted it down.

"Thank you," said Guin.

"You're welcome. Just handle the Sadlers with kid gloves. They've been very generous to the charities here."

"I wasn't planning on accusing him of anything. I just want to find out why he changed his mind about investing with Mandelli."

"Maybe he saw the light."

"Maybe."

They ended the call, and Guin immediately sent an email to Sadler, asking if he would meet with her. Then she stared at her computer.

What was the name of that resort in the Hamptons Washburn had worked at? Was it the Maidstone? No, that wasn't it. But she was sure it started with an M. Then she remembered. It was the Mecox. She immediately entered *Mecox Resort Hamptons* into the search box.

"Bingo!" she said.

She scrolled through the results, clicking on an article from a few years ago. She began to read and frowned.

CHAPTER 36

Guin got up Monday and looked out her window. It was another beautiful, blue-sky, sunny morning. She thought about going for a beach walk. But again, she had work to do, namely the Santa meet-and-greet piece. Though surely, the article could wait a bit. She went back and forth with herself and headed to the kitchen. She'd make some coffee and then decide. She gazed out the window while the coffee steeped. As much as she wanted to go for a walk, work won out.

She sat in front of her computer, staring at the blank document. But she was having a hard time focusing. She told herself to just start typing, but it was no use. She kept thinking about Mandelli and the hotel and Glen.

"Maybe I should go for a walk," she sighed. Walks always helped clear her head. "I mean, it's not like I'll be gone for that long."

She quickly changed and headed out the door. But instead of going to the beach, she walked down West Gulf Drive. She didn't want to be tempted by shells. Forty minutes later, she was back at her desk, feeling more clear-headed. She opened the document again and began to type. This time, the words flowed. And by noon, she had a first draft.

Guin took out her phone, not having checked it in several hours. She was pleasantly surprised to see an email from Tim Sadler in her inbox. She immediately opened it.

He was available at four that afternoon. Did she mind coming to his house?

Guin didn't mind at all and immediately wrote him back, saying she would be there. She just needed the address. He wrote her back a few minutes later. His place was on Bay Drive. Guin hadn't been to Bay Drive before, but she would find it. Guin thanked him and said she'd see him at four.

"Well, that was easier than I thought it would be."

Feeling lucky, she called over to the San Ybel and asked for the Maintenance Department.

"One moment please," said the operator.

Guin waited to be connected.

"Maintenance," a man answered, a different one than she had spoken with last time. What was his name again, Nick?

"Yes, I'd like to speak with Luis Garcia. Is he there?"

Guin had no idea if he was back at the hotel, but it was worth a shot.

"Who's calling?"

That was a good sign.

"Tell him Guinivere Jones."

"Does he know you?"

"I'm with the *Sanibel-Captiva Sun-Times*."

There was a long silence.

"Luis doesn't want to speak with any reporters."

"Who am I speaking with, please?"

"Manny."

"Hi, Manny. Look, I understand why Luis might not want to talk to a reporter. But you can tell him it can be off the record. That is, whatever he says to me will be confidential. Can you tell him that? Also, tell him he can speak to Hermione Potter about me. She and I are friends."

Silence.

"For what it's worth, I don't think he's responsible for that light coming loose."

Still nothing.

"Are you still there?"

"I'm here," said Manny.

"Look, can I just give you my number and have you pass it along to Luis?"

Guin waited.

"Okay," said Manny.

Guin breathed a sigh of relief.

"Thank you, Manny."

She gave Manny her number and spelled her name for him. Then they ended the call. Guin hoped Manny would pass along the message, but she wasn't sure that he would. Well, if she didn't hear from Luis by tomorrow, she'd pay a visit to the Maintenance Department.

At four o'clock, Guin was standing in front of Timothy Sadler's grand Bay Drive home. Despite living on Sanibel for several years, Guin had never been to this part of the island. Though she had seen the large bayfront houses while driving over the Causeway.

She rang the doorbell, and a few seconds later an attractive woman around Guin's age answered the door. Guin guessed it was Sadler's wife.

"Can I help you?" asked the woman.

"I have an appointment to see Mr. Sadler."

"And you are?" said the woman.

"Guinivere Jones. I'm with the *Sanibel-Captiva Sun-Times*. He's expecting me."

"Ah, yes. I recognize the name. Come in." She opened the door, allowing Guin to enter. "I'm Tori, by the way, Tim's wife."

"Nice to meet you."

Guin glanced around the palatial entryway.

"Tim's in his office," said Tori. "I'll get him." She walked over to the stairway and yelled for Tim to come down, telling him he had a visitor.

"Tell her I'll be right there!" Tim yelled back.

"Excuse the shouting," said Tori. "We should probably install an intercom system."

"It's fine," said Guin. "My mother and stepfather are always shouting across their apartment to each other. However, I think in their case it's because they're both a bit hard of hearing."

Tori smiled.

"Can I get you something to drink?"

"I'm good. Thank you."

They stood in the entryway, waiting for Tim. Tori sighed.

"This is so typical. He gets on his computer and then loses himself. Can I give you a tour of the house? Then we can go wrest my husband away from his computer."

"That's okay," said Guin. "I don't mind waiting. And you're probably busy."

"I love giving tours. Come."

Guin had to admit she was interested in seeing the house. The views alone must be spectacular. She followed Tori into the living area.

"Wow," said Guin, taking in the view of the Causeway and Pine Island Sound. "I may never leave."

"I felt the same way when the real estate agent showed us the house. It is pretty breathtaking. Do you like to cook?"

"Sometimes," said Guin.

Tori smiled again.

"I know how you feel. But when you see the kitchen… Come. I'll show you."

Tori led Guin to the kitchen. It was huge and had two ovens, one of the largest refrigerators Guin had ever seen, a large island, an eating nook, and views of Pine Island Sound from the windows.

"I designed it myself," said Tori, seeing Guin's appreciative gaze.

"I take it you like to cook," Guin said.

"Tim and I both do. We took it up after we sold the company. We wanted something we could do together, and we both liked to eat, so…"

Guin walked around, admiring the granite—or were they marble?—countertops.

"Let me show you the rest of the place. Then I'll make sure Tim stops doing whatever it is he's doing."

She led Guin around the rest of the first floor, which had a powder room, a guest room with an en suite, and an office that Tori said was hers.

"Tim's office is upstairs, as is the master," she said as they climbed the stairs. They walked down a short hallway and Tori led them into a large bedroom.

"This is the master," she said.

Guin stepped inside and had to stop her jaw from dropping. There was that amazing view again—and one of the biggest beds she had ever seen.

"Come, let me show you the bathroom."

Guin followed Tori, wondering if the house could get any more amazing. Then she saw the master bathroom. It was huge and contained a jetted tub, a large shower with multiple shower heads, a separate toilet area with a bidet, and double sinks.

"Wow," said Guin. "Was it like this when you bought it?"

"Goodness, no," said Tori. "The bathroom—really the whole place—looked like it hadn't been touched since the eighties or early nineties. You should have seen it. We knew we'd need to remodel. But we fell in love with the view. And it had plenty of space."

"So you re-did the whole place?" That must have cost a fortune.

"We did," said Tori. "It took over a year, but I think it turned out rather well."

Guin eyed the neat tile work and high-end fixtures. She

wished her bathroom looked like this.

"Let me show you the closets."

They left the bathroom and Tori opened a nearby door.

"This one's Tim's," she said. Then she opened another door. "And this one's mine."

Guin stared. Carrie Bradshaw would have been in ecstasy. Guin herself was ready to move in. Tori's closet was straight out of *Sex and the City* and was about the same size as Guin's first apartment in New York City.

"It's huge," said Guin.

"We had to get rid of a bedroom to do all of this, but I think it was worth it, don't you?"

"Definitely." *I guess a lot of people need saddles*, she said to herself. How else could the Sadlers have afforded to do all of this?

"There you are!" It was Tim.

"I was just showing our guest around while you were busy doing whatever it was you were doing."

"Watching the *Closing Bell*," he said to his wife. He turned to Guin. "Sorry to keep you waiting."

"No worries. Your house is amazing. It's like something out of *Coastal Living* or *Architectural Digest*.

"Actually, a crew from *Coastal Living* was just here," said Tori. "We're going to be in the spring issue."

"Come," said Tim. "I'm afraid I only have a few minutes. I have to do a call at five."

"Thank you for the tour," Guin said to Tori. "You have a beautiful home."

Tori smiled.

"Thank you. We think so."

Guin then followed Tim to his office.

"Now, what can I do for you?" he said, taking a seat behind a big antique-looking desk. Guin wondered if his wife had picked it out.

"I wanted to know about your relationship with the

Mandelli Group. How did you hear about them? Did they approach you?"

"In a way. I met Tony at the Hampton Classic last summer." The Hampton Classic Horse Show was a leading horse-jumping event held in Bridgehampton over Labor Day weekend. "A mutual friend introduced us."

"I see," said Guin. "And the two of you hit it off?"

"You could say that. We chatted for a while, and he invited me and Tori out for dinner."

"Did he know you had a place on Sanibel?"

"We may have mentioned it."

"Did he ask you to invest money with him?"

"Not right away. At the time we met I was in the process of selling my company."

"But he did eventually ask you to invest with him."

"Yes."

"When?"

"A few months ago, I think."

"And did he mention the San Ybel?"

"Yes. That's why he wanted the money. He was putting together an offering for the place and wanted to know if I was interested."

"And what did you tell him?"

"I told him I might be interested. We had never stayed at the San Ybel, but we had heard good things about it. And it seemed like a good opportunity."

"Then what happened?"

"I told him to send me an investment packet."

"And did he?"

"He did. I also did my own research."

"And you decided to invest."

"I did."

"Even knowing his track record?"

"You mean the bankruptcies."

Guin nodded.

"Tony explained them to me and said he had learned from his mistakes." Guin doubted that but didn't say anything. "And some of his recent ventures had done quite well."

"Can I ask how much you committed?"

"I'm afraid that's confidential."

"So, you made a commitment to invest but then changed your mind. Why?"

"I received a letter."

"A letter? From whom?"

"It was anonymous, signed *A Friend*."

Guin looked skeptical.

"I know. I took it with a grain of salt initially too. But some of the things the letter writer said…"

"Like what? I assume it was something about Mandelli."

"Again, I'm afraid that's confidential. But…"

"But whatever he said made you change your mind."

He nodded.

"And when did you receive this anonymous letter?"

"I forget exactly. Maybe a couple of weeks ago?"

"And how do you know Ms. Lamb?"

"I met her through Tony."

"Did you know she was a reality TV star?"

Tim smiled.

"Not at first."

"Was she working for Mandelli when you met her?"

He nodded.

"So how did you find out?"

"Tori told me. She loves *The Bachelor* and immediately recognized her."

"When did Tori meet her?"

"About a month ago. Mandelli and Ms. Lamb—or should I say Ms. Lambert?—were here on the island and invited me to have dinner with them. Tori insisted on joining us."

"They didn't invite her?"

Guin wondered if that had been on purpose, so that Honey could work on Sadler.

"I think it was an oversight. Anyway, Tori immediately recognized Ms. Lambert and began chatting her up. The two of them were thick as thieves by the time dinner ended."

Interesting, thought Guin.

"And you never found out who sent you that letter?"

"No."

"And why were you meeting with Ms. Lambert?"

"I'm afraid that's confidential. But I assure you, I wasn't cheating on my wife. Tori knew about it. And now I must end our chat. I need to get ready for my five o'clock call."

Guin got up and thanked him for his time. Tori was waiting for her outside his office.

Had she been eavesdropping?

"You and Tim have a good chat?"

"We did," said Guin. Though she still wanted to know why Sadler had been meeting with Honey. Should she ask his wife?

"I couldn't help overhearing you asking Tim about Tony Mandelli," said Tori. "For the record, I was relieved when he changed his mind about investing with him."

"Oh? How come?"

"I didn't think it wise."

"How come?" Guin asked again.

"I didn't like the man. He seemed a bit of a Slick Willy to me."

Guin didn't disagree.

"Did your husband tell you about the letter he received?"

"He showed it to me."

"And you agreed with the letter writer?"

"I did."

"And how did Mandelli react when your husband told him he had changed his mind?"

"He was furious and threatened to sue Tim."

"When was this?"

"I don't recall exactly."

But it had to be recent. Did that give Tim Sadler a motive for killing Mandelli?

"Was Mr. Sadler relieved when Mr. Mandelli died?"

"Relieved?"

"Sorry. That was a poor choice of words. I meant, with Mr. Mandelli being dead that meant he couldn't sue him, yes?"

"Not according to Audra Linwood. She's insisting that Tim honor his commitment. I'm afraid I need to run. Shall I see you out?"

Guin knew that meant it was time for her to leave. Tori escorted her to the front door.

"By the way, were you and Mr. Sadler at the holiday lighting event last weekend?" Guin asked her.

"No, we had other plans. Why?"

"Just curious."

Tori opened the front door, and Guin thanked her for the tour.

"My pleasure," said Tori.

Guin stood in the driveway, staring up at the house. She had a feeling the Sadlers were hiding something, but she had no idea what.

CHAPTER 37

Guin was eating dinner when her phone began to ring. It was a local number but one she didn't know.

"Hello?" she said, picking up.

"Ms. Jones?"

"Yes?"

"This is Luis Garcia."

"Oh, Mr. Garcia! Thank you for giving me a call."

"Manny said you wanted to speak with me."

"I do. Though I'd rather speak in person if possible. I could meet you at the San Ybel. Will you be there tomorrow? I'd also like to speak with your wife."

"Why do you want to talk to Maria?"

"I want to ask you both about Mr. Mandelli."

"I don't know."

"I don't want to cause any trouble. As I told Manny, I won't print anything you tell me if you don't want me to. I'm just trying to find out what happened that night."

"I had nothing to do with that light falling. Nor did Maria. She wasn't there."

"I believe you. But I still want to talk to you. I understand Mr. Mandelli behaved inappropriately around your wife and some of the other maids."

"What Mr. Mandelli did to Maria and the other women was not right."

"I agree. You must have been very angry when you

found out."

"*Sì.* But I did not kill him."

"How is Maria? Is she all right?"

"She is better."

"And where were you when the light fell?"

"I was outside, fixing the decorations."

"Was there a problem?"

"Some of the lights were not working."

"Did anyone see you?"

"It was dark where I was working."

"Do you recall where you were working or which decoration you were working on?"

"It was one of the candy canes."

Guin tried to picture where all of the candy canes were. As she recalled, they were scattered around the property. Had there been one outside the ballroom?

"Do you remember which one?"

"It was one of the ones near the front of the hotel."

But Luis said it had been dark where he was working, and the front of the hotel had been brightly lit. Was he lying?

"I understand you inspected the ballroom that afternoon."

"*Sì.* Ms. Hermione wanted to make sure everything was shipshape."

"And was it?"

"*Sì.*"

"And you checked the rigging where the spotlights were?"

"I did."

"And none of the spotlights felt loose to you?"

"No."

Guin wondered if he was telling the truth, if he had really checked or if he could have been the one who loosened the light. She got the sense he was hiding something.

"So if you checked the lights beforehand and you and Maria were nowhere near the ballroom when the light fell, why did you run away?"

There was a long silence.

"That woman. She told the police she had seen me backstage."

"You mean Ms. Lamb?"

"*Sí.*"

"But surely you told the police it couldn't have been you."

"I did. But if no one saw me… Who do you think the police would believe, me or the pretty white lady?"

Guin wanted to say that she knew Detective O'Loughlin and that he wasn't racist. But Honey was an actress and could be quite convincing. And if she had sworn that she had seen Luis backstage just before the accident…

"But if Ms. Lamb didn't say it was definitely you, just that she saw a maintenance worker backstage…"

"That is not what she told the police."

"She said it was you?"

"*Sí.*"

Guin frowned. Why would Honey say that? When she had spoken with Honey, Honey gave only a vague description of the man she had scene backstage.

"So you ran."

"Maria, she was scared."

"Scared that they would arrest you?"

"*Sí.*"

"But you know that running only made you look guilty."

"We realized that after. That is why we returned."

"I thought the police found you."

"Maria's brother-in-law, he is a policeman in Miami. He said if I called the police here, told them why we left and that we would come back, it would be okay. He said he would speak for us."

Ah. So that's why they hadn't been arrested. At least not yet.

"I assume you met with Detective O'Loughlin?"

"*Sì.*"

"What did he say to you?"

"He told us not to leave the island again without telling him." Guin thought she heard someone speaking to Luis. "I need to go," he said.

"Just one more question. Was there anyone else at the hotel, someone who was on duty that night or could've slipped in unnoticed, who could've climbed up the ladder backstage and loosened that light?"

There was a long pause.

"Maria is calling me. Good night, Ms. Jones."

The line went dead, and Guin frowned. She felt sure that Luis was hiding something or covering for someone. But who? She was tempted to reach out to the detective, to ask him about Luis and Maria. She thought about calling him but sent him a text instead, saying she wanted to talk, purposely keeping the text short and vague.

She wasn't expecting a response, at least not right away, so was surprised when he texted her back a minute later.

"I've been wanting to talk too. You free for dinner tomorrow?"

Guin stared at her phone. Had the detective just invited her out for dinner? Why? Did she have plans tomorrow? Not that she could think of. But did she really want to have dinner with him? Then again, she was curious to know what he wanted to talk about.

"What time and where?" she replied.

He suggested an Italian place on the mainland at seven.

"Fine, I'll see you then."

Guin put down her phone. Then she immediately picked it back up and speed-dialed Shelly.

"You'll never guess who just invited me out to dinner."

"George Clooney?"

"George Clooney? Why would George Clooney invite me out to dinner?"

"You said I'd never guess."

Guin shook her head. Leave it to Shelly.

"Guess again."

"I don't want to guess. Just tell me."

"The detective."

"O'Loughlin?"

"He's the only detective I know. Okay, not technically true, but you know what I mean."

"So, why did he ask you out?"

"I'm not sure. I texted that I needed to speak with him—about the case. Though I didn't say that. And he suggested we meet for dinner."

"Huh," said Shelly. "You think he wants to get back together?"

"I don't know. I don't think so, but…" What else could he want to talk to her about? She doubted he wanted to discuss the case.

"What if that's it?"

"I'll tell him the truth, that I have no intention of getting back together with him. That I'm with Glen now."

"Good for you!"

"Yes, well."

"Be strong. Remember that he dumped you for a baby."

"Thanks for reminding me. And that baby is his grandson."

"Whatever. You're better off without him."

"I thought you liked the detective."

"He wasn't good for you. Glen is."

Though Shelly had been fine with Guin dating the detective before.

"So, where are you going to meet him?"

"Some Italian place on the mainland."

"Well, let me know how it goes."

"I will."

"Good. Anything else?"

"Not really."

"Okay. Thanks for letting me know. I should get back to work."

"How's the jewelry-making going?"

"Slowly."

"I'd love to see your latest pieces."

"I'll show you when I'm done."

"Okay."

They said goodbye and Guin looked down at her food. It was cold now. She frowned. Well, she wasn't that hungry anyway.

Guin rose early Tuesday and went for a walk on the beach. She had a lot on her mind, including trying to figure out why the detective had invited her out to dinner. She was also thinking about Luis Garcia. Had he been telling her the truth? She was starting to form a theory, which she was planning on running by the detective later.

Guin was so lost in thought that she collided with a fishing line.

"Oh, sorry!" she said to the fisherman, taking a step back.

"You okay?" he asked her.

"Yep. Just wasn't paying attention."

"You shellers," he said, shaking his head. "Always looking down instead of in front of you." Though he didn't say it in a mean way.

"I know. We should be more careful. So, you catch anything?"

"Not yet, but it's still early."

"Well, good luck."

"Thanks. And watch where you're going."

"I will."

Guin felt a bit embarrassed as she continued her stroll down the beach. She was usually more mindful. But she had a lot on her mind.

She paused by the headless palm tree just past Beach Access #7 and stared out at the Gulf. There were birds flying over the water, including several brown pelicans. One of them dove in. No doubt it had spied a fish. A moment later she saw a dolphin. Then she saw another. She stood there watching the dolphins, waiting for them to surface. A few minutes later, she turned around and headed east toward home.

She made herself coffee as soon as she got back. She thought again about what Luis had told her. Then she picked up her phone and called Craig.

"You home?"

"No, I'm out fishing."

"You on a boat or at the beach?"

"Actually, we're over at Ding."

By *Ding* he meant the J.N. "Ding" Darling National Wildlife Refuge.

"How is it over there?"

"It's okay."

"You catch anything?"

"Not yet."

"You got a minute?"

"What's up?"

"I spoke with Luis Garcia, who works in Maintenance at the San Ybel. He's the one who supposedly checked the rigging before the lighting event."

"And?"

Guin relayed their conversation.

"And you think he's hiding something or covering for someone?"

"I do."

"Any idea who?"

"I have some ideas. You learn if any of Mandelli's business associates or former girlfriends happened to be on the island at the time of the holiday lighting event?"

"I asked, but I haven't heard anything."

Guin heard shouting in the background.

"You need to go?"

There was more shouting.

"Yup."

"Okay. I'll catch you later."

She was going to mention the detective, but it could wait.

Guin stared out the window. Who else did she need to follow up with? She called over to the San Ybel and asked to speak with Honey—and was surprised to learn that Honey had checked out.

"When?" Guin asked the woman.

"This morning."

Where had she gone? Had the police given her permission to leave? She thanked the woman for the information and immediately texted the detective, asking him if the police had given Honey permission to leave Sanibel.

"No, why?" he replied a short time later.

"The hotel said she checked out this morning."

The detective didn't reply. And Guin wondered if he hadn't known that she'd checked out. Was she flying back to New York? Or had she just switched hotels? But why check out of the San Ybel? Unless they had kicked her out. After all, they had moved her out of the Presidential Suite. Who would know?

She called the hotel again and asked to speak with the general manager. Surely, Washburn would know if Honey had been asked to leave. Maybe they had needed her room. It was the hotel's busy season. But where had she gone?

"One moment. I'll connect you," said the operator.

The phone rang several times, then a woman answered.

"Laurence Washburn's office."

Guin recognized that voice.

"Marjorie?"

"Speaking."

"Hi, Marjorie, it's Guin Jones. Is Mr. Washburn available?"

"I'm sorry, he's not. Would you like to leave a message?"

"I really need to speak with him. Does he have any time this morning?"

"He's very busy, but I'll take a look at his schedule. Can you hold?"

"Sure."

Marjorie didn't get back to her for several minutes.

"Sorry to keep you waiting. He could possibly see you at three. Though he has a three-thirty."

"I'll take it. I don't need much time."

"Okay, I'll put you down for three."

Guin was hoping to speak to him sooner, but she would have to wait. She thanked Marjorie and asked if there was any more news about the sale.

"The Thompsons are meeting with their lawyer later," Marjorie said in a hushed tone.

"Does that mean they're planning on breaking their contract with the Mandelli Group?"

"Marjorie?" It sounded like Mrs. Thompson.

"I need to go," said Marjorie.

Before Guin could say another word, the call ended.

Guin stared out her window. She knew Mrs. Thompson hadn't been eager to sell the hotel to the Mandelli Group. Could she have somehow been involved in Mandelli's death? It was hard for Guin to picture her climbing a metal ladder and loosening that light. And Honey had said she had seen a man backstage, not a woman. But she could easily picture Mrs. Thompson asking Luis or someone to loosen the light or put a little something into Mandelli's drink.

CHAPTER 38

Guin was going to send Glen a text. Instead, she called him.

"What's up?" he said.

"You still have those pictures you took in the ballroom the night of the holiday lighting ceremony?"

"I do. Why?"

"Can you forward them to me?"

"Sure. But why?"

"I want to see who was in the room around the time the light fell."

"You looking for anyone in particular?"

"Maybe."

"You don't want to tell me?"

"Not just yet. Can you just send me the pictures?"

"I'm a bit busy right now. Can I send them later? I have to go through and separate them from the others."

"Can you send them to me before two?"

Glen sighed.

"I'll try."

"Thank you."

Guin wished Glen would just send her the photos now. Actually, she wished she had thought of getting the pictures days ago. Oh well, better late than never.

Finally, a little before noon, she received an email from Glen with a .zip file attached. She clicked on the .zip file and extracted the photos. Two of the photos caught her eye. She zoomed in to be sure what she was seeing. Had the police seen the same things? She wondered. She would have to ask the detective when she saw him later.

Guin arrived at the San Ybel a little before three and went straight to Laurence Washburn's office. But he wasn't there, and the lights were off. Strange. She went next door to the Thompsons' office. Marjorie was at her desk, talking to someone on the phone. Guin waited for her to get off. Finally, she was free.

"Do you know where Mr. Washburn is?" Guin asked her. "We had a three o'clock."

Marjorie didn't answer right away. She seemed a bit nervous.

"Is something wrong?"

"The police were here."

"They were? Did they want to speak with Mr. Washburn?" Marjorie nodded.

"Did they arrest him?"

"I don't know. I just know that he left with them."

"When was this?"

"A couple of hours ago. I was at lunch. Ms. Potter told me."

Guin would go speak with Hermione as soon as she was done here.

"Why didn't you call and tell me he couldn't make our appointment?"

"Sorry, it's been a bit busy around here."

Guin immediately felt guilty. No doubt Marjorie was being bombarded with calls and work and was overwhelmed.

"Do you know why the police wanted to speak with him?"

"You might ask Ms. Potter. She was here when it happened."

"I'll do that. Thanks."

Guin left Marjorie and headed to Hermione's office, but she wasn't there. Could the police have taken her in for questioning too? Though her lights were on. And she couldn't have told Marjorie about Washburn if the police had taken her in for questioning too. She was probably just away from her office.

Guin was typing a text to Hermione and was about to hit "send" when she saw Hermione coming down the hall.

"Hermione!" Guin called.

"I'm a bit busy, Guin."

"I just had a couple of questions. They'll only take a minute."

Hermione sighed.

"Let me guess, Marjorie told you about Laurence."

"She did. Did they arrest him?"

"I don't know. I don't think so. I didn't see any handcuffs."

"So he went willingly."

"He didn't put up a fuss if that's what you mean."

"Did you happen to hear what they wanted to talk to him about?"

"I assumed it had something to do with Mr. Mandelli."

"I'm sure it did. Did you know that the resort Washburn worked at in the Hamptons, the one he got fired from, was owned by the Mandelli Group?"

"No, I didn't," said Hermione. "How do you know that?"

"I looked up the hotel."

Hermione didn't say anything.

"So he never mentioned that he had worked for Mandelli?"

"No. But… It was obvious he didn't like the man. Though he tried to hide it."

"You said he had been a rigger back when he worked at the circus."

"That's right."

"So it wouldn't have been a big deal for him to have climbed the ladder backstage and gone up into the rigging."

"Well, maybe thirty years ago it wouldn't have been. But he's not a young man anymore."

"But he's still in good shape. Maybe it's like riding a bike; you never forget."

Hermione looked skeptical.

"You don't seriously think Laurence loosened that light? He played Santa for goodness sake!"

"I know. And I hate to think he was responsible. But there's a picture of him in the ballroom that evening. He's standing near the stage, looking right at Mandelli."

"That doesn't prove anything."

"But he matches the description of the maintenance worker spotted there."

"I still can't believe it. Laurence would never do such a thing."

"Maybe he hadn't planned on it. Maybe he just saw Mandelli there, playing Santa with Ms. Lamb, and something snapped."

Hermione's phone had been ringing, but she had been ignoring it. Now it was ringing again.

"I should get this. It could be important." She took out her phone and swiped. "Hermione Potter." She nodded her head and told the caller she'd be right there. Then she put her phone back in her pocket.

"Is everything all right?" Guin asked her.

"Just the usual. I need to go. I hope you're wrong about Laurence. He's a good man."

"I hope I am too." But Guin had a feeling she wasn't.

Guin stood in the lobby. Had the police arrested Washburn? Only one way to find out. She sent texts to both Craig and the detective. Would the detective still keep their dinner date? Though it wasn't a date, she reminded herself.

She waited a few minutes, to see if she received a reply. When she didn't, she headed to the parking lot. As she was about to get into her car, her phone began to vibrate. It was Craig. She immediately answered.

"Yes?" she said.

"I got your message," Craig replied.

"And? Do you know if they arrested Washburn? I heard they took him in for questioning."

"They arrested him."

"What was he charged with?"

"Second-degree murder."

Guin froze.

"Second-degree murder?" That was a serious charge. If Washburn was convicted, he could spend years in jail.

"So they think Washburn deliberately loosened the light and wanted to kill Mandelli? Maybe he was just trying to frighten him."

"Maybe."

"More to the point, I thought the medical examiner said Mandelli died from a heart attack brought on by drugs. That it wasn't the light."

"I didn't get the details. Just reporting what I heard."

"You hear about Honey?"

"What about her?"

"She checked out of the hotel this morning."

"You think O'Loughlin told her she could leave?"

"I don't know. I doubt it. I texted him, but he didn't get back to me. Though I'm supposed to see him later."

"You think she made a run for it?"

"Maybe. You think the police were about to arrest her too?"

"Don't know."

Guin wondered. She had seen Honey leaving the stage

with a glass, the one Mandelli had been drinking from, in one of the photos Glen had sent her. That glass could possibly prove that Honey had drugged him.

"Can you find out?"

"I can try."

"Thank you."

"Did you say you were seeing O'Loughlin later?"

"I did. He invited me to have dinner with him."

"Hm."

"You don't think it's a good idea?"

"I didn't say that."

"But I could tell from your tone."

"I barely said anything."

"I could still tell. You think it's a bad idea?"

"I didn't say it was a bad idea."

"Come on, Craig. Tell me."

"I think you're a grown woman who can make up her own mind about who she wants to have dinner with. Even if that someone treated her badly."

Guin rolled her eyes.

"Well, at least I know where you stand."

"You asked."

"I did."

"Anything else?"

"No. Just let me know if you hear anything about Honey."

Guin had spent too long trying to decide what to wear to her dinner with the detective and was running late. Hopefully, the detective was too. She had sent him a text earlier to confirm that they were still on, but she hadn't received a reply. She sent him another text after she got dressed, saying she might be a few minutes late. Again, no reply. Was he blowing her off? Well, she would soon find out.

She drove across the Causeway and made her way to the restaurant, which was on McGregor Boulevard. She parked her car and went inside. The place was dimly lit, and she didn't see the detective at the bar. She approached the hostess and told her she was meeting someone.

"This way," said the hostess, leading Guin to a booth near the back.

As they approached, Guin saw the detective seated there with what looked like a Scotch in his hand. She had never seen him drink hard liquor. And by the looks of it, he had drunk most of it already. Had he been there long? She wasn't that late.

"Enjoy your meal," the hostess said. Then she slipped away.

"You going to sit?" asked the detective.

For a second, Guin thought about telling him this had been a mistake and leaving. But she had business to discuss with him.

"So," she said, taking a seat. "Did you arrest Laurence Washburn?"

"You want a drink?" the detective asked her, signaling to a server.

The server came over and the detective ordered a beer. Guin gave him a look. A Scotch *and* a beer? That wasn't like him. Was he nervous? The server looked at her, and Guin ordered a glass of white wine and asked for some water.

"You didn't answer my question," Guin said after the server had left.

"Sounds like you already know the answer."

"Craig said he was being charged with second-degree murder. So they think Washburn deliberately loosened the spotlight to kill Mandelli? You have any evidence?"

"He confessed."

Guin stared at him.

"He confessed?"

The detective nodded.

Guin had thought Washburn was the one who had loosened the clamp and the cable, but she didn't want to believe it.

"What about Honey? Did you give her permission to leave?"

"No."

Guin was about to ask him another question when the server appeared with the detective's beer and her wine and asked if they were ready to order. The detective told him to give them a minute.

Guin resumed her questioning.

"Was she making a run for it? Did you catch her? Is she in custody?"

"She's been detained."

"What does that mean?"

"What do you think it means?"

Guin scowled.

"Did you find the glass, the one Mandelli had been drinking from? I saw Honey carrying it off the stage."

"No, but we found traces of cocaine in the suite they shared as well as an empty bottle of sleeping pills."

"And that wasn't enough to arrest her?"

"No. It's all circumstantial. Without the glass, we don't have a strong enough case. Even then…"

"But you said you found cocaine and sleeping pills in the suite she and Mandelli shared. Were the pills hers? I assume you also found fingerprints."

"The empty bottle belonged to Mandelli."

"Were her fingerprints on it?"

"It had been wiped clean."

"And you don't find that suspicious?"

The detective didn't say anything.

"How do you know she didn't have her own bottle?"

"We didn't find one."

"She could have gotten rid of it. What about the cocaine? Did you ask her about it?"

"We did."

"And?"

"She claimed to know nothing about it."

"She's lying."

"Can you prove that?"

Guin scowled.

"I'm hungry," said the detective, picking up a menu.

Guin looked at him and then picked up the other one.

CHAPTER 39

"So why did you ask me to have dinner with you?" Guin asked the detective after they had ordered.

The detective took a sip of his beer, and Guin waited. She knew he was a man of few words who found it hard to discuss personal matters.

"There's something I needed to tell you."

Guin patiently waited for him to go on.

"When I told you I was going to Boston to take care of my grandson… It wasn't the whole truth."

Guin remained quiet. She could tell that whatever it was he wanted to say to her was hard for him.

"I have cancer."

"Cancer?" She hadn't been expecting him to say that. "Why didn't you tell me? When did—"

He cut her off.

"Let me finish."

Guin closed her mouth.

"I got diagnosed in June."

Guin was unable to stop herself.

"Why didn't you tell me? What kind of cancer? Are you okay?"

He gave her a look, and Guin fell silent again.

"Prostate. I was… having problems. So I went to see a doctor. I didn't tell you because…" Guin could tell he was struggling and forced herself to keep her mouth shut.

"Because I was afraid you would…"

Guin had never seen him like this.

"Because you were afraid I would what?" she asked softly.

"I was afraid you wouldn't want me," he said.

Guin stared at him. Wouldn't want him? Because he had prostate cancer? Was he serious?

"Why wouldn't I want you? I know lots of people who've had cancer, including prostate cancer. It's not contagious, at least as far as I know. Not that I have a prostate, but… I don't understand."

"I know it's not contagious. It's just that I couldn't… you know."

He looked down at his beer.

"You couldn't what?"

Then it hit her. Was that why the detective had wanted to end things?

"Because you couldn't have sex? Is that it?" He nodded. "You think that was the only reason I was interested in you?" He didn't say anything, and Guin felt insulted. Though, to be fair, it wasn't like they had in-depth conversations about literature when they were together. "Well, for the record, that wasn't the reason I wanted to be with you." The detective gave her that look of his. "Okay, that was part of the reason, but not the main reason. Still, I don't understand. Prostate cancer is treatable. I know plenty of men who've had prostate cancer and recovered their ability to, you know."

"I realize that. But at the time… I didn't know if I'd ever be able to…"

"I assume you told your family, about the cancer, that is."

He nodded.

"Joey was the one who suggested I get treated up there. He knew some oncologist."

"Well, I wish you had told me."

"I know. I should have."

They sat in silence, neither knowing what to say. Then Guin spoke.

"But why not take a leave of absence instead of quitting your job?"

"To be honest, I'd been thinking about retiring for a while, ever since Frankie was born. I wasn't lying when I said I wanted to make it up to Joey. I wasn't there for him when he was little and needed a father. I figured maybe this was God's way of giving me another chance."

"By giving you cancer? How bad was it?"

"Stage three."

Guin stared. Stage three was bad.

"Are you okay now?"

"I'm in remission."

"That's good, yes?"

"For now. But it can come back."

Again, neither said anything. The server came over with their fried calamari, but neither was in the mood to eat it now.

Over dinner, Guin asked the detective about his treatment, but he was loath to talk about it. So she asked him about his family, specifically his grandson. That seemed to loosen him up. Or it could have been the second beer. He told Guin that he had wanted to take Frankie to a Red Sox game over the summer, but his daughter-in-law had vetoed it.

"Of course she did!" said Guin. "Frankie was too little."

The detective had frowned and said it was never too soon to take a kid to a baseball game and that he had gotten Frankie a little Red Sox jersey instead.

Guin had smiled at the story.

"You can take him when he's older."

"That's what Joey said. But what if I'm not around?"

"You'll be around."

"You don't know that. Look at the chief."

Guin assumed he was referring to his former boss.

"But he was a smoker. You're not."

"Still."

Time to change the subject.

"So, does it feel odd being back in Boston?"

"At first it did. But now it almost feels like I never left. But enough about me. How've you been?"

Guin regarded him. Did he really want to know?

"Good," she replied. "Busy."

"You still like working for the paper?"

"I do."

"You ever miss New York?"

"Sometimes. But Sanibel is my home now."

"And you and the photographer…"

"You mean Glen?" Though she knew that's who he meant.

The detective nodded.

"What about him?"

"You two serious?"

"We are."

"He make you happy?"

Guin looked at him, studying his face. He had asked her the same question at the barbecue. Had he forgotten? Or was he hoping she would give him a different answer?

"He does," she replied. And she meant it. Unlike the detective, Glen always asked her how her day was and what she was thinking. And he always listened to her answer.

They finished their food, and the busboy cleared away their plates. A few minutes later, their server returned, asking if they wanted anything else. Some dessert, perhaps? They had homemade tiramisu and ricotta cheesecake.

Guin looked over at the detective.

"You want to share something?"

"I'm good, but you go ahead."

She thought about getting tiramisu but decided to pass.

"That's okay."

"Any coffee? Perhaps a cappuccino or espresso?" said the server.

"Guin?"

She shook her head.

"Nothing for me, thanks."

"Just the check," the detective told the server.

The server returned a minute later with the check, which the detective insisted on paying.

"Thank you," said Guin.

Then they got up to leave.

"Thank you for dinner, and for telling me about…" she said as they stood outside. He didn't say anything. "So, you still planning on leaving after you wrap up the case?"

"I'm heading back to Boston Friday."

"Oh," said Guin.

The detective was looking at her, and Guin felt herself grow warm.

"Will you come back?" She didn't know why she asked that.

He shrugged.

"Maybe."

"What about your friend, the former chief?"

"He's in hospice. His family's with him."

"So, that's it? You're leaving, never to return?"

The detective smiled that crooked smile of his.

"Never is a long time." He was looking at her in that way of his again. "Goodbye, Guin. Take care of yourself."

Guin nodded. For some reason, she couldn't speak. He looked at her for a few more seconds, then he turned and walked away. Guin watched him go. Then she headed to her car.

She sat in the Mini, the key in her hand. She had finally gotten the closure she had wanted. But instead of feeling better, she felt sad. Had she wanted the detective to beg her to take him back? If she was being honest, a part of her had. Though she told herself she would have turned him down.

She went to put the key in the ignition but grabbed her phone instead and entered Glen's number.

"Hey," she said when he picked up. "You busy?"

"Just editing some photos. Why?"

"You mind if I came over?"

"Now?"

"Yes. I'm in Fort Myers."

"What are you doing in Fort Myers? Having dinner with a friend?"

"In a manner of speaking. Okay if I stop by?"

"You know you're always welcome. You sure you're all right? You sound a bit sad."

"I just miss you."

"I miss you too. Shall I put up some coffee? Or do you want decaf?"

"I should probably have decaf. Or do you have any herbal tea?"

"I do. I'll boil some water."

"Great. I'll be there soon."

CHAPTER 40

The next couple of weeks went by quickly. Guin was busy covering holiday events around Sanibel and Captiva, including a big announcement being made at the San Ybel. Ginny claimed she didn't know what the big announcement was, but Guin had a feeling.

She arrived at the hotel with Glen, standing where they had stood less than three weeks before. Hermione had been made interim GM in Laurence Washburn's absence. (He had given his notice after being arrested. Though he was currently out on bail.) She stood on the stage with Hugo Blanchet and the Thompsons. This time, there were smiles on everyone's faces.

Hermione welcomed everyone. Then she introduced the Thompsons. Fred did most of the talking. He thanked everyone for joining them, spoke about how he and Linda came to purchase the hotel and what it meant to them, and then said that although the San Ybel would always hold a place in their hearts, it was time for the resort to have a new caretaker, someone who could bring the hotel into the modern age while still keeping its spirit alive. Then he introduced Hugo Blanchet.

Blanchet thanked the Thompsons and gave a speech about the hotel, how he had fallen in love with it at first sight. He promised great things were on the horizon and spoke about his vision for the place. He also said that no one would be losing their job. If anything, they would need to hire more people.

His speech was met with polite applause. Change didn't come easily to Sanibel or Sanibelians. But Guin sensed that Blanchet meant what he said. And she would be keeping an eye on the resort as it underwent renovation.

Guin glanced around, half expecting to see Honey (she still couldn't think of her as Henny) somewhere. But she had heard that Honey had gone back to New York. Guin was convinced that Honey had somehow been involved in Mandelli's death. But Honey had hired a hotshot lawyer who claimed the police didn't have enough evidence to hold her, and she had avoided arrest. If only the police had found that glass! Guin wondered what had happened to it.

At least Washburn wouldn't be spending Christmas in a jail cell. His trial was scheduled for the spring. And Guin hoped he wouldn't have to spend the rest of his life behind bars. While he may have loosened the light, she doubted that he had drugged Mandelli. He certainly hadn't forced Mandelli to snort coke or drink. Mandelli had weakened his heart on his own.

It was now Christmas Eve. Although Guin loved Christmastime, she was feeling a bit melancholy. Both her brother and mother were away. Not that the three of them usually spent Christmas together. But it felt like everyone was either with their family or on vacation. And here she was, alone, having Christmas with her cat. Though that wasn't technically true. Glen was coming over later, and the two of them would be cooking dinner together. Then tomorrow they'd be having Christmas lunch with his family at the assisted living facility.

"Snap out of it, Guin!" she told herself. Then her phone began to ring. It was her brother.

"Ho ho ho!" he said.

"Ho ho ho yourself. Where are you?"

"At Owen's friend Monty's place on St. Martin."

"Nice place?"

"Fabulous. The view is to die for. Owen and I are thinking of renting a place here next year."

"Wow."

"You should join us."

"Maybe I will."

"Really?"

"Sure, why not?"

"Huh, you okay? You sound a bit blue."

"I'm fine."

"Is Glen there?"

"Not yet. He's coming over later. It's just me and Fauna."

"Well, that doesn't sound depressing."

"So, you and Owen having fun? What have you two been up to, lounging at the pool? Going skinny-dipping in the sea?"

"Sadly, no. I've been working most of the time."

"But it's almost Christmas."

"Tell my clients that."

"What about Owen?"

"He discovered some new artist and is trying to sign him."

"On St. Martin?"

"They have artists here, just like everywhere else."

Guin felt chastised.

"When you going back to Brooklyn?"

"Never."

"Seriously."

Lance sighed.

"We were supposed to go back before New Year's but now we're thinking of staying a few extra days. The sea air agrees with us."

Guin smiled. She could just picture her brother on the

beach, the wind blowing through his curly, reddish-blond hair, so similar to hers.

"What are you doing for New Year's?"

"I don't know. You know I'm not a big fan. I'm fine staying home."

"With Glen, I assume. And what are you two doing for Christmas?"

"I told you, we're making dinner together here tonight. Then tomorrow we're having lunch with his parents."

"Right. How domestic of you. Speaking of parents, have you spoken with our mother?"

"Not yet. Have you?"

"I just got off the phone with her."

"Is she having a good time in Bath?"

"I suppose. She's not really happy unless she has something to complain about." Too true. "You should give her a call."

"I was planning to, tomorrow."

"Good."

Guin heard someone speaking to her brother.

"I need to go," he said. "Merry Christmas!"

"Merry Christmas!" said Guin.

"And Guin?"

"Yes, Lance?"

"I hope you get what you want this year."

Guin hoped so too.

The doorbell rang and Guin went to get it. It was Glen. He had a bag of groceries in one hand and... was that a cat carrier in his other hand?

"May I come in?" he said.

Guin nodded and let him in.

"Is that a cat?" she said, looking at the cat carrier.

"Using those keen powers of observation, I see," he said with a smile.

He put down the bag of groceries and the cat carrier.

"What are you doing with a cat?"

Guin knelt and looked inside the cat carrier. Inside was a somewhat scared-looking white cat.

"It's a long story," he replied. "The short version is my neighbor, Mrs. Hillsborough, had a bad fall and had to go to the hospital."

"Oh no! That's terrible. Will she be okay?"

"I think so. She fractured her hip and is going to be out of commission for a while. So she asked me to look after Spot while she's in rehab."

"Spot?"

"You'll understand when you open the cat carrier."

Guin wondered if it was wise to let Spot out. Fauna might not like having another cat in the house. But Fauna was nowhere to be seen, and she didn't like keeping the animal cooped up in the cat carrier.

She unzipped the carrier, but the cat didn't budge.

"Hey, Spot," Guin cooed. "Would you like some food and water?"

She got out Flora's old bowl and put a little food in it. Then she showed it to Spot. Spot sniffed at it. Then he slowly made his way out of the cat carrier. Immediately, Guin understood why Mrs. Hillsborough had named him Spot. While he was mostly white, he had a large black spot on his back and another smaller black spot on his head.

Spot took a few steps and began to sniff the air.

"He probably smells Fauna."

Tentatively, Spot made his way over to the food bowl and began to eat. Guin smiled.

"I have Spot's bed and his toys in the car," Glen said. "I'll go get them."

"Wait!" said Guin. "You're not planning on leaving Spot here, are you?"

Glen looked at her.

"Is there a problem?"

"But Mrs. Hillsborough asked *you* to look after him."

"Yes, but you know what my house is like. I have all that photo equipment. And I don't know the first thing about cats."

"You've taken care of Fauna."

"That's different."

"How?"

"I took care of her here."

Guin frowned.

"Speaking of Fauna, what if she doesn't like Spot?"

"Doesn't like Spot? Just look at that sweet face. She's going to love him."

Guin wasn't so sure about that. Though Spot did have a sweet face.

"I'll be right back."

As soon as he left, Fauna appeared. She eyed the visitor and hissed at him. Spot looked momentarily surprised but didn't run away. Guin wondered if the two of them would get along. Did that mean she was contemplating letting Spot stay there?

Just then Spot came over and started rubbing himself against her legs and purring. Guin knelt and petted him. The purring grew louder. Guin smiled. He did seem like a sweet cat.

"I see the two of you are getting along," said Glen, smiling down at them.

"Yes, well," said Guin, getting up. "I don't think Fauna's so happy about it."

They looked over at Fauna who was growling at the new feline. But Spot was ignoring her.

"He seems pretty mellow."

"He is," said Glen.

"How old is he?"

"Three, I think. Mrs. Hillsborough says he's a lap cat. Just likes to sit around and be petted."

"Hm," said Guin.

"So, you'll help her out?"

Guin sighed.

"It's just for a few weeks, yes?"

Glen nodded.

"Just until she's back on her feet."

"Okay," said Guin. "But if Fauna hates her…"

"I'll take Spot. But I'm sure the two of them will become best buds in no time."

Guin wasn't so sure about that, but she figured Spot could hold his own.

"So, shall we get cooking?"

"What are we making?"

Glen had said it was a surprise.

"Duck."

"You got duck breasts?"

"Nope, I got a whole duck."

"You bought a whole duck?"

"I originally wanted to get a goose or a pheasant, but I settled for duck."

"Goose or pheasant? What is this, *A Christmas Carol*?"

Glen smiled.

"I thought we'd make something special for Christmas."

"Yes, but duck?"

"I thought you liked duck."

"I do, but… a whole duck?"

"Come on, it'll be fun. I also got some French beans and figured we could make some rice to go with."

"Okay," said Guin. "Duck it is."

"And we can't forget about dessert."

"What are we making, figgy pudding?"

Glen smiled again.

"No. Though I thought about it. How does chocolate mousse sound?"

"Is that a trick question?" Guin loved chocolate mousse.

Another smile.

"Good. We should make the mousse first so it can set. You ready?"

"As ready as I'll ever be."

Ever since they had taken that cooking course in Italy over the summer, Glen had become obsessed with cooking and trying new recipes. Not that Guin was complaining. She loved that he liked to cook. She also liked when they cooked together.

"You have an apron?"

Guin went and got him one and pulled out one for herself.

"Okay! Let's do this!"

Dinner had been delicious. And even though she had been full from the duck, Guin ate her entire ramekin of chocolate mousse. Now they were lying in bed.

"I can't believe I ate that entire chocolate mousse," she said, her head resting on Glen's chest.

"I can."

She whacked him.

"Hey, what was that for?"

"You know very well."

She settled against his chest again, listening to his heartbeat.

"You should take the rest home with you."

"I have a better idea. Why don't you give some to Shelly? Didn't you say her kids were home?"

"That's a great idea. I'll text her in the morning."

She snuggled in closer, and Glen laid a hand on her arm.

"You know, when we're in Paris, you can have chocolate mousse all the time."

Guin had forgotten about Paris. They were scheduled to go in a few weeks. Guin still couldn't believe Ginny was sending them there. They would have a limited budget. Still, Paris!

"You looking forward to it?" Guin asked him.

Glen looked down at her.

"It's Paris! And it'll be even better being there with you."

Guin smiled. Glen was stroking her hair, and she suddenly felt sleepy. She closed her eyes and before she knew it, she had drifted off to sleep.

Guin was awakened early the next morning by two pairs of feline eyes staring at her.

"You two in cahoots?" she asked them. She looked around. Where was Glen? She got up and made her way to the kitchen. Was that coffee she smelled?

"Merry Christmas!" said Glen.

"Merry Christmas," said Guin. "How long have you been up?"

"Not long."

"Thanks for making coffee."

He poured her a mug, which she gratefully took, and waited for her to taste it.

"Mm, good," she said.

He smiled.

"Now that you're up, I have something for you. I would have put it under the tree but…"

Guin didn't have a tree. She had been worried Fauna would knock it over, even one of those fake ones, so she hadn't gotten one.

"What did you get me?"

He smiled and reached into his pocket.

"Wait," said Guin. "I got you something too. I'll go get it."

"You didn't have to get me anything."

"I know, but I wanted to. Be right back."

She went into her closet and removed the box she had wrapped a few days before and carried it into the kitchen. Glen eyed it.

344 Jennifer Lonoff Schiff

"What's in there?"

"Open it and find out."

He undid the bow and carefully took off the wrapping paper. Then he opened the box.

"Oh, wow. You shouldn't have."

In the box was a large camera lens.

"I hope you didn't get it already."

She had heard Glen talking about the lens and worried he might have bought it for himself.

"No, I was going to wait until after Christmas, to see if it went on sale."

"Well, now you don't have to."

He looked at her.

"Thank you. I don't know what to say."

Guin smiled.

"You don't have to say anything."

"Now let me give you your present."

He reached into his pocket and withdrew a small box.

"Here," he said, holding it out.

Guin eyed the box.

"What is it?"

"Open it and find out."

Guin removed the wrapping paper and opened the box. Inside was a jewelry case. No, a ring box. Guin felt her heart pounding inside her chest. She opened the box. Inside was a beautiful sapphire and diamond ring. It looked old.

"It's beautiful," she said.

"It was my grandmother's."

Guin stared at the ring, afraid to touch it.

"Glen, I…"

"It's a promise ring."

"A promise ring?"

"I know you're not ready to make a big commitment. It's just my way of saying, I promise to be there when you're ready."

Guin felt herself tearing up.

"It's beautiful," she said a second time.

"Let's see if it fits."

Guin took out the ring and slipped it onto her ring finger. It fit perfectly. Glen smiled.

"It's perfect," he said.

And Guin had to agree.

Acknowledgments

First, I'd like to thank *you* for reading this book. If you enjoyed it, please consider reviewing or rating it on Amazon and/or Goodreads.

Next, I'd like to thank my first readers, Robin Muth and Amanda Walter. Amanda and Robin have been with me from the beginning of my writing journey, and I value their insights and typo spotting. Thanks, too, to my mother, Sue Lonoff de Cuevas, a former professor of English and Writing, for proofreading the manuscript; Rita Sri Harningsih for designing a gorgeous cover; and Polgarus Studio for formatting the interior. It really does take a village to produce a book.

And as always, thank you Kenny for listening to me moan and groan and for supporting and feeding me.

About the author

Jennifer Lonoff Schiff is the author of the popular Sanibel Island Mystery series and the novels *Tinder Fella* and *Something's Cooking in Chianti*. When not busy writing or editing, Jennifer can be found on the beach looking for seashells, with her nose in a book, or playing with her two cats.

For more information about Jennifer and her other books, visit www.ShovelAndPailPress.com.

Made in the USA
Monee, IL
15 May 2023